D1403419

The Sense of Death

Matty Dalrymple

WILLIAM KINGSFIELD PUBLISHERS

Matty Dalrymple/William Kingsfield Publishers
www.mattydalrymple.com

Cover design: Derek Murphy

The Sense of Death / Matty Dalrymple
ISBN-13: 978-0615919775
ISBN-10: 0615919774

In memory of my father, Thomas W. Dalrymple,
who planted the seed.

In gratitude to my husband, Wade Walton,
for letting me believe it was possible.

In gratitude to my sister, Mary Dalrymple,
for letting me believe it was time.

The sense of death is most in apprehension;
And the poor beetle that we tread upon,
In corporal sufferance feels a pang as great
As when a giant dies.

William Shakespeare
Measure for Measure

Chapter 1

Ann Kinnear followed her brother, Mike, the distraught mother, and two bodyguards down the alley of the Baltimore slum, wearing the sweatshirt of a girl very likely dead. The first day there had only been one bodyguard—the giant who was leading the way today. However, an encounter with an angry prostitute and her pimp had convinced the group that one bodyguard for three clients who were very clearly strangers to the neighborhood was not a desirable ratio and today the giant had arrived with a colleague who made up in attitude what he lacked in stature. Today had been largely uneventful.

"Uneventful" was both good news and bad—good in that they were not dealing with switchblade-armed pimps but bad in that they were no closer to the goal that the distraught mother had hired Ann to reach—locating her missing daughter. The girl's last online post suggested that this area of Baltimore was where she was headed when she disappeared, but the police had exhausted every option for locating a runaway—hospitals, jails, halfway houses, drug dens. That had been three months ago, and the fact that the mother was now willing to hire Ann Kinnear to continue the search suggested that she recognized that she was less likely with each passing day to find her daughter alive.

They were mid-way through the second of the search grids the mother had mapped out and the seeming hopelessness of the search and the growing despair of the mother were making it hard for Ann to concentrate. They were periodically trailed by a small knot of children who yelled obscenities and then rushed away shrieking when one of the bodyguards turned toward them. At each cracked concrete front stoop or packed-dirt, garbage-strewn backyard, they stopped for a moment for Ann to look and to sense. She just wanted the day to be over so she could return to her safe and sterile hotel room in the Inner Harbor and fall into bed and sleep for days.

Near the end of an alley amid an assault of frenzied barking from a three-legged, mixed-breed dog chained to the back stair railing, Ann caught a glimpse of what she was searching for.

There was something in the yard near the foundation of the building, a faint lavender flicker that brightened as they approached. It snaked out from beneath a dented metal trash can, hovering over ground strewn with overflow which was clear only in the area reachable by the dog. The light stretched toward them then jerked to a stop, seemingly chained to its spot like the dog. The mother stepped up beside Ann and the light brightened beseechingly.

"What is it?" the mother asked, almost too tired to allow herself to be hopeful.

"A light. Do you see a light?" Ann felt a familiar lurch in her stomach.

Mike, at her other elbow, scanned the yard. "I don't see anything," he said, glancing at the mother.

"I don't see anything either. Should I?"

"No," said Ann, still watching the light. "Take a step forward. But watch the dog." The mother took a step forward—the dog lunged at the end of its chain, barking insanely.

The light pulsed and extended toward them like an arm outstretched.

"She's here," said Ann.

The mother turned back to Ann. "My daughter? She's

here?"

Ann turned to her, her eyes stricken. "Yes, she's here. In the yard. Under the trash cans." She slipped off the sweatshirt and handed it to the mother. "It's the best I can do. I'm sorry."

She turned away and began walking toward the street at the end of the alley, then broke into an awkward run before lurching behind a pile of sodden cardboard boxes. They heard a retching noise and the big bodyguard glanced at Mike.

"She'll be OK," said Mike. "You stay with Mrs. Chen. Make a note of which yard this is. And you," he inclined his head toward the bantam bodyguard, "come with me." The small one looked at the giant who nodded. Mike touched the mother's arm. "Mrs. Chen, I have to go see to Ann. You call the police. Let them know we found your daughter. I'll call you tomorrow."

The mother nodded, her eyes still fixed on the filthy yard.

Mike squeezed her shoulder then he and the smaller bodyguard followed Ann down the alley. The giant took out his cell phone, snapped a few pictures of the backyard and the surrounding buildings, then took the mother's elbow and led her the other way down the alley, the children still watching but suddenly silent.

The next morning the police dug up the body of Jocelyn Chen from the back yard of the Baltimore row house.

Chapter 2

Biden Firth slammed his fist down on his mahogany desk, making the ice cubes in his drink jump. He sat breathing heavily for a moment and then slammed his fist down again and then a third time. As he sat with his hands still clenched, a movement caught his eye and he looked up to see the nanny, Esme, standing in the doorway, her fingers twisted together in front of her.

"I'm sorry, Mr. Firth, I thought something had … fallen."

Biden tried to relax the grimace on his face and slow his breathing. "No, Esme, everything's fine. Close the door on your way out. Please," he added. His mother had always told him it was important to be polite to the help.

"Yes, Mr. Firth," said Esme, and pulled the door closed softly behind her.

Biden unclenched his fists and placed his hands palms down on the desk blotter. He stared at them and, after a minute, pulled a letter opener from a wooden holder on his desk. With his left hand still flat on the blotter, he grasped the handle of the letter opener with his right hand and drove the opener into the blotter between his thumb and first finger. Pulling the knife away he examined the dent the opener had left on the blotter, then drove the opener down again, between his first and second fingers. This time he misjudged and the opener grazed his index finger.

"Fuck!" he yelled, jumping to his feet. Holding his hand out in front of him he went to a bar built discreetly into the bookshelves in the corner of the room and put his hand under the faucet, watching the water as it circled pinkly down the drain. When the throbbing subsided he pulled a paper towel from under the sink and blotted his finger, then examined it. The letter opener, not being sharp, had gouged rather than cut the skin and a ragged flap of skin hung from the inside of his finger. "Fuck," he muttered to himself and, giving the finger a last blot, he dropped the stained paper towel into a small trash can under the sink.

He retrieved his glass from the desk and, opening a silver ice bucket next to the sink, dropped an ice cube into his glass, then added more Glenfiddich with a shaking hand. He returned to his desk and sat staring straight ahead for a moment and then sank forward with his elbows on the desk, his head in his hands. His face was even paler than normal, his fingers messing his short, dark, usually carefully combed hair.

The cause of his distress was a call from his father, Morgan Firth.

"Biden, I got a call from some guy named Miles Walters, said he was a buddy of yours from Penn," said Morgan.

Biden's stomach flipped. "Yes?"

"Do you know why he was calling me?" said Morgan, his volume rising. "He says you owe him $270,000."

"Yes?" said Biden, a sweat breaking out on his forehead.

"Goddamn you, Biden, don't make me pry every goddamn piece of information out of you one piece at a time! Why is this guy calling me and telling me you owe him money?"

Biden rose from his chair, striking a pose of nonchalance. "He's opening a restaurant. In Northern Liberties. I made an investment in it but I didn't like the way it was going so I decided not to give him any more."

Morgan's volume rose another notch. "A restaurant? A

restaurant is not an investment, you idiot, it's a money pit! You told him you'd give him $270,000 for his restaurant?"

"No," said Biden. He had, in fact, told Walters he would give him $350,000 and had already paid out $80,000.

"Well, what *did* you tell him?"

"I told him I'd contribute. I don't think I ever specified an amount."

"That's not something you *think*, Biden, it's something you *know*. Does this guy have anything that would contractually obligate you to give him more money?"

Biden wasn't sure. "No," he said. "He's hiring a very well-known chef."

"I thought you didn't like the way it was going."

"I didn't," said Biden. "I'm just saying he got a good chef."

Biden heard a deep sigh over the phone line and imagined his father shaking his head in disgust. It was a sight he was well accustomed to.

"Biden, restaurant people talk. They talk to newspapers. They talk to *real estate investors*. If this guy says the son of Morgan Firth legitimately owed him money and didn't pay, that's not the kind of publicity I want. People deal with me because they know I'm on the up-and-up. If you have jeopardized that, you are going to be in a world of hurt."

Biden didn't say anything.

"Did you hear me, Biden?"

"Yes."

"Are you going to take care of this?"

"Yes."

"Do you need Culp"—the Firth family lawyer, fondly known as Culpability Culp—"to get involved?"

"No. I'll take care of it."

"Do that. I'm going to call this Walters guy back in a week and make sure it's put to bed."

"Jesus, Dad, I said I'd take care of it," said Biden angrily.

There was a moment of silence and Biden knew what was coming. Morgan Firth's volume went up one final notch. "Don't you dare act angry with me, Biden, I have had it up to here with bailing you out of the shit you get yourself wrapped up in and I'm not going to do it anymore." Over the phone, in the background, Biden heard a woman's voice—his mother, Scottie. "Who do you think," said his father, his voice aimed away from the phone receiver. "It's Biden." There was another pause as he heard his mother's voice again. "No, everything is not all right. I'll tell you when I'm done here." There was a pause while, Biden assumed, his mother left the room. "One week," said Morgan into the phone, "and when I call Walters you better have gotten this worked out." And he slammed down the phone.

Biden slammed his own phone down and fell back into the desk chair. Then he pulled his cell phone out of his pocket, found Walters' number in the contacts list, and dialed it, then disconnected before Walters answered. He had been intending to ask what the fuck Walters thought he was doing calling Biden's father, but he knew what the answer would be— Walters had been calling Biden himself for the past month, asking where his money was, yelling about contractors and employees needing to be paid. When Biden stopped answering Walters' calls, and told his housekeeper, Joan, to tell Walters he wasn't home the one time he had actually come to the Rittenhouse Square townhouse, Walters had left a message on voicemail that he was going to go to Biden's father.

"I'm thinking your father would rather cover your debts than see the lawyers get involved," Walters had said. "I don't like getting family involved, Firth, but I'm going to make sure you pay up the money you committed."

The money Biden had already given to Walters had come from a trust fund that his wife Elizabeth's grandfather had set up for her. Biden's name was on the account because they mainly used it for house-related expenses. The gracious old townhouse just off Philadelphia's Rittenhouse Square had been a wedding gift from his parents, so the expenses were mainly for furnishing and decorating it, Elizabeth's area of expertise, and maintaining it, the payments for which Biden handled. The house had been renovated shortly before they moved in and the initial onslaught of decorating expenses had subsided in the last couple of years so that, aside from the periodic demands that Elizabeth put on the account for a new piece of furniture or painting, the money just accumulated in the account.

Biden had been withdrawing twenty or thirty thousand dollars at a time in a schedule of payments to Walters. He had sat in the shell of the building on North 2nd Street, discussing the location of the bar and the equipment that would be installed in the kitchen. He had felt like an insider. He looked forward to the day when he could take Elizabeth to the restaurant and be greeted with the deference appropriate to a major investor. They would have their own table, and Alain Broussard, the chef Walters had lured away from Etoile, would come to their table to greet them, maybe even sit down with them for a few minutes before hurrying back to the kitchen.

Then one day Walters had called Biden to tell him his check had bounced and when Biden called up the account there was only $100 left in it, a withdrawal of the remainder having been made by Elizabeth the previous week. She had never said anything to him about it.

The knowledge that Elizabeth had known about his withdrawals and had never given him a chance to explain had set him up for the humiliation at the hands of Walters, a humiliation that still made his face burn. His father's derision—his assumption that he, Biden, had done something stupid—and Biden's inability to confront Walters was too much.

Now, his drink on the desk before him and his head in his hands, Biden sat for so long that the watery February afternoon light began to give way to dusk. He heard Elizabeth come in the front door and go to the kitchen, at the back of the house, and then go upstairs and some time later he heard Esme leave. Shortly after that he heard steps descending the stairs and a knock on the door. He sat back in his chair and smoothed his hands over his hair and was preparing to say "come in" when the door opened and his wife entered the library.

Elizabeth was a stunningly beautiful woman in her early thirties, with dark, straight hair that fell to her shoulder blades. She was tan despite the time of year, thanks to a recent visit with acquaintances in the Keys. She was wearing a cream-colored silk blouse cinched at the waist with a wide brown leather belt, camel-colored silk pants, and brown leather boots with very high stiletto heels. A large solitaire diamond pendant on a gold chain glinted at her throat. She was petite and whip-thin, thanks to the ministrations of a personal trainer in the gym she had outfitted on the top floor of the townhouse. She stood—posed, one might say—at the door, her hand resting on the knob.

"Working?" she asked.

"No," said Biden.

Elizabeth glanced at the glass on Biden's desk. "I'll have one of those." She crossed the room and sank into a leather couch near the fireplace. Biden returned to the bar and made a scotch and water and put it on the table next to her.

"Biden, coaster," she said, and Biden returned to the bar

for a coaster, moved his wife's drink onto it, and wiped the moisture off the table with a clean handkerchief. He sat down at the other end of the couch. They sat in silence for a minute, sipping their drinks, Biden looking into the empty fireplace and Elizabeth glancing around the room.

It was a handsome room, lined with built-in bookshelves filled with a mixture of old and new hardcover books and objets d'art. A large oil painting of a hunting scene, painted a century and a half before in nearby Chester County, hung over the fireplace, and smaller oils of the same era decorated the walls not covered with shelves. A pair of wing chairs flanked the couch and a grouping of two antique chairs and a table provided seating in front of the windows that looked onto the street. Across the room from the windows was a large mahogany desk set at an angle. Several richly colored Persian rugs covered the floor.

Elizabeth stood, crossed to one of the bookshelves, and adjusted the placement of a jade elephant. "We should leave by 6:30," she said.

Biden nodded.

"Joan had to run an errand but she'll be back by then. Sophia's asleep." Sophia was their two-year-old daughter.

Biden nodded again.

"The Jurgensens will be there."

"Great."

"They're buying a house in Bermuda."

"Great," said Biden again, and drained his drink. He returned to the bar for a refill.

"Take it easy, Biden, it's going to be a late night," said Elizabeth.

Biden dropped ice cubes into the glass with a clatter. "Let's skip the dinner," he said, knowing that there was no way in hell his wife would miss the charity dinner scheduled for that evening—a chance to see and be seen by

Philadelphia's most wealthy, a chance to show off whatever dress she had bought for the occasion which would, of course, never be worn again.

Elizabeth crossed to where Biden stood, put her glass down on the bar, and patted his cheek. "Take it easy on the scotch. I'm going to go change." She headed for the door.

"Elizabeth, we need to talk," said Biden.

"Not now, Biden."

"Now, Elizabeth," he said with unaccustomed force.

Elizabeth turned at the door and looked at him quizzically.

"You took all the money out of the house account," he said.

She examined him for a moment then shut the door and said, "Yes, I did."

"Why?"

"Because you were making withdrawals without discussing them with me first."

"I've never discussed the withdrawals I make with you before."

"I was always able to confirm that withdrawals from the house account have been spent on the house. Except for the past few months."

"You've been checking up on me?"

Elizabeth laughed humorlessly. "Trust yet verify."

"I can't believe it …" said Biden.

"*You* can't believe it?" she said incredulously. "So, what were you spending the money on?"

"It was a surprise."

"It certainly was."

"It was a surprise for you."

"What was it?" she said sharply and, when he didn't answer, turned back to the door and said, "Get ready for dinner, Biden."

"I was trying to make some money," he said angrily. "I was trying to make some money to keep you in the lifestyle to which you have become accustomed," he added nastily.

She turned back to him. "I had 'become accustomed' to a certain lifestyle long before I met you, Biden," she shot back. "I thought you would be able to support that lifestyle. If not, you shouldn't have asked me to stop working."

There was a long silence, Biden looking down into his glass, Elizabeth looking first at him and then toward the window, her arms crossed. The street lights had come on outside. She crossed to the window and pulled the curtains shut.

"I need some money," muttered Biden.

"Good luck with that," she said coldly.

He paused. "Maybe your father ...?"

"Don't even think about it. It is not my family's responsibility to bail you out of your financial difficulties."

"There are worse things than having financial difficulties," said Biden, beginning to sound petulant.

Elizabeth walked over to where he stood and took his glass from him. She leaned toward him and, almost whispering, said, "No, Biden, there are not. A person's financial standing determines his standing in his community and is an indicator of his success, of his worth. Having money ensured that your daughter would have the best in life because that's what she deserves. It's what I deserve too. I expect you to be able to continue to provide that. If you can't, then I'll go back to work and do it myself."

Biden looked into his wife's eyes and saw nothing but cold appraisal and contempt.

"You're a bitch," he said, and she flung his scotch into his face.

Biden's hand shot out and slapped his wife across the

face. She dropped the glass which bounced on the thick carpet and put her hand to her cheek and glared at him with undisguised hatred.

"You're pathetic," she said, and turned once more toward the door. "Can't you do anything right?"

Biden felt a stab of pain like a needle in his eye and with a cry he grabbed Elizabeth's arm and spun her around. He thought he was going to hit her again but instead he found himself shaking her, her head whipping back and forth. There was a moment when the pain of his anger receded before the shock of what he was doing and he loosened his grip, and in that moment she drove her knee into his crotch and twisted away as he gasped and doubled over. Elizabeth ran for the door and was through it before he recovered, but she hesitated in the entrance hall and that's where he caught up with her, tackling her like the football player he had been in high school. His 185 pounds landed on top of her barely hundred pounds and he felt the breath whoosh out of her body. He flipped her over so she was facing him and now her face was filled not with contempt but with terror. He straddled her and then closed his hands around her neck and tightened, his thumbs pressing into her Adam's apple, his fingers digging into the back of her neck. He was going to choke off every slight, every insult she had ever thrown his way.

She was thrashing beneath him trying to get air, her feet banging into an antique sideboard and rattling the dishes in it. Her eyes were bulging, her body jerking spasmodically beneath him.

"Shut your eyes!" he yelled, and banged her head against the marble floor. Her eyes, huge, stayed on his face. "Shut them!" he shrieked and banged her head against the floor again, and then he wasn't looking at her eyes anymore, just tightening his fingers still more and listening to the thumps as her head hit the floor again and again.

It seemed to take forever for Elizabeth to stop struggling and even when she was motionless he still sensed a flicker of life in her. *I could stop now*, he thought, and then realized that there was no going back. He kept his hands tight around her throat as he fought back his rising gorge.

Eventually, when he could sense no life left—not a hint of breath, not a flutter of a heartbeat—he let go and her head bounced on the marble floor one last time. She was not the beautiful Elizabeth she had been a few minutes before, hers was a grotesque parody of a human face, her tongue and eyes protruding, her legs splayed out behind him.

Dimly he heard Sophia crying from the second floor for the nanny—"E-mee! E-mee!" He pushed himself to the wall of the entrance hall and leaned against it, burying his head in his hands. His blood pounded in his ears and his breathing was fast and shallow, his body covered with a cold slick of sweat.

After a minute, when his breathing had slowed somewhat, he crawled over to Elizabeth. "I can't do anything right?" he said, gazing into her glazed eyes. "We'll see about that, you bitch." Then he leaped to his feet.

How long until the housekeeper got back? It would be easier to explain a blocked entrance than a body—he went to the front door and slipped on the chain. Then he ran to the back of the house and down the stairs to the garage and popped open the trunk of his Mercedes. Running up to the master bedroom, past the room where his daughter was still crying, he pulled a large bath sheet from the linen closet and, returning to the garage, spread it on the bottom of the trunk. Returning to the entrance hall, he gathered Elizabeth's body up, carried it to the garage, dumped it into the trunk, and slammed the trunk shut.

He stepped back, breathing heavily, the image of her

jumbled limbs searing his brain. He steeled himself, then popped the trunk open again. Her legs were twisted, her hands obscenely caught between her thighs. He arranged her legs as best he could, and folded her hands across her chest. Then he slammed the trunk closed again and ran up the stairs to the kitchen.

Elizabeth's purse and keys were on the counter where she always put them, next to the charger that held her cell phone. A stopwatch ticking in his head, Biden considered, then grabbed the purse from the counter. He went to the coat closet and pulled out the coat he knew she had been wearing earlier in the day, and, carrying these down to the garage, opened the trunk again and threw them in without looking.

He grabbed a flashlight from the workbench at the back of the garage and, returning to the entrance hall, knelt and examined the floor. There was no blood that he could see. He found a few strands of Elizabeth's hair which he flushed down the powder room toilet.

Was there anything else incriminating to be dealt with before Joan arrived? Nothing that he couldn't explain. He went to the front door and took the chain off, then climbed the stairs to the second floor.

Sophia was screaming now, not used to having her needs ignored. He started for the master bedroom and then retraced his steps to her room. She was standing in her crib, little fists around the bars, hair a messy halo, her face red. When she saw Biden she quieted with a hiccup, a look on her face not of comfort but of confusion. Biden gazed back from the doorway. What could a two-year-old have heard? What would she remember? What did it matter? She couldn't tell anyone anyway. He turned from the door and gritted his teeth against her wail.

In the master suite he dried his face on a hand towel then,

in the walk-in closet, threw his wet shirt and sweater into the laundry hamper and put on fresh clothes. As he pulled the sweater over his head, he heard, over Sophia's wail, the front door close and steps climbing the stairs. He met the housekeeper, Joan, in the hallway.

"I was just going to check on her," he said.

"I'll check," said Joan, taking off her coat and hanging it over the banister. She started for Sophia's room then turned. "Everything all right, Mr. Firth?"

"Absolutely," he said with a bright smile. He turned to the stairs and the smile turned to a grimace. Normal, he must act normal—he would never say "absolutely" and he rarely had cause to smile.

In the library he could still smell the spilled Scotch. Biden picked up the unbroken glass and put it in the sink at the bar—Joan checked the bar periodically to take away dirty glasses and restock with clean ones—and then used some paper towels from under the bar to dab at the Scotch that had soaked into the carpet. As he finished this, there was a knock at the library door. He dropped the paper towels into the wastebasket by his desk.

"Come in," he said.

Joan came in, carrying Sophia who was red-eyed but quiet.

"Are you and Mrs. Firth going to the dinner tonight?" she said, glancing at her watch.

"No, my wife and I had a bit of an argument," said Biden. "I don't think we will be going to the dinner tonight."

"Oh," said Joan. "Would you still like me to stay tonight?"

"Yes, that would be helpful."

"Certainly," Joan said and left the room.

If he hadn't killed her, what would he be doing now? Biden looked up the number of the hotel where the charity dinner was being held. He called and asked the concierge to deliver a message to the host and hostess of the event that Mr. and Mrs. Firth would not be able to attend this evening's event; unfortunately Mrs. Firth was not feeling well.

What else would he be doing? Trying to call her, he supposed. From the phone on his desk he dialed her cell and heard the faint ringing coming from the kitchen. *She didn't take her phone with her*, he coached himself, *she left in a hurry*. Then he found some maps of the Philadelphia area and New Jersey in one of the room's built-in cabinets and, spreading them open on his desk, began scanning them, committing the parts he needed to memory.

Biden went up to his bedroom in the early hours of the morning, Joan having retired to the small apartment on the third floor long before. He sat on the edge of the bed, pulled off his shoes, and fell back on the pillow, lying on top of the covers. After a minute, though, he pushed himself up and forced himself through his normal nighttime routine—stripping and throwing his clothes in the hamper, pulling on pajama bottoms. His hands shook as he squeezed toothpaste onto his toothbrush and for a moment he thought about going downstairs for another drink. Instead he rinsed with Listerine, climbed under the covers, and switched off the light.

Early in their marriage, Elizabeth had been interested in sex. To tell the truth, Biden had never been as interested in sex as he gathered other men were—or as interested as Elizabeth seemed to be—but he hardly objected when Elizabeth had slipped into bed in a skimpy silk nightie and ran her hands—or her mouth—over his body. He reciprocated, too, and, based on the reactions he got, he figured he must have been doing a good job. When Elizabeth had gotten pregnant she didn't initiate sex as often and, in the last months of the pregnancy, didn't initiate it at all, but he could hardly blame her—she couldn't have felt sexy looking like that, with her thin body distorted by her bulging stomach. Why did small women always have big babies? After Sophia was born, however, he looked forward to getting back to their pre-pregnancy pattern but it never happened. One of the few times he had tried to initiate sex she had barely looked up from the book she was reading.

"Biden, please," she said, turning a page, her face creased with annoyance.

"You used to like it," he said in a voice he hoped mixed reproach and conciliation.

Elizabeth snorted. "Yes, well ..." And eventually he stopped waiting for her to finish the sentence and turned over and switched off the light.

Now he lay with his arms at his sides on top of the covers. This is how a body would be laid out for a viewing, he thought. This is how Elizabeth would be laid out if there was a viewing of her body. But there would never be a viewing. Not if he could help it.

Chapter 3

The next morning Biden dressed in old jeans, a blue t-shirt, a plain sweatshirt, and worn sneakers. He wished he had a baseball cap but the closest he could find was a golf hat which he thought would make him more conspicuous, not less.

He got his gym bag down from the closet shelf and put a t-shirt, underwear, socks, and a toiletry bag in it. He didn't actually plan to stay anywhere overnight—he just needed the bag and a couple of the things in it—but if someone happened to look in it, it would be best if it were stocked like an overnight bag. Acting normal and keeping it simple—that was what was going to let him get away with murder.

Downstairs in the library he called his credit card company and told them that he was afraid his wife might have misplaced her card and asked if it had been used since five p.m. yesterday; they assured him it had not. He called the Rittenhouse Hotel where Elizabeth had gone once before when they had an argument and asked if they had an Elizabeth Firth or Mrs. Biden Firth staying there and was told that they were not at liberty to share that information. He called the Sofitel and got the same response.

All things a concerned, but not overly concerned, husband might do.

He hardly felt like eating but since he rarely skipped breakfast he buzzed Joan on the intercom and asked her to bring eggs, toast, juice, and coffee to the library. While he waited, he paged through the *Philadelphia Chronicle*, paying special attention to the restaurant reviews—he wasn't ready to give up on his restaurant ambitions yet.

There was a knock on the door and he called "Come in" as he began making room on his desk for the breakfast tray. He glanced up and started, the blood draining from his face, as Elizabeth entered the room carrying the tray.

"Good morning, Biden, we missed you last night," she said and Biden realized it was Amelia Dormand, Elizabeth's mother—Jesus, they looked alike. Amelia put the tray down on the desk, picked an extra coffee cup on a fine china saucer off the tray, and began to take a sip, then stopped and looked closely at Biden. "Good heavens, are you all right? I thought Bob said it was Elizabeth who wasn't feeling well."

Biden panicked for a moment—what the hell was she talking about?—then remembered the excuse he had given for missing last night's dinner. He had forgotten that Elizabeth's parents had also planned on attending.

"Yes. I mean no, not really. We're both fine, just had a ... an argument. Weren't in much of a mood for a party."

"Ah, I see. Well, that's understandable," said Amelia, her voice carefully neutral. She paused. "Is she upstairs?"

"No. She got angry and left. I wanted to skip the dinner." He had to keep the story as close to what had actually happened as possible, they would likely find out about the missing trust fund money eventually—for all he knew, Elizabeth had told her mother. "And other things," he added.

After a beat, Amelia asked, "Do you know where she is?"

"I'm thinking maybe the shore house, she did that once before ..."

"Yes, but in February? It doesn't sound so appealing. Have you tried calling her?"

"She didn't take her cell phone."

Amelia knit her brow. "That certainly doesn't sound like Elizabeth. Maybe she went to a hotel—"

"I tried the Rittenhouse and the Sofitel but they won't give me any information."

"I know one of the concierges at the Rittenhouse, he might tell me." She took a distracted sip of coffee. "Although if she's hiding out maybe she doesn't want to be chased after." She smiled slightly. "Or maybe she does. Who can tell with Elizabeth."

"I think I'll go down to the shore house, I feel like taking a drive."

"Well, it can't hurt—let me know. When you see her, remind her we were supposed to have brunch with her grandmother this morning," she said with mock severity. "That on its own might have been enough to make her leave the state."

Biden produced an unconvincing smile.

"Don't let me keep you from your breakfast." Amelia turned to go but when she left the library rather than turning right toward the front door she turned left toward the back of the house. Biden, alarmed, followed her, reaching the hall in time to see her disappear into the kitchen and, after muffled goodbyes to Joan and Esme, reappear in the back hall and head for the door to the garage. He caught up with her as she was descending the stairs.

"Where are you going?" he asked, more abruptly than he intended.

Amelia turned, surprised. "I parked in back."

"Oh. Sure." He stood at the top of the stairs with his hands in his pockets. Normal.

Amelia continued down the stairs, skirted the Mercedes on her way to the back door, then stopped and peered in the window of Elizabeth's Porsche. "She was supposed to get a present for her grandmother—I don't suppose she left it in her car." She opened the passenger door and looked in the back seat, then circled to the driver's side and, popping open the trunk, checked there as well. "No. No granddaughter, no present." She sighed. "It's going to be a long brunch."

She glanced toward the Mercedes and Biden bit the inside of his cheek, tasting the iron tang of blood.

"Let me know when you hear from her," Amelia said with a small wave, and she slipped out the back door.

Biden heard her car, parked just outside the garage doors, start up, and saw her drive down the alley. He crossed the garage and locked the door behind her. He returned to the library where his coffee was cooling and his juice was warming on the desk—his stomach churned, he couldn't even think of eating now. Leaving the tray on the desk, he got a navy pea jacket and leather gloves from the coat closet, picked up the overnight bag, then went to the kitchen where Esme was feeding Sophia and Joan was polishing a glass with a dish towel.

"I haven't heard from Mrs. Firth—I'm going to drive out to the shore house and see if she's there. I might end up staying there tonight. Can one of you stay if I'm not back?"

"Yes sir, that's no problem," Joan replied.

"If she calls, let me know right away."

"Yes sir."

Biden went down the steps from the back hall to the garage and, steeling himself, opened the trunk. He made a point not to look at her face. A stray ray of light from the small windows in the garage doors glinted off her engagement ring which looked garish against the lifeless gray of her hand where it rested on her stomach. He wished he had covered her body. He grabbed her purse, stuffed it into the gym bag, slammed the trunk closed, and almost screamed when he saw Joan standing at the top of the garage stairs.

She held something out. "Mrs. Firth left her cell phone, do you want to take it with you?"

"Yes." He came to the stairs and took the phone from her. She turned back to the kitchen and closed the door as he climbed in the car and hit the automatic door opener.

Biden drove across the Schuylkill River to one of the churches near the University of Pennsylvania campus and found a parking space among the church goers. With his gloves still on he opened the gym bag and his wife's purse and took out her wallet. He removed the cash — nearly $500 — and put it in the glove compartment. He wiped the handle of the purse with the t-shirt and, replacing the purse in the gym bag, got out of the car and began walking west.

As he walked, the surroundings deteriorated until, after about a dozen blocks, he was in a neighborhood he would never go into at night and, in fact, felt uncomfortable in in broad daylight. The streets were nearly deserted and the few people he passed appeared drunk or perhaps exhausted after a graveyard shift.

He glanced into the garbage-strewn alleys he passed until he saw what he was looking for. He turned in between a closed pawn shop and a boarded up row house and, lifting the lid of the dumpster, pulled the purse out of the gym bag, dropped it in, and quietly closed the lid. His heart thumping, he stepped out of the alley and glanced around — no one in sight. Trying not to hurry he continued in the same direction he had been walking, turned at the next street, and then returned to his car one block over from his original route. Better not to risk being seen passing twice by someone looking out of their grimy front windows.

When he got back to the car he made his way to I-95 and headed south, exiting when he saw signs for the wildlife refuge at Tinicum, near the Philadelphia International Airport.

Even in February there were a few cars in the parking lot near the visitors' center — what idiot goes bird watching on a freezing February morning?—so he began skirting the borders of the refuge, relieved to see that it was not enclosed by a fence. In many places there were tightly packed, rather worn-looking houses directly across the street from the refuge but in others the border of the refuge wandered away from the houses and here he found a few places where construction on streets had begun but then been abandoned, the weed-infested stretches of pavement blocked by concrete barriers.

Next he negotiated the streets around the sports complex and crossed the Walt Whitman Bridge, heading toward Long Beach Island through the Pine Barrens. Traffic was light but the road was by no means deserted and the pine woods on either side of the road were less dense than he had remembered—a body lying on the ground away from the road wouldn't be easy to spot but a person carrying a body would be visible from the road for dozens of yards. Even at night, who knew what passing headlights might be able to pick up? Tinicum was still looking like the best option.

Near Long Beach Island, he stopped at a mom-and-pop sporting goods store he had once visited when he was looking for snorkeling gear. A bell jingled and a painfully thin teenager looked up from the magazine he was reading spread out on the checkout counter.

"Help you?"

"No." Biden turned his head away from the boy. "Thanks."

The store was small in comparison to the giant sports stores of suburban shopping centers. Biden found a pair of waders but had almost given up on the other item on his mental shopping list and was loath to ask the clerk, wanting to have as little interaction with him as possible, when he spotted it—a sleeping bag in a dark green carrying sack enclosed in dusty plastic.

He brought the items to the checkout counter where the

clerk—Bud, according to his plastic name tag—flipped his magazine closed. Based on the cover, surfing was Bud's sport.

"Find everything?"

"Yes."

Bud punched the price of the waders into an old-fashioned register and turned the dusty sleeping bag over in his hands.

"Know how much this was?"

Biden named a figure he thought sounded reasonable; it must have sounded reasonable to Bud as well because he punched it into the register and gave Biden the total. Biden peeled bills off the roll of money he had removed from Elizabeth's purse.

"Cash?" said Bud, mildly surprised. He gave Biden his change. "Bag for that?"

"Yes."

Bud packed the waders and the sleeping bag into the largest plastic bag he could find. "Receipt in the bag?"

"I'll take it," said Biden. Bud handed over the bag and the receipt.

"Nice day," said Bud, returning to his magazine. Biden dropped the receipt in a trash can on the way out.

Back in the car he crossed the East Bay Avenue bridge over Manahawkin Bay, the only way onto the long narrow strip of land that was Long Beach Island. Long Beach Boulevard was practically deserted, with only a few restaurants open, catering to the local after-church lunch crowd. Elizabeth's cell phone vibrated periodically on the seat beside him and he glanced at it disinterestedly, recognizing most of the names that appeared on the caller ID as friends of Elizabeth's and, once, her mother.

He arrived at his in-laws' shore house around 1:30. It was a large, airy house on the bay, with the ocean, on the other side of Long Beach Island, just a few blocks away. In back was the dock where Bob Dormand kept his boat in the summer; in the winter it would be in storage. The house itself looked as if it were in storage, its storm shutters closed and the gravel yard speckled with leaves.

Biden used a keypad to open the garage door, pulled the car in, and closed the door behind him. He got the shopping bag from the sporting goods store out of the back seat and pulled the tags off his purchases, using the bag to collect the trash. He had to keep everything together—no good leaving a scrap of paper behind that could tie him to the evidence, should it ever be found. He removed the sleeping bag from its nylon carrying sack, unzipped it, and spread it open on the floor.

Pulling on the leather gloves, he steeled himself and opened the trunk. Averting his eyes as much as possible, he slipped his hands under her shoulders and knees and tried to lift her out. It was like trying to move a piece of furniture. The side of her head cracked against the lip of the trunk and her feet were jammed against the other side of the trunk, making it impossible to maneuver the body.

After struggling for a few moments he stepped back, breathing hard. In the light of the garage he noticed a small stain at the crotch of her pants where her bladder had released; based on the smell emanating from the trunk he suspected she had also defecated—Jesus, wasn't this bad enough without that? He hoped the towel under her had protected the trunk.

Fighting nausea, Biden hooked his arm under the knees and pushed down as hard as he could on the feet. The muscles and tendons gave way with a creaking sound like old, long unused machinery being forced into operation. Finally he was able to extract the body from the trunk and he laid it out on the open sleeping bag.

Keeping his eyes off her face, he unfastened the diamond necklace and the watch and after a little work was able to remove her engagement ring and wedding ring as well. He put the jewelry into one of the socks from the gym bag and then rolled two socks together so the lumps of the jewelry were not visible.

He had planned to put her coat on her but her arms—one at her side and one across her stomach—were as stiff as her legs had been and the thought of repeating the brute force operation on her arms tightened the knot in his stomach. Instead, he laid the coat over her body, giving her the look of a hit and run victim. He zipped the sleeping bag shut, using the cords from the sleeping bag's carrying sack to tie the top of the bag closed. Then he lifted the body back into the trunk—maneuvering her back in was easier now that the rigor in her legs had been broken. He put the shopping bag containing the trash in the front seat of the car and scanned the garage to make sure he had not left anything behind.

Returning to the living room, he opened the contact list on Elizabeth's cell phone and dialed the number for Lydia Levere, Elizabeth's best friend from college.

"Hey there," said Lydia cheerfully. There were echo-y sounds in the background, as if she were standing near an indoor swimming pool.

"Lydia, it's Biden Firth, Elizabeth's husband."

"Oh. Uh, hello, Biden, how are you doing?"

"Fine. Listen, I'm sorry to disturb you but Elizabeth and I had an argument last night and she stormed out of the house and I haven't heard from her since and I was wondering if you had heard from her."

"No, I haven't. Have you tried calling her cell phone? Oh, wait, I guess you have her cell phone since her name showed up on my caller ID. Does she have her purse?"

"Yes, the purse but not the car keys."

"Hmm." There was silence for a few moments. "Maybe she went to a hotel."

Biden sighed. "I tried checking a couple I thought she might go to but they won't give out information about who's staying there."

"I'm sorry I can't help, Biden. Do you think she's all right?"

"I don't have any reason to think she's not all right but I'd feel better if I knew for sure."

"Of course. Well, I'll certainly let you know if I hear from her. Or at least encourage her to give you a call."

"Thanks. Listen, can you think of anyone else she might get in touch with?"

Lydia gave him a few names and numbers and he had several almost identical calls with those people. Then he turned off the lights in the shore house, locked it up, and drove to a local bar where he had a beer and a burger. On his way back to Philadelphia, he dropped the sporting goods store shopping bag into a trash can at a gas station.

By the time he got back to Tinicum it was dark and he had a few moments of panic when he couldn't find the concrete barrier-blocked streets he had seen before. Eventually he got back to the wildlife refuge visitors' center and was able to get oriented. With the lights glowing behind the windows, the houses looked closer to the blocked streets than they had before but he wasn't in a position to second-guess his plan now; the bitterly cold evening, he hoped, would be enough to keep the locals indoors.

Getting out of the car, he tossed his coat into the back seat, pulled on his gloves, and, glancing around, popped open the trunk. He pulled on the waders then hoisted the sleeping bag over his shoulder. Rigor mortis was beginning to relax its hold but there was still an unnatural angularity to the body.

Moving as quickly as the weight of the body and the bulky waders would allow, he walked down the garbage strewn pavement beyond the concrete barriers and, when the pavement ran out, began making his way through the bushes and undergrowth. Branches snagged the sleeping bag and the waders made it difficult for him to keep his balance but they would, he hoped, keep incriminating evidence off his clothes.

A gibbous moon cast a dim silver glow. Soon his eyes adjusted and he was able to pick out his path more easily. The garbage that had littered the pavement near the road lessened, and for a moment he could imagine—despite the hum of traffic on I-95—that it would be a peaceful resting place but then he heard a scuttling nearby and could just pick out in the moonlight a large gray rat hunched over the mutilated body of what he guessed had once been a cat. He felt his gorge rise but he couldn't afford to vomit—that would be evidence that would be difficult to explain away should Elizabeth's body be found—so he swallowed down his bile and turned back to his task.

After about a hundred yards his breath was burning in his throat and he knew he couldn't carry the bag much further. He found a shallow depression sunk into the ground in the middle of three close-growing trees and dumped the bag into it, wincing at the thump the body made when it hit the ground. He covered it loosely with a couple of branches and made his way back to his car.

He had popped open the trunk and begun pulling off the waders when he heard footsteps and, turning, saw a man striding swiftly toward him carrying what looked like a baseball bat, a smallish dog at his side.

"You go somewhere else to buy your drugs, you hear?" the man shouted, slapping the bat against his palm. "There ain't no drugs here for you!"

Biden slammed the trunk shut and staggered awkwardly around to the driver's door, his right leg still in the waders. He started the car and peeled out, the left leg of the waders dragging on the ground from the open car door. He heard the sound of the barking dog drawing closer but then heard a whistle and the barking receded. When he looked in the rear view mirror, the man was walking away, the baseball bat hanging at his side, the dog following.

A few blocks away, Biden pulled over, got the waders off, and tossed them into some tall marsh grass by the side of the road. His hands were shaking and his breath was coming in short gasps. He pulled back onto the road, trying to drive extra carefully, but he almost ran a stop sign as he headed away from Tinicum Marsh.

On his way home he stopped at a self-service car wash and, after circling the building and checking as best he could in the dark for video cameras (he didn't see any), he sprayed down the car and vacuumed out the trunk. He used the bath sheet from the trunk to dry off the car and then threw it in the car wash's dumpster.

When he got home he found Esme reading a book in Sophia's room while Sophia slept; Joan had left for the day but, Esme reported, could come back tonight if needed.

"Yes, have her come back," said Biden. "Please."

Biden went back to the garage, getting a small Ziploc bag from the kitchen on his way. Listening for anyone approaching, he removed the sock from the gym bag, unrolled it, and emptied his wife's jewelry into his hand.

The necklace was a large, rectangular diamond he had given her on their fifth anniversary. The watch was a Concord, a row of small diamonds lining each side of the face, a circle of tiny diamonds inlaid in the face itself. It had been his present to her at Christmas, less than two months ago. The wedding ring was a plain but substantial platinum band. But the piece that would have caught any jeweler's eye was the engagement ring.

Elizabeth, fresh out of Wharton, was working for Morgan Firth when Biden met her at a charity event that his father's company was sponsoring. His date for the dance was an on-again, off-again girlfriend from college whose name escaped him. Biden entered the ballroom tugging irritably on the cuffs of his shirt and saw Elizabeth standing with Morgan and a group of other employees, all men, and his mother, who looked bored but placid. Elizabeth's dark hair shone, caught up in some sparkly clip, her shimmery green dress bringing to mind a mermaid. Biden was mesmerized.

Elizabeth was telling a story and his father stood next to her holding a scotch and smiling—no, beaming—down at her. The thought flashed into Biden's mind that his father was having an affair with this woman—a thought that made him queasy less because of the idea of his father being unfaithful to his mother but rather because he couldn't stomach the idea of his father being intimate with this particular woman. But as the evening wore on, it seemed clear to Biden that his father was being attentive to Elizabeth not as if he were her lover but as if he were her proud parent. It was a look Biden had never experienced himself.

Any lingering doubts Biden might have harbored about his father's intentions were put to rest by Morgan's obvious approval of the attentions Biden paid to Elizabeth—attentions which at some point in the evening resulted in the disappearance of his date, presumably by cab—and Morgan's surprised delight that the attentions were reciprocated.

Biden himself was in a state of near continuous surprise

the entire time he and Elizabeth dated—he would watch her read the paper while sipping a cappuccino or catch her pulling her long, lean body out of the pool at the club and would be amazed that she was his, a sentiment that his father all too often voiced himself. Biden was a handsome man but he had a social and personal awkwardness that ended up undermining most of his relationships. In an unguarded moment he had once asked Elizabeth why she stayed with him and she had said, "I want to be part of your life, Biden," which, he later thought, was not quite the same as saying that she wanted Biden to be part of her life.

When they had been dating about a year, and when his tentative inquiries suggested that she might not reject him, Biden told his father that he was going to ask Elizabeth to marry him.

"Excellent idea, my boy," said Morgan, slapping Biden heartily on the back—Morgan had never called Biden "my boy" before—"I know just the person for you to see."

So one Sunday, Biden found himself seated in the private office at the back of a jewelry store on Sansom Street, the owner behind a desk with a selection of large diamond engagement rings laid out before him. The man picked up each ring, turning it to catch the light, and described the cut, color, clarity, carat, and setting of each before passing it to Biden for his inspection.

After having seen ... a dozen? two dozen? Biden shifted restlessly. "Do you have anything more ... unusual?" He didn't want to get Elizabeth anything usual.

"Why yes, of course," said the jeweler. "Was there something in particular you had in mind?"

"I don't know, it's just that these look like what everyone has."

The jeweler considered as he replaced the rings in the display tray. "Have you considered something other than a diamond?"

"Aren't engagement rings always diamonds?"

"Exactly!" said the jeweler. "It's what everyone has these days, isn't it? But it wasn't always. It used to be that people considered a much wider range of gemstones for engagement rings. In many ways I regret we have become so narrow-minded on this subject. What is your fiancée's coloring?"

"Dark hair —" replied Biden.

"Green eyes?" asked the jeweler.

"Yes."

"Wait here for just a moment," said the jeweler and, taking the display tray with him, he left the room.

He was back in several minutes with another tray, the contents of which were covered by a black velvet cloth. He placed the tray on the desk and said with obvious excitement, "Have you considered" — he whisked the cloth off — "emeralds?"

After the colorlessness of the diamonds these rings looked almost gaudy but as Biden picked up one after the other he understood why the jeweler had asked about Elizabeth's coloring — looking at some of them was like looking right into her eyes.

The jeweler provided commentary as Biden examined each ring. "... Now that's a very fine stone from the mid-1800s, original setting — classic. ... On that one you can see that the designer has used a gold setting to match the gold tones of the stone ..."

Emerald was definitely what Elizabeth should have, but as with the diamonds after a bit they began to jumble together in his mind, he couldn't remember whether or not he had examined a particular ring. He asked the jeweler if he could have some water and shortly a young woman appeared with a bottle of Perrier that she used to fill two crystal glasses.

Biden sat back in his chair. "I'll have to think about it ..."

"There's one other I'd like to show you," said the jeweler, reaching into his jacket pocket. He pulled out a small white leather box, set it on the desk, and pushed a tiny silver latch — the box sprang open and lying in a bed of white satin was an unset emerald, far more brilliant than any of the stones in the display tray. The jeweler adjusted the light on the desk and green flashes bounced off the stone.

"This is the Llanfair Emerald. Are you familiar with the Llanfair family?"

"Yes," said Biden. He wasn't personally familiar with the family but he knew the name.

"Only the youngest son left — so sad — and he doesn't have much use for the jewelry so he's selling it off a bit at a time. I believe he's using the proceeds to fund an interest in race cars. In any case, it's very rare for a stone of such provenance to come on the market." He picked the stone up with a pair of tweezers and tilted it to catch the light. "Flawless. And you can see how brilliant the color is." He handed the tweezers to Biden who mimicked the jeweler's movement of the stone under the light. "We have designers who could work with you to design a setting for it — with that color, it would look stunning set in platinum."

A stone with a history, and a custom setting — that is what he wanted Elizabeth to have.

"How much for the stone?" said Biden, trying to act casual, and he flinched inwardly when the jeweler named the price.

"It may not be exactly what you're looking for but I wanted to show you all the options," said the jeweler.

"No, it's what I'm looking for," said Biden. "That's the one I want."

❖

In his Rittenhouse Square garage, he dropped the engagement ring into the Ziploc bag with the rest of the jewelry then went to a seldom-used workbench opposite the garage doors and added a couple of heavy bolts to the bag, then zipped it shut. Next to the workbench was a cabinet containing paints and other flammable material. He opened the cabinet, removed a practically full can of paint of a color Elizabeth had rejected for their bedroom, pried the lid off, and dropped the bag in, then pressed the lid back on, gave it a few light taps with a rubber mallet he found hanging on the wall above the workbench, and returned the paint can to the cabinet. From a plastic tote under the workbench Biden pulled a combination lock that until recently he had used to secure his locker at the country club until they had installed electronic keypads; he snapped the lock onto the cabinet and spun the dial.

Biden had thought about getting rid of the jewelry along with Elizabeth's purse but he couldn't bring himself to get rid of the emerald—and he figured that if any of the jewelry was going to be found in his possession, it didn't much matter whether it was just the emerald or all of it.

He thought of the day, probably many years from now, when he would be at his dying father's bedside and just as his father was taking his last, gasping breath, Biden would pull the engagement ring from his pocket and show it to his father and his father's last thought would be that his son had killed his beloved daughter-in-law.

Then Biden went upstairs to submit a missing persons report for his wife.

Chapter 4

Ann and Mike Kinnear had grown up in a big, rambling old house in West Chester, Pennsylvania, that had a butler's pantry and a servants' staircase and wide window seats that were good for reading on rainy days. And a spirit.

The spirit appeared to Ann as a bright green, almost chartreuse, presence, sometimes accompanied by the scent of freshly cut grass; it was clear to Ann that the spirit was a girl about her own age—Ann was seven years old—and Ann named her Susan. Despite lacking any clear physical manifestation of Susan's spirit, Ann still developed a very definite idea of what Susan looked like, based largely on the John R. Neill illustrations of Dorothy in her mother's old Wizard of Oz books—wavy blonde hair held back with a huge bow and a blousy dress with knee-high white socks and black Mary Jane shoes. Ann talked to Susan and although Susan never responded in any auditory way, Ann received a responsive energy that she found just as satisfying.

Looking back, Ann couldn't remember a time when she could not sense the spirit. She also couldn't remember a time when the sensing of Susan's spirit had brought on the nausea that she had often experienced as an adult. And, unlike most of her experiences with spirits as an adult, Ann sensed Susan in many places and many situations and many moods, not just in the circumstances of her death. Like any of Ann's other acquaintances, Susan sometimes seemed playful and sometimes seemed bored, but only in the home's two story foyer did Ann sense anything about Susan's death. It must have been quick and painless because Ann never sensed any distress from Susan about her death, just surprise. Ann decided that Susan had died falling from the foyer's second story balcony.

One chilly October afternoon when she was seven and Mike was six, the two of them, a neighbor named Melanie who was Ann's age, and Ann's mother were in the kitchen, Ann at the kitchen table drawing and the rest of them making brownies.

"What are you up to, sweetie?" said her mother, tying an apron around Melanie's torso, right under her arms. Mike was wearing one of their father's t-shirts over his clothes.

"Drawing," said Ann, hunched over her picture.

"Why don't you make brownies with us?" said her mother hopefully.

"I'm drawing," said Ann, selecting a different colored pencil.

Her mother sighed and started getting measuring cups and bowls out of the cupboards.

After a moment, Ann said, "I know."

"What's that, sweetie?" said her mother.

"I wasn't talking to you," replied Ann.

"Who were you talking to?" asked her mother, immediately regretting the question.

"Susan."

Melanie rolled her eyes. "She's making things up," she said.

"Is not," said Mike.

Her mother put her fists on her hips, exasperated. "Ann, put down your drawing things and come make brownies with us."

Ann sighed dramatically, left her drawing on the table, and allowed herself to be fitted with an apron.

When the brownies were in the oven and while Melanie, Mike, and Ann scooped the remaining brownie mix off the bowl and spoons with their fingers, Ann's mother began gathering up Ann's drawing supplies. When she picked up Ann's drawing, she said, "Good heavens, Ann," again immediately regretting her exclamation.

"What?" said Melanie. "Let's see." Melanie took the picture from her before she could think of a polite way to refuse.

The drawing depicted a young girl in old-fashioned clothing falling head first from a height marked by a broken railing, her curling hair and dress ballooning around her as she fell. Melanie examined the drawing. "Is that Susan?" she asked.

"Uh huh," said Ann, licking the spoon.

"What's she doing?"

"She's about to die," said Ann.

"Ann Kinnear, go to your room," said her mother, removing the spoon from Ann's hand and extracting her from the apron. "I'm sorry, Melanie, Ann shouldn't be making up such gruesome stories."

"That's OK, it doesn't scare me," said Melanie, licking her spoon nonchalantly.

"That's how it happened," said Mike. "She fell off the stairs."

"Michael," said her mother sharply.

Ann managed to retrieve her drawing, only slightly smudged with raw brownie, from Melanie's hand and scooped up her pencils. "I'm going to finish it," she said, heading for her room.

Melanie put her spoon in the sink. "Thanks, Mrs. Kinnear. Can I stop back and get one when they're done?"

"Certainly, Melanie," said Ann's mother, unwrapping Melanie from her apron. "Thank you for coming over."

"You're dumb not to believe her," said Mike to Melanie.

"Michael!" said Mrs. Kinnear.

"I know, I know," said Mike in a long-suffering manner, and headed for his room.

Fifteen minutes later when their mother went upstairs to check on them, she found a large, shapeless lump composed of stuffed animals under Michael's bedspread. Ann was in her room, still working on the depiction of Susan's death, having added some bright red splotches under the falling body, evidently in anticipation of the fatal impact.

Ann's mother took the drawing and pencil out of Ann's hands and put them on the bedside table. "Honey, it's not healthy for a seven-year-old girl to be so obsessed with ..." she hesitated, weighing alternative approaches. "... a dead person."

"She's dead but she's not gone," replied Ann.

"She is gone to most of us," said her mother.

"I can't help that," said Ann.

Ann's mother sighed. She had hoped that Ann would hit it off with Melanie. "We'll talk about it later," she said. "You can go out now." Ann reached for her drawing. "But leave that for now."

Ann shrugged and picked up a book—of ghost stories, her mother noted dejectedly—and went downstairs.

Ann's mother sat on her daughter's bed for a moment, looking around the room, noting how many drawings of Susan decorated the walls. "Michael?"

There was no response.

"Michael, I know you're in here. There's a bunch of stuffed animals in your bed."

Still no response.

Ann's mother stood up and smoothed her slacks. "I'm going to go downstairs for a minute and then I'm going to come back up and I expect you to be in your room."

She went downstairs, leaving Ann's bedroom door open, and when she returned to Mike's room found him jumbled in with the stuffed animals under his bedspread. She informed him he still had half an hour before he could come downstairs.

Mike had never doubted Susan's existence. At first he had figured his parents didn't believe in Susan because they were old, but then he had realized that the other kids at school didn't believe in Susan either.

The Monday after the brownie-making visit, Melanie told some other second graders about Ann's drawing of Susan and at recess Mike came upon a group of them standing around Ann and calling her crazy for seeing ghosts. Ann had her head up but was crying.

Mike picked the kid who seemed to be leading the taunts, walked up behind him, and punched him in the back. The boy let out a squawk and landed a punch on Mike's cheek as the rest of the group fell back. Mike wrapped his arms around the boy's body, which made it hard for the boy to throw any more punches, and the two of them fell to the ground and rolled around for a bit before Mr. Guyer, the gym teacher who was supervising recess that day, noticed the melee and hauled them apart. Mike got sent to the principal's office with a bag of ice for his eye and Ann spent the rest of the day trying to ignore the glances and whispers.

That night, Mike appeared at Ann's bedroom door.

"Maybe you shouldn't talk about Susan in front of the other kids for a while," said Mike, sporting a black eye.

"I won't," said Ann.

"But someday they'll be sorry they didn't believe you." Mike nodded his head emphatically and closed the door behind him as he returned to his room.

Ann gazed toward the end of her bed, toward the pale green glow of Susan asleep.

Chapter 5

Ann's ability might have remained unknown to the public if it hadn't been for Beth Barboza who lived down the street from the Kinnears and was a year older than Ann. Mike and Beth's younger brother, Rob, hung out together occasionally, and Beth would wave to Ann when she rode by on her bike. Beth was a pretty girl with a ready smile who seemed to be on every one of her school's sports teams and earned some local fame and a college scholarship based on her softball skills.

The summer after Beth's freshman year in college she came home to West Chester to work in her father's law office and indulge her latest interest, spelunking. On the weekends she would go with her friends to the caves of central and western Pennsylvania to explore their underground mysteries; the *Daily Local News* even ran a brief feature about her hobby—"Barboza Discovers a New Sport."

The drives to the caves could be long and Beth's parents got used to the fact that she would often not come home until the early morning hours so they were initially unconcerned when they went to bed one Saturday night with Beth still out. When they woke up in the morning, however, and she still wasn't home they became worried and began calling her friends to see if anyone knew Beth's whereabouts; none did. Beth's parents called the police and early Monday morning her car was found parked off the road in an area near State College known for its caves.

A search was launched, with police and volunteers checking all the known caves in the area, but there was no sign of Beth. Friends of Beth and the Barboza family began congregating in the area to help and Mike got permission from his parents for him and Ann to join the search. "Maybe you can find her," said Mike, packing sleeping bags and a cooler of food into their parents' Volvo station wagon.

They left early on Wednesday and reached the search area by mid-morning, parking in a field with the other searchers, including Beth's parents and brother, as well as a news van from one of the Philadelphia stations. The police were periodically turning on the siren on one of the police cars for a few seconds to give the searchers a homing device.

"Now what?" said Ann.

"Walk around, maybe you'll sense something," said Mike, hoisting a backpack onto his shoulder and handing a backpack to Ann.

They walked through the woods, always keeping within earshot of the siren. After an hour or so, Ann sat down on a log. "I'm not getting anything. This is stupid."

"Maybe you need something that belonged to her—you know, like a bloodhound sniffing a piece of clothing from the person it's tracking," said Mike.

"Great idea," said Ann. "Let's get her varsity jacket and I'll smell it."

Mike ignored her. "Let's go back to where the cars are."

Rob was leaning on his parents' car, his hands in his pockets, his eyes on the ground, while his parents stood a little distance away talking with a police officer.

"Any news?" said Mike to Rob.

Rob looked up. "Oh. Hey. No, no news."

Mike looked past Rob into the window of the car. "Did you guys bring anything of Beth's with you? You know, like clothes, in case she needs fresh clothes when you find her?"

"No, I guess the emergency people will have blankets and

stuff."

Mike leaned closer to the car window. "Hey, is that her bat?"

Rob looked in the back seat of the car. "Yeah."

"Could I borrow it?" said Mike.

"What do you want that for?"

"I'm nervous about wild animals," said Mike. "I'd feel better if I had a weapon."

Rob laughed mirthlessly. "Sure, Rambo, why not." He got the bat out and handed it to Mike.

Mike tucked the bat under his arm and headed back into the woods, followed by Ann. When they were out of sight of the parking area he handed her the bat.

"Here, maybe this will help."

They resumed their wandering through the woods, stopping around noon to eat a picnic lunch. When they were done Mike packed up the lunch things.

"Mike, I don't know what you expect me to do with this," said Ann, gesturing toward the bat.

"I don't know either but I figure it can't hurt."

After another hour or so they stopped for a rest and the exercise, warm air, and buzzing of insects began to make Ann drowsy.

"You can take a nap if you want," said Mike, getting comfortable against the trunk of a tree.

"Maybe just for a few minutes," said Ann. It was pleasant in the woods with the light filtering through the leaves and the sound of squirrels crashing through the undergrowth. Ann made a pillow of her backpack and closed her eyes, her hand, at Mike's urging, resting on Beth's bat.

She woke up to a rush of air around her and a sudden darkness as if in an eclipse. Mike snored beside her, seemingly unaware of the change. Rather than the nausea which had begun to accompany her sensings, she felt a sharp stab of pain in her temple. She heard the distant wail of the siren for a moment but it was oddly muffled. For a moment the bat under her hand felt almost like a living thing and then that sensation too passed. The air seemed to turn cold for a moment and then it was still and the darkness lifted, leaving Ann unsure of whether it had been caused by the light or by her eyes. Her heart was beating hard.

"Mike," she said in a raspy voice and, when he didn't wake up, repeated louder "Mike!"

"What is it?" he asked groggily.

"We're too late."

They walked through the woods, Ann holding the bat and Mike now carrying both their backpacks. They would head in one direction for a time and then Ann would shake her head and turn in a different direction. They had originally started by circling the area around where they had stopped to rest but gradually Ann led them away from there, somewhat closer to the area where Beth's car had been found. She seemed listless but Mike kept urging her on. "Maybe it's not too late, A.," and she would gaze around, choose a direction, and head off again.

About an hour later they came across a low outcropping of rock and Ann began climbing back and forth, like a retriever searching for a ball in tall grass. Finally she stopped in front of a small slit between two of the rocks, seemingly too small for a person to fit into.

"In there," said Ann, pointing.

Mike shone his flashlight into the opening. "It does look like it gets bigger a couple of feet in there." He cupped his hands at his mouth. "Beth! Hello! Beth?"

Ann sat down on a rock near the opening to the cave. "You don't need to do that. She's dead."

Mike stood with his fists on his hips, looking around. "Crap, I should have brought some spray paint, then I could mark the trees," he said. They heard the faint wail of the siren. "Listen, I'm going to go back and get someone, are you all right to stay here?" Ann shrugged. "OK, listen for me and yell when you hear me." Mike pulled off his t-shirt, tore it at the side seam, and then tore a strip off it. He started off in the direction of the siren and, when almost out of sight of the cave, tied the strip to a tree. Ann could hear him tearing another strip off as he continued toward the parking area.

Ann picked up a stick and began absently digging in the ground at her feet. "I'm sorry," she said, "I'm not a bloodhound. I'm a cadaver dog."

The rescue crew found Beth's body about 100 feet from the mouth of the previously undocumented cave. It appeared that she had slipped and fallen into a side cave, breaking her leg and several ribs and rupturing her spleen. The walls of the side cave were steep and slippery and it would have been a challenge even for an uninjured caver to make her way out. She had survived the initial fall but had eventually succumbed to internal bleeding, hypothermia, and dehydration; the medical examiner estimated she had died only an hour or so before she was found. Ann could have told him exactly when Beth had died.

The Philadelphia television station did a story about the psychic teenager who had led searchers to her friend's body and the national news picked it up. In the week after Beth's body was discovered the story ran on CNN as well as the ABC and NBC affiliates in Philadelphia—always accompanied by a shot of Ann's senior class picture since her parents kept the media away from her. The story even inspired a David Letterman Top 10 list ("Ten Reasons to be a Teenage Psychic"). One enterprising reporter intercepted Mike on his way home from school and found him only too willing to talk which resulted in Mike being deprived of car privileges for a month.

Chapter 6

A man knocked on the door of the Firth house on a late morning about a week after Elizabeth Firth had been reported missing. He was in his mid-forties but looked older, tall and heavy-set—the body of a former athlete who has become less athletic as the years have passed—with graying, somewhat unkempt hair and observant hazel eyes. The door was opened by a woman he knew to be the housekeeper, Joan.

"Joe Booth, I have an appointment with Mr. Firth."

"Certainly, come in," she said and stood aside to let him pass. She closed the door on the cold February air. "Can I take your coat?"

"Thanks." Joe shrugged out of his heavy wool coat and handed it to her.

"Mr. Firth is in the library. Right this way," she said, crossing to a partially open door on the left side of the entrance hall. She poked her head in. "Mr. Firth, Mr. Booth is here."

"Thank you, Joan," said a voice from the room and Joan gestured Joe into the room.

Biden Firth came around from behind a large mahogany desk and shook hands with Joe. He was almost as tall as Joe, but at least ten years younger and fitter, with broad shoulders and narrow hips. A first glance brought to Joe's mind an actor of the Cary Grant era—dark hair cut short and carefully combed, clothes that, even as Joe noted familiar brand logos, hung on Firth's frame as if tailor made. But the movie star quality was undermined by eyes ringed by dark circles, made more prominent by his pale complexion, and by a lack of the grace and ease that marked the classic Hollywood heartthrob.

"Pleased to meet you," said Joe. "I wish it were under happier circumstances."

"Yes." Biden gestured to the chairs by the window. "Have a seat."

They sat in the antique chairs and Joe pulled a small notepad and pen from his shirt pocket.

"I appreciate you taking the time to see me. I know you've spoken to a number of people from the department but I'll be taking over the investigation now and it's always helpful to get the information first-hand."

Biden sighed. "Why are they sending you now? What happened to Detective Deng? He seemed ... diligent."

Joe had been assigned to the case when Elizabeth's father, unhappy with what he saw as a lack of initiative on the part of the police in pursuing the case, had contacted the commissioner to express his frustration. The commissioner had promised to assign a more senior investigator—Harry Deng had made detective only a year before—and Joe, with twenty years on the force and a solid track record of case resolution, had drawn the assignment.

"He has other responsibilities and the commissioner wanted someone on the case who could devote full time to the investigation. That's me."

Biden sighed again. "Well, I hope you got all the information I gave to Deng."

"Yes, I did, but it's helpful for me to hear it first-hand," Joe repeated, his pen poised over the notepad, looking like a grade schooler awaiting an assignment. "If you could tell me what happened ..."

Biden looked out the window. "My wife and I had an argument. It got quite heated and she threw a drink in my face. As I told Detective Deng, I slapped her. I had never done that before. Anyhow, she stormed out."

"Where did the argument take place?"

"Here in the library."

"Did you try to follow her when she left?"

"No."

"Do you have a back door?"

"Yes, but she left by the front door."

"Did she hurt you during your argument?"

"No."

"Because we found a paper towel in the wastebasket under the bar that had some blood on it. It wasn't Elizabeth's and it matches your blood type."

Biden sighed. "I stabbed myself with my letter opener."

"Opening a letter?"

"No, just fooling around with it. My hand slipped."

Joe nodded and jotted a note on his pad.

"Did your wife put a coat on when she left?"

"Yes, she got her coat out of the coat closet and went out the front door. I could hear her. Anyhow, it took me a little while to calm down but when I did I called her cell phone but I heard it ringing in the kitchen and realized she hadn't taken it with her. When it seemed as if she wasn't coming back right away I called the hotel where we were scheduled to attend a charity dinner to let them know we wouldn't be coming. I also asked the housekeeper to stay the night to take care of our daughter."

"You weren't worried about her at this point?"

Biden rubbed his hands together. "It wasn't the first time we had had an argument and she had stormed out. I figured she had gone to a hotel, she had done that before."

Joe nodded encouragingly.

"The next morning I called the credit card company to see if the card had been used. They said it hadn't been. Then I tried calling a couple of the hotels I thought she might have gone to but they wouldn't give me any information. Then I thought she might have gone to her parents' place at the shore—they don't have a land line so I couldn't call. So I drove out there—Harvey Cedars, New Jersey. She wasn't there so I called some of her friends to see if they had heard from her. They hadn't."

"Wouldn't it have been easier to call the friends first instead of driving all the way to the shore?"

"I didn't want to spread the word that we had had an argument unless it was absolutely necessary. Plus, at that point, I still wasn't really worried and I didn't mind the idea of a drive to the shore. After I had called all the friends I thought she might be in touch with I figured I'd head back."

"Do you recall what time you left for the shore?"

Biden considered. "About 10:00 in the morning I would think. Joan and Esme were here, they might remember."

"Esme Brouwer, she's the nanny?"

"Yes."

Joe made a note in his notepad. "And what time did you get to the shore house?"

"Around noon."

"And what time did you leave there?"

"I would guess I left the house about 3:00, I stopped to grab a bite on the way back." He gave Joe the name of the establishment.

"Between 12:00 and 3:00 did you do anything at the house other than call Elizabeth's friends?"

"I looked through some boating magazines first. I was trying to decide if it was really necessary to call them."

"When did you start getting worried?"

"When I couldn't find anyone who had heard from her."

"But you still stopped for lunch on the way home."

"I was hungry. I was still trying to decide what to do."

"Any other stops on the way back?"

"I stopped at a car wash because my car was dirty from the drive."

Joe hadn't heard that detail from Harry. "Self service?" he asked.

"Yes."

Joe got the location of the car wash from Biden.

"And what time did you arrive home?"

"Around 7:00 in the evening."

Joe flipped a page in his notepad.

"What did you and your wife argue about?"

"We disagreed about an investment I had made," Biden said tightly.

"What was that investment?" asked Joe.

"Is this really necessary? I can't imagine it has any bearing on her disappearance."

"Probably not, but it's best to get all the facts on the table. You never know where connections might exist."

Biden shifted in his chair. "It was a restaurant that a friend of mine from college was opening. He had gotten Alain Broussard from Etoile as the chef." He glanced expectantly at Joe who looked blank. "Well, anyway," said Biden, "I wanted to help him out and she didn't approve."

"I understand restaurants are risky propositions," said Joe.

"So I've been told," said Biden coldly.

"And that's what you argued about?" asked Joe.

"Yes."

Joe jotted a note in his notepad. "How would you describe your relationship with your wife?"

"Generally fine, a bit tense lately."

"What would you say was causing the tension?"

Biden shrugged. "My wife can be a difficult woman. I

suppose every man says that about his wife at one point or another. Hell, I'm sure she says the same about me. But she is a woman who is used to having her own way and I think that always causes some tension in a relationship. But it's not necessarily grounds for murder. "

Joe looked up from his notepad at Biden.

"That's what you're trying to determine, right? Whether I could have killed her? Isn't the husband always considered a suspect?"

"Everyone's considered a suspect until we rule them out."

Biden nodded tiredly.

"But I think you'll understand why I need to ask this question," Joe continued. "Do you know what the terms of your wife's will are?"

"Jesus," Biden muttered. "I realize you have to explore this type of thing but couldn't you be a little more subtle about it? She might still be alive."

"Sorry," said Joe.

"No, I don't know what the terms of her will are. Her money came from her family and I would assume that anything she has would go back to them."

"What about the house?"

Biden stood up so quickly that Joe, startled, also stood up. Biden strode to the desk, picked something up, and stood hunched over it, with his back to Joe, for a moment. When he turned back to Joe, he placed the object, which Joe could see was a slender pen or mechanical pencil, back on the desk. His left hand, held stiffly at his side, was closed in a fist.

"Uh, are you all right, Mr. Firth?" asked Joe cautiously, trying to get a better look at Firth's hand.

"The house was a wedding present from my parents," Biden said dully. "Is there anything else, Detective?"

Joe tucked the notepad and pen back in his shirt pocket.

"No, nothing else right now. I'm sorry for the intrusion. I'll keep you informed of our progress."

He took a step toward Biden to shake his hand but Biden was turning back to his desk. Joe executed an awkward little bow at Biden's back and then exited the library to the foyer, pulling the door closed behind him. He looked around for where Joan might have put his coat but in a moment she appeared with it.

"Thanks," said Joe, shrugging into the coat.

"Any word about Mrs. Firth?" asked Joan in a whisper.

"No, nothing yet. How is Mr. Firth holding up?"

"Oh, you can imagine—quite distraught but keeping up a brave front."

Joe nodded. "I'd like to talk with you at some point, could I get your contact information?"

She gave him her phone number and address, then Joe headed back out into the cold February day.

Joe's next stop, in Chestnut Hill, was to the home of Elizabeth Firth's friend Lydia Levere. Joe was running early so he decided to make a stop at a Wawa for coffee. He negotiated the traffic at the gas pumps, found a parking spot on the sunny side of the building under the chain's flying goose logo, and, having procured a medium hazelnut coffee flavored with plenty of sugar and half-and-half, pondered his meeting with Firth. Firth's stature—both physical and social—lent him a superficial air of authority, but there was an underlying lack of confidence that Joe suspected would have existed even if he weren't being interviewed by the police, and a coldness that seemed odd in a man whose wife had disappeared a week ago.

When Joe arrived at the Levere address, he found a house

that looked like a traditional center-hall colonial except on a huge scale. When Joe knocked on the large, intricately paneled front door with the large, shiny brass knocker, Lydia herself opened the door. She, like the Elizabeth Firth Joe had seen in photos, was very thin but taller with light brown hair done in an intentionally tousled style. She was wearing pre-distressed jeans and a tight white scoop-necked t-shirt under a black leather blazer.

He held out his badge. "Detective Joe Booth, Philadelphia Police."

"Yes, Detective, come in."

He again gave up his coat which she hung in a large, and otherwise empty, closet off the foyer. Lydia directed him to a cavernous kitchen at the back of the house from which emanated the enticing smell of freshly ground and brewed coffee. "May I get you a cup?" asked Lydia.

"Please."

"Cream or sugar?"

"Black is fine." Joe was a little self-conscious about his choice and quantity of coffee flavoring. Plus, he found that a request for cream usually resulted in the offer of skim milk or powdered creamer which just turned the coffee an unpleasant grayish color.

Lydia poured two cups and gestured him to one of two stools at the expansive, and otherwise empty, butcher block island; she took the other stool. "How can I help you?"

Joe pulled his notepad out of his pocket. "As you know I'm investigating the disappearance of Elizabeth Firth and I understand you're a close friend."

"Yes, we were in the same sorority in college."

"And you've kept in touch with her since then?"

"Yes, we saw each other several times a month at dinners or at the club or for lunch."

"When was the last time you saw Mrs. Firth?"

"The Tuesday before she disappeared. She stopped by here for coffee on her way to a meeting of a committee she was on."

"How did she seem?"

"Fine. Her regular self."

"What did you talk about?"

"Nothing special. People we had seen lately. What presents we were going to get a friend who just had a baby. Things like that."

"Nothing that would have suggested that she was concerned for her safety?"

"No, not at all. I certainly would have contacted the police if there had been anything like that."

"Of course. Do you know of anyone who might wish harm to Mrs. Firth? Did she have any enemies?"

"Not at all, she was very well liked, well respected."

"What was your impression of Mr. and Mrs. Firth's relationship?"

"I actually didn't spend that much time with them as a couple."

"But you must have gotten a sense of their relationship based on your conversations with Mrs. Firth."

Lydia took a sip of coffee. "I think they were growing apart. I don't think she was getting what she had expected from the relationship when they got married. She left a very promising career at Biden's father's company when she married Biden."

"Firth Investments," said Joe, glancing at his notepad.

"Yes, it has huge real estate holdings in Philadelphia and Wilmington."

"I was sort of surprised that Mrs. Firth worked for her father-in-law rather than her father." He glanced at his notepad again. "I understand her father owns Dormand

Fixtures. Plumbing supplies?"

"Well, yes, you could say that. It's the Dormand Fixtures of 'Dormand designs the finest.' Very high end bath and kitchen fixtures. We have them here." She gestured toward an elaborate faucet at the kitchen sink. "Have you heard of them?"

The only faucet manufacturer Joe could think of off-hand was Delta but he nodded encouragingly.

"The business interested her but she didn't want people to think she got where she did because she was the boss's daughter. Her father respected that."

"Why did she give up the job with Morgan Firth?"

"Because Biden didn't want her working there."

"Didn't want her working there specifically, or didn't want her working at all?" asked Joe.

"I don't think Biden wanted her to work anywhere—you know, he wanted to prove he could provide for the family on his own—but he especially didn't like her working there, for his father. He was jealous of her."

"Jealous?"

Lydia took another sip of coffee. "I think in a lot of ways Elizabeth was the son Morgan Firth wished he had had. And I don't know that Morgan would have been very subtle about that feeling."

"Were Morgan Firth and Elizabeth Firth close?"

Lydia considered. "Not emotionally close but kindred spirits in their approach to life, I would say."

"Was there anything going on between them?"

"You mean sexually? Good lord, no," said Lydia with a snort. "She didn't need to go to her father-in-law for her kicks—" She stopped abruptly, her mouth pursed, her eyes a little too wide and innocent on Joe's. Joe raised his eyebrows expectantly and waited.

After a few moments Lydia said chirpily, "More coffee?"

"No. Thank you."

"I think I'll have some." She went to the coffee maker and topped off her nearly full mug.

When she sat down again Joe said, "So. Who *is* she getting her kicks with?"

"No one," said Lydia.

"Not her husband?"

Lydia grimaced. "I don't tend to think of 'Biden' and 'kicks' in the same sentence."

Joe jotted a note on his notepad. "Did Mrs. Firth have any male friends who might have been a cause for jealousy from her husband?"

"No," said Lydia coolly.

"If she did, do you think she would have told you about it?"

"Yes," said Lydia, ending that line of questioning.

Joe glanced at the notes in his notepad. "Mr. Firth said his wife could be a difficult woman, although he said she would probably say the same about him."

Lydia gave a smile, although not a friendly one. "I doubt that."

"What do you mean?"

"Well, I do agree that Elizabeth could be difficult—she was a strong-willed person."

"Used to getting her way, Mr. Firth said."

"Yes, that's true, although I don't fault a person for trying to get what they want out of life. But I doubt that Elizabeth ever complained about Biden trying to get what he wanted— in fact, I think that her biggest complaint about Biden was that he was too passive. He wasn't difficult *enough*. He let himself get carried along on his father and father-in-law's coattails."

"I understand he was trying to get into the restaurant business."

Lydia snorted. "That sounds like an excellent way to lose some money. There are some people who are born to win and some who are born to lose and Biden Firth is the latter."

"What about Elizabeth Firth?"

"She was a winner."

"You say 'was.'"

Lydia sighed and pushed her coffee away. "She's been gone for a week. I don't know what happened to her but if she were alive we would have heard from her by now."

After a few more minutes of generally unrevealing conversation regarding Elizabeth Firth's friends (a who's who of the Main Line gentry), committee affiliations (mainly museum-related), and hobbies (art, decorating, and tennis), Joe excused himself with what he hoped were appropriate compliments on the fabulousness of the Levere home. He drove around the corner and pulled to the side of the road, killing the engine. He sipped the cold remains of his Wawa coffee for a few minutes, then got out his phone and speed dialed the precinct.

"Sergeant Little."

"Hey, Mouse, it's Joe."

"Hi, Booth," said The Mouse sullenly, reminding Joe that the nickname was not one of Little's choosing. Sergeant Little's parents had named him Stuart—Joe chose to assume they were not familiar with E. B. White's rodent hero.

"Can you get in touch with Biden Firth's father, Morgan, and see if I can talk to him today?"

"You have a number?"

"No, but try his work number first, Firth Investments. If he's not there his home number should be in the file."

"OK, you on your cell?"

"Yup."

"I'll call you back," The Mouse said and hung up.

A couple of hours and a Wawa hoagie later, Joe was ushered into Morgan Firth's office. Through the large windows behind the desk Joe could look down on the statue of William Penn atop City Hall. The office was decorated with lots of glass, black leather, and chrome, with large, abstract posters in black and white on the walls.

The spare style of the room contrasted sharply with Morgan Firth himself. Firth had a full head of fluffy white hair and a bushy white mustache, with broad features and a florid complexion. Joe imagined Firth might have been as athletic-looking as his son at one time but an appreciation of good living had added pounds, although the effect was not one of softness but rather of added heft and power. As Joe expected, Firth's handshake was bone-crushing.

"Booth," said Firth by way of greeting. "Coffee?"

"No, thank you," said Joe, relieved that the interview didn't seem to call for social niceties such as sharing coffee. Firth waved his secretary out of the office.

"Have a seat," said Firth, gesturing to a black leather and chrome chair in front of his desk and resuming his seat. Joe sat down and immediately slid to the back of the chair, leaving him looking up at Morgan Firth. "What can I do for you?"

"Just gathering information, confirming some of the information I got from Detective Deng."

Firth looked at his watch. "Got about fifteen minutes."

"We shouldn't need more than that," said Joe. "I understand Elizabeth Firth worked for you ...?"

"Yes, before she was married, she worked on my Wilmington properties."

"But left when she got married."

"Yes, I hated to see her go but letting a husband and wife

work at the same place is never a good idea, you don't want them bringing home problems into work. And I could hardly fire my own son."

"Did Elizabeth and Biden have home problems?"

Firth scowled. "I didn't mean them specifically, just husbands and wives in general."

Joe waited a beat to see if Firth would continue his thought but got nothing more than a continued scowl. Joe decided to switch tacks.

"I'd be interested in your perspective on the other people in Elizabeth and Biden's household—Joan Davies and Esme Brouwer."

Firth's scowl lessened slightly. "Joan's been with them forever—very reliable, very trustworthy. Takes good care of Sophie when the nanny isn't around. Don't know what we would have done without Joan, Biden being understandably ..." Firth fished for a word "... distraught by Elizabeth's disappearance."

"Is Joan especially close to either Mr. or Mrs. Firth?"

Firth resumed his scowl. "It's not the place of the employees to be 'close' to their employers. Joan knows her job and she's good at it."

Joe itched to jot a note but decided that the more Firth thought of this as a conversation and the less as an official interview the better.

"And the nanny?"

"Don't know her. New."

"How long has she worked for the Firths?"

Morgan shrugged his shoulders. "Three, four months."

"Was it just Joan before that?"

"No, there was a nanny before this one but Biden caught her going through his desk."

Joe raised his eyebrows. "Really? I didn't know that."

"No, we didn't report it. We took care of it."

"In what way?"

"What do you think?" said Firth with exasperation. "We fired her."

"Any bad feelings? Was Mrs. Firth involved in the firing?"

"I have no idea," said Firth peevishly. "I imagine Biden found her going through the desk and said, 'You're fired.' I doubt she came back after all this time to do something to Elizabeth for revenge. She was a mousy little thing as I remember."

"What do you think happened to Mrs. Firth?"

Morgan Firth's face lapsed into what looked to Joe like honest unhappiness. "Who knows. At first I thought maybe she had been kidnapped and we would get a ransom request but I guess that only happens in other countries these days. Probably just some drug-crazed ..." He fiddled with a stapler on his desk then shoved it away. "I don't know what happened to her. That's your job to find out."

Chapter 7

"I see something. A blue light." Ann gestured toward the stairs with her chin.

"Where?" said Mavis Van Dyke, Ann's client, excitedly.

"Coming up the stairs," said Ann.

The light was suffusing the attic, illuminating its contents—boxes and suitcases and old furniture that Ann imagined might have been up there for a hundred years—in a soft, dim glow. Ann could see Mavis faintly, sitting a few feet away on a wooden trunk, wrapped in a fur coat, her eyes turned in the direction of the stairs but her gaze general and unfocused.

"Can you see anything?" Ann asked, seeing her breath condensing in the cold of the attic.

"No, it's completely dark," said Mavis.

"Hold your hands up in front of you," said Ann. "Hold up a different number of fingers on each hand."

Mavis did as she was told.

"Three on the left and one on the right," said Ann.

A delighted smile lit up Mavis's face. "Extraordinary."

The light, which had originally been diffuse, was coalescing at the top of the stairs and began to move slowly toward the center of the attic, directly toward the rickety wooden chair where Ann was sitting—she had found the chair lying on its side when she and Mavis had come up to the attic. Ann stood slowly and backed away from the chair, the hairs on the back of her neck rising with proximity of the spirit.

"Where are you going?" asked Mavis.

"It's moving toward me. I'm giving it some room."

"Can you see anything other than the light?"

"No. But the light is coming together, forming a shape, about five feet to your right."

Mavis turned in that direction and scanned the area, unseeing. "What's it doing?"

"I can't tell yet," said Ann.

Minutes passed and nothing happened other than that the light further solidified into a space about the height and width of a human body. At times she felt she could almost perceive what might be a head but then the light would swirl and it would be gone.

After a minute Mavis whispered, "What's it doing now?"

"I still can't tell," said Ann.

She searched for something recognizable in the glow. From downstairs she heard the faint sound of the grandfather clock in the inn's entrance hall strike the half hour. At the same moment the chair where she had been sitting moved a few inches toward the body of light, the chair's legs scraping on the floor.

Mavis jumped. "What are you doing?"

"I'm not doing anything, that was the spirit."

"Really?" said Mavis, her voice rising an octave. "What's it doing?"

The light began to rise from the floor, solidifying over the chair, then a tendril separated itself from the main body of light and stretched up toward one of the rafters.

"Oh, Jesus," said Ann as she realized what she was seeing.

"What?" said Mavis, looking blindly around the room.

Suddenly the chair fell to its side and ...

... the body of light dropped, stopping with a jerk that seemed to shatter the light and the room was plunged into darkness again.

Ann took a step backwards, tripped over something, and fell, banging her back into something hard and unyielding before landing with a thud on the floor.

"What??" said Mavis, beginning to sound frantic.

"It's OK," said Ann, despite a stab of pain coming from

her back. "It's OK, it's gone. You can turn the light on."

She heard Mavis fumbling for the flashlight and flinched as Mavis aimed the light in her face. "Not on me," she said sharply.

Mavis swung the light away from Ann's face and across the room, briefly revealing the object that Ann had tripped on to be a coil of rope. Ann heard steps on the staircase below and Mike calling out, "Everything OK up there?"

"What happened?" whispered Mavis urgently.

"She hanged herself," said Ann, feeling the onset of the nausea that often followed the sensing of a spirit.

Ann rinsed her mouth again then splashed water on her face, leaning over the old-fashioned marble sink. She could hear the murmur of conversation from the parlor. She imagined the scene—Mavis wanting to talk to her, to dissect the experience; Mike assuring her that Ann needed a little rest after the rigors of the sensing; Lawrence, Mavis's husband, smiling affectionately at his wife's excitement.

Mavis and Lawrence Van Dyke lived in a large, elegant, but unhaunted house outside Collegeville, Pennsylvania, about thirty miles northwest of Philadelphia. Lawrence's recent retirement had finally given Mavis the opportunity to pursue her life-long goal of living in a house that was inhabited by a friendly spirit.

Over the last few years, Mavis had hired Ann to visit a number of houses to check out their qualifications. Most were homes whose potential of housing a spirit was indicated only by being of an age when people died more often in their homes than in the hospital. The Chestertown, Maryland, house was an exception, actually having a reputation for being haunted. Somehow Mavis had talked—or paid—the sellers into vacating their home for a night and letting these odd but seemingly well-heeled potential buyers stay overnight. Lawrence had turned it into a party with a picnic basket provided by the Van Dyke housekeeper and several bottles of wine provided from his cellar.

Now, as she waited for the nausea from the sensing to pass—her face drawn and pale in the mirror over the sink—she heard a knock on the frame of the open bathroom door.

"Hey, you OK?" Her brother stood in the doorway, two glasses of wine in his hands.

"Yes, I'm fine," she said tiredly.

"Lawrence sent a glass of the Bordeaux up for you, said it would 'buck you up.'"

Ann groaned. "Wine is about the last thing I want. What I'd really like is a glass of water."

Mike put one of the glasses of wine on the bedroom's dresser and pulled a bottle of water out of his pocket. "Voila."

Ann took the bottle gratefully. "Thanks." She downed most of the bottle in one draft while Mike poured Ann's rejected wine into his own glass.

"So the spirit is someone who hanged herself in the attic?"

"That's what it looks like."

"Male or female?"

"I don't know." She paused. "Female."

"Any specific details?"

"No. Just the drop and the jerk."

"And the chair moving."

"Yes, that's probably what people were hearing—a scraping sound from the attic, always at the same time. That and the fact that I'm betting if someone stood the chair up it was always on its side again in the morning."

"Well, the whole thing got Mavis pretty flustered. She's claimed one of the bottles of Bordeaux as her own."

"She didn't even see anything," said Ann irritably.

"I guess your color commentary was enough," he said, and grinned at her.

She smiled back wanly. "Is she upset?"

"Are you kidding me?" said Mike, turning to go back to the inn's parlor. "She hasn't had this much fun in years."

Chapter 8

The day after his interviews with Biden, Lydia, and Morgan, Joe was back at the Firth house to interview Joan Davies and Esme Brouwer; Biden himself was away from home. Joe decided to interview them individually in what he thought of as the living room and he suspected the Firths thought of as the parlor, across the hall from the library where he had interviewed Biden Firth.

Harry Deng had spent what seemed to Joe from Deng's notes like an inordinate amount of time with Miss Brouwer and when Joe met her he suspected why—in her early twenties, she was extremely pretty, with light blonde hair held back in a ponytail from a round, rosy face, startlingly light blue eyes, and a well rounded figure that just escaped plumpness. She wrung her hands a lot during the interview and answered his questions in a charming Dutch accent. Joe toyed with the idea of the husband killing the wife in favor of the younger, more pliant lover but Esme's apparent respect for Elizabeth Firth, her apparent nervousness about Biden Firth, and her obvious concern about her job security began to undermine his liking for this theory.

"So," said Joe, "you heard a noise coming from the library."

"Yes."

"And you went to see what it was."

"Yes."

"And what did you find?"

"Mr. Firth."

Joe sighed inwardly. "And what was Mr. Firth doing?"

Esme twisted her fingers. "Nothing?"

Joe sighed outwardly. "Miss Brouwer ..."

"Nothing," said Esme with more conviction. After a pause she added, "Looking mad."

"How so?"

"Red face. I think the sound I heard was him banging the desk. I couldn't see what else it could be. But he told me everything was all right and close the door."

Joe played around with other lines of questioning for a bit and then excused her to her obvious relief, asking her to send Joan in.

Joan Davies was in her early fifties, tallish, with regular features, hazel eyes, and striking auburn hair tinged with gray—not beautiful, thought Joe, but probably what people had in mind when they described a woman as handsome. She sat on the couch with her hands clasped but relaxed, her eyes serious and steady.

"I wanted to speak with you and Esme because oftentimes when someone disappears, understanding the environment they live in and the events leading up to the time of their disappearance can be helpful."

"Yes, of course."

Joe walked Joan through the time between the last time she had seen Mrs. Firth and when Biden Firth had reported his wife missing; he experimented with different approaches but there were no deviations from the account that she had given Harry Deng—the reported argument between Mr. and Mrs. Firth that kept them from attending the charity dinner, the fact that Mrs. Firth's cell phone was at the house although her purse and coat were gone, the timing of Mr. Firth's departure from and return to the house the next day, the stained and scotch-scented shirt in Mr. Firth's laundry basket.

When that line of questioning seemed to have played itself out, Joe asked, "Why don't you tell me how you came to work for the Firths."

"I started working for them when they moved into this house, right after they were married," she said.

"Do both the husband and the wife generally interview candidates for a housekeeper position?" asked Joe, casting about for an approach that might prove fruitful.

"I've only worked for two other families before the Firths and in both those cases the wife did the final interviewing after the agency had done screening interviews."

"Is that what happened in the case of the Firths?"

"Actually, in this case Mr. Firth's mother, Mrs. Morgan Firth, hired me. My previous employers were retiring to Arizona—they were friends of Scottie Firth so she already knew me slightly and, I believe, got a strong recommendation from them. I believe both Mr. and Mrs. Firth—the Biden Firths—were quite busy preparing for their wedding and Mrs. Firth was busy wrapping up her employment with Firth Investments."

"It sounds like your previous jobs were long-term."

"Yes, I worked for the family before the Firths for twelve years and for my first family for eight years."

"What are the Firths like to work with?"

"Very fair."

Joe expected more, but Joan merely looked at him, awaiting the next question.

"That's it? 'Very fair'?" he asked after a few seconds.

"Don't underestimate the importance of fairness," said Joan a bit severely.

"No, of course not," said Joe. "Have you become friendly with them?"

"No, they aren't that type. Fair, but not familiar."

"Demanding?"

Joan shrugged. "Not unreasonably demanding."

"Which one is more demanding?" asked Joe with a conspiratorial smile.

"Mrs. Firth," said Joan promptly but without apparent rancor. "Of course she has more to do with directing the running of the house so that's to be expected."

"Other than the argument that Mr. Firth told you about that kept them from going to the charity dinner, did Mr. and Mrs. Firth argue?"

"Well, yes, of course, all married couples argue, don't they," said Joan with apparent mildness but Joe caught a twitch in her hand out of the corner of his eye.

"Recently?"

"I couldn't say."

"Miss Davies, this isn't a social conversation, it's part of a criminal investigation. Your discretion would be admirable in other circumstances but it's not helpful here."

She paused then said, "Yes. Fairly recently."

"What did they argue about?"

"I don't know. They never argued in front of me or Esme but sometimes I could hear raised voices from behind closed doors."

"Were the arguments getting more heated or more frequent lately? Over the past few weeks or months, say?"

Joan considered. "No, I wouldn't say they were more frequent as recently as that. Only perhaps more frequent over the last year or so."

Joe nodded and jotted a note in his notepad. "Any signs of infidelity?"

He glanced up quickly and saw a jumble of emotions—shock, confusion, indecision, strained composure—cross Joan's face. She looked down at her hands and said, "I'm sure I wouldn't know."

He put his pencil down. "Joan, you're the worst liar I've ever seen."

Her head came up, her face red, and she began to sputter out a retort but Joe interrupted her. "I've heard rumors, I need to know if they're true."

To Joe's surprise Joan asked, "What rumors did you hear?"

"They were shared in confidence."

"Shared in confidence with a police detective?" asked Joan, looking at Joe skeptically. Joe revised his opinion of her upward—she might not be a good liar herself but she also was not as gullible as he had first thought.

"I hear that Mrs. Firth may have ..." he cast about for a word that seemed appropriate to use with Joan "... strayed."

Joan raised her eyebrows and a slight smiled played at her lips. "'Strayed'?"

Joe shrugged. "You know."

Joan sighed and looked over Joe's shoulder out the front window. After a few moments she said, "I only know of one—a personal trainer who used to come to the house. And that was over a year ago." She thought for a moment. "Fifteen months ago."

"How did you know?"

"They were up in the exercise room having a session," said Joan. "They were laughing a lot—I could hear them, I was on the second floor putting away laundry. Then Mrs. Firth came down and said that Stephan—that was the trainer—wanted some kind of special sports drink that was only available at a store in Ardmore and asked me if I could go get some. She had the name of the drink and the store written on a piece of paper. I got my coat and purse and got to my car and then realized I had forgotten the paper and when I went back I heard them." She had been looking at her hands but now glanced up at Joe with just a hint of a teasing smile on her face. "*You* know." She looked back down at her hands and then back at Joe. "That's all."

"Did the relationship go on long?"

"I don't know. He stopped coming to the house not long after that."

"Were there others?"

"Not that I know of."

He tapped his pencil on the notepad a few times. "Did Mr. Firth know?"

Joan sighed. "I don't know."

Joe got the trainer's full name and the interview continued for a few more minutes with Joe probing the marital relationship angle. When that line of questioning grew stale he switched to a discussion of the Firths' relationship with their daughter. It appeared there was little friction between them when it came to parenting since, as far as he could tell, in general it was Joan and Esme doing the parenting. He asked briefly about Esme but didn't unearth anything interesting—the two woman seemed on good terms with each other.

"So who's looking after Sophie these days?" Joe asked, already knowing the answer.

"Oh, I've been staying at the townhouse since Mrs. Firth disappeared. There's an apartment on the third floor. Quite nice. It would be convenient if it became a permanent arrangement because then I wouldn't have to rent my own place. Even when Mrs. Firth gets home, of course," she added hastily.

Chapter 9

It was a week after his interview with Joe Booth and Biden was feeling antsy. At first he had spent most of his time in the house, feeling somehow that staying out of the public eye was safer. He had been surprised that being in the library and walking through the entrance hall or going into the garage didn't seem to bother him, then it did start to bother him. He would be sitting at his desk reading the paper and suddenly have to jump up—usually he used the opportunity to get himself a drink—or he would need something from the garage and would have Joan get it for him. He wasn't sleeping well, and switching to the guest room hadn't helped. Joan and Esme did their best to keep Sophia entertained and quiet, but when she did cry the sound cut through him like broken glass.

Now on this last day of February—cold and clear, more like December—he had to get out of the house. He decided to go to the restaurant on North 2nd Street and try to work things out with Walters. He hadn't heard from Walters since the conversation with his father and he assumed Walters had heard about Elizabeth's disappearance and realized that Biden had other things on his mind than payments on some gentleman's agreement investment. And of course even his father was not so crass as to ask him about the situation with his wife missing. Biden was sure he could find some other source to fund his restaurant investment, he just needed to smooth things over with Walters until he decided what that was.

On his way to the restaurant he fought what had now

become a near continuous urge to take his car to the car wash—the Ultra option with the interior vacuuming. That detective, Booth, hadn't been happy to hear he had taken it to the car wash on the way back from Long Beach Island—the first one, Deng, hadn't asked if he had made any stops and Biden hadn't volunteered any information. Sometimes when he was home and sure Joan was occupied with Sophia, he would go to the garage with a high powered flashlight he had gotten for the purpose and search the trunk for any traces. And who knows what might be in other parts of the car that he wasn't even thinking to look for. He had thought about selling the car but was afraid of making the police even more interested in it—for all he knew the police might not even let him get rid of it.

With these thoughts nagging at him, he was surprised and annoyed to see when he reached the restaurant a sign over the door giving the name of the establishment as Waterman's. Waterman had been the last name of a favorite uncle of Miles but Biden had argued that it made it sound like a seafood chain. Biden favored a French name and he thought it might not be too late to convince Miles.

He pulled the Mercedes in behind a contractor's truck in back of the restaurant. He could hear hammering coming from the second floor of the building and, closer by, the sound of voices which faded as the speakers moved away from one of the open windows on the first floor. The door which would be the service entrance was unlocked and he went in.

The kitchen was quite far along, with an electrician working on wiring for the grill. Biden passed through the kitchen into the service area, following the sound of the voices. A painter was applying a rich mustard yellow to the walls of one of the several small rooms where diners would be seated. In the room beyond, which had already been painted,

Miles stood with a woman who was holding up fabric swatches to the wall.

"It'll be great," she said. "French country, very warm. Plus it would cost a fortune to change it now."

Miles Walters fidgeted with a clipboard. "But will it look good in dim light?" he said. "It might be too ... I don't know ... *yellow*."

"I like it," said Biden. "I always liked that color."

Miles and the woman turned and Biden realized the woman was Miles's wife whose name he couldn't remember.

"Firth," said Miles, looking surprised.

"I thought I'd stop by and see how things were going."

Miles and his wife exchanged glances. "Going fine," said Miles.

Biden wished the wife would go back to choosing fabric or whatever it was she had been doing. He said to Miles, "I thought we could talk about, uh, that thing we had been talking about." He flushed. No doubt the wife thought he was an idiot. What was her name?

Miles and his wife exchanged looks again and Miles shrugged. "Sure."

"I'll just check on the electrician," she said, looking more curious than irritated, and headed back to the kitchen.

"So, what brings you around?" said Miles, swinging the clipboard at his side between his forefinger and thumb.

"I guess you heard about Elizabeth," said Biden.

Miles stopped swinging the clipboard. "Yes, sorry to hear that. Any news?"

"No, nothing yet. I'm sure the police are doing their best." He began unbuttoning his coat. "I'm sure you can imagine I haven't been able to concentrate on anything else lately."

"Sure," said Miles.

"Well, I wanted to talk about the investment, see if we can't work out something that will be beneficial for both of us."

Miles tossed the clipboard onto a nearby card table. "Let's not go there, Biden. 'Fool me once—'"

"What do you mean?"

Miles squinted at Biden. "Have you talked with your dad?"

"He did tell me you had spoken to him about our arrangement," said Biden coldly.

"You didn't leave me any choice," retorted Miles. "You made a commitment—"

"I know, that's why I'm here," said Biden, exasperated. "To work it out."

"Your dad took care of it," said Miles. Biden's face froze and he said nothing so in a moment Miles continued. "He called about a week after I talked to him, asked me if I had heard from you. I said no, so we worked out a deal."

"What deal?" said Biden, his voice taut.

"It's really not any of your business," said Miles, clearly losing patience with the conversation.

"It is my business," said Biden, and he felt his hands forming into fists. "I gave you $80,000."

Miles shrugged. "Go ask your dad, Biden. But don't come to the restaurant anymore. You're out of it." And he picked up the clipboard and followed his wife back to the kitchen.

Biden stood in the empty dining room, surrounded by sawhorses and drop cloths, and felt a familiar anger—his father was making a fool of him once again—bring a burn to his face and churn to his stomach. He strode to the front door and jerked the knob but the door was locked and he couldn't figure out how to unlock it. He was calculating the least humiliating way he could make his exit when he heard the sound of metal on metal and then the wail of a car alarm coming from the back of the building.

When he got there, Miles, the wife, and the painter were standing in the back door. They stepped aside to let him through to the sight of the electrician climbing out of the truck whose back end was embedded in the grill of his wailing Mercedes.

"Holy Christ," muttered Biden, fumbling with his key chain and stabbing at the button to quiet the alarm.

"I couldn't see you parked back there," said the electrician, looking dejectedly at the damage to the Mercedes.

"If you looked before you backed up—" began Biden, anticipating the inconvenience of having his car in the shop. He hated to have other people mess with his car—the cheap paper floor mats they put down in a vain attempt to keep the mechanics' muddy footprints off the carpet, the cloying floral smell of the products they used to clean the car when he took it in for service ... a small smile replaced his scowl. "Accidents happen," he said. "I'll need a tow truck."

Chapter 10

On a blustery morning in April, Ella Franklin was scrambling eggs for breakfast for her and her husband, Edwin, in their Tinicum Township row house. Edwin sat at the table sipping black coffee and reading the *Daily News*. Ella heard the scratching at the door that meant that their terrier mutt, Dolly, was back from her patrol of the neighborhood. The police had warned the Franklins about letting Dolly roam free but she did love visiting the neighbors (and the Franklins had never heard any of the neighbors say that they didn't love Dolly's visits), not to mention exploring the wildlife refuge which was practically next door.

Ella put down the spatula, wiped her hands on the dishtowel, and opened the door. Dolly trotted in with something in her mouth, headed for her dog bed in the corner, and flopped down with her back to the room.

"Edwin, she's got something," said Ella and went back to the stove.

"Now what," said Edwin, levering himself up from the table and crossing to Dolly's dog bed. "Give it up, Dolly," he said, bending down. Dolly gave a slight growl and hunched protectively over her prize. Edwin pulled Dolly up by her collar so he could see what she had and, when he did, jumped back so suddenly that he banged into the corner of the kitchen table, sloshing coffee onto the newspaper.

"DOLLY, DROP IT!" he yelled, and Dolly, who had never in her life had Edwin yell at her, promptly dropped it and slunk behind Ella.

"What in the world …" Ella said, turning from the stove then her words died as she saw what Dolly had brought in.

"What is that?" she whispered.

"I think it's a hand," said Edwin, his voice quavering.

Ella clapped her hand over her mouth, then ran to the bathroom.

Edwin scooped Dolly up, put her in the laundry room and shut the door, then grabbed the phone and dialed 911.

Chapter 11

Joe Booth showed his badge to the guard at the gate and was waved through to the building housing the Delaware County Medical Examiner's offices.

Roger Stanislaus, the ME, was tall and aristocratic looking, of an indeterminate age, with fine, faded blond hair combed back from a high forehead and wire rim glasses that he would push up on top of his head when looking at something up close. He had a slight accent that Joe was never able to place more specifically than to assume it was European. His clothes were classic and, Joe suspected, not off the rack.

Joe found Roger in the office area adjacent to the labs, flipping through a manila folder in consultation with one of his assistants. The assistant could hardly have looked less like Roger—short and stocky, with red hair pulled back in a pony tail, and tattered jeans emerging from the bottom of a lab coat which had "Pete" embroidered on the chest. Roger glanced up and, seeing Joe, said, "Detective Joseph Booth, it's been too long!" Not even Joe's mother called him Joseph. Roger's colleague rolled his eyes.

"Yup, too long, Roger. You've got something for me?"

"Yes indeed," said Roger, handing the manila folder to the other man. "Take care of that, will you, Peter?"

"Sure," said Pete, who nodded to Joe and then disappeared into a back room.

Roger removed his coat—a fine wool with microscopic black and white checks—and hung it on a wooden hanger on a coat rack in the corner, replacing it with a spotless white lab coat from another hanger on the rack. "I do believe we have found your missing young lady."

"Elizabeth Firth?"

"The very same. I knew her, you know. Not well. Spoke with her a few times at charity events."

Joe recalled having seen a photo of Roger in *Philadelphia Magazine* a few years before, escorting a wealthy-looking older woman to a charity dinner. Joe pictured Roger eliciting shrieks of horror and delight from his table mates with stories gleaned from his "day job."

"Sorry to hear she was someone you knew," said Joe.

"Yes, well, these things happen," said Roger cheerfully. "Come with me." He pushed through a swinging door into a room with a stainless steel examination table in its center—empty, Joe noted with relief—and a bank of refrigerated compartments for storing bodies along one wall.

Roger picked a manila folder out of a rack on the wall, scanned it quickly, then crossed to the compartments and slid one open. On it lay a plastic body bag like many others Joe had seen but the contours of this one looked flatter than normal.

Roger flipped through some papers in the folder. "We determined her identity based on dental records. The body was in a sleeping bag but that didn't prevent animal predation. Also the decomposition was pretty advanced. Want to see?"

"No," said Joe hastily. "They found her in Tinicum Marsh?"

"Yes, but not in the marshy area, in a dry area."

"Buried?"

"No, on the surface."

"I don't suppose she had just decided to take a camping trip in the wildlife refuge," said Joe, wishing Roger would slide the compartment shut.

"Not unless she decided to tie herself into the sleeping bag when it was time for bed," said Roger with what sounded to Joe like a chuckle although, he thought, it might have been an aborted cough.

"What was the cause of death?"

Roger sighed. "Hard to say. No evidence of gunshot or knife wounds, no significant broken bones. There were a couple of hairline fractures of the skull but I don't think they would have been enough to kill her, although possibly enough to knock her out. If I had to guess I'd say she had been choked—there was damage to her larynx but I couldn't say definitively that it happened when she was killed."

"Was she dressed?"

"Yes, she was fully clothed. There was a coat stuffed into the bag with her."

"Any ideas why she wasn't wearing her coat?"

"Oh, I can come up with all sorts of ideas, all pure speculation. She was mugged and the mugger had her take her coat off so he could search her pockets. Or he planned to rape her and was having her disrobe but got interrupted. Or she was indoors somewhere and had taken off her coat before she was killed and the killer had to get rid of it."

"Or she was killed at her own home and someone took her coat out of the closet to make it look like she had left the house on her own."

Roger cocked an eye at Joe. "You know, I like that idea best because I thought it was odd that there wasn't a scarf or gloves with the body. Especially the scarf. The coat had a low V neckline and the blouse she was wearing was low cut and you would think that she would have wanted something around her neck—she disappeared in February, right? But maybe the killer used the scarf to choke her and kept it as some kind of souvenir."

"Or was just in a panic and didn't think about it."

"Also a possibility," conceded Roger, "although not as interesting." He glanced back at his notes. "However she died, at some point she was in the trunk of a car. There were carpet fibers from the trunk of a car, some on the body and some on the sleeping bag, mainly around her head and feet. I'm guessing there was something like a garbage bag on the floor of the trunk that kept fibers from getting on the mid-section of her body and the sleeping bag but that didn't cover the area where her head and feet were resting."

"So if there were fibers on the body as well as on the sleeping bag, it sounds like she wasn't in the sleeping bag the whole time she was in the trunk of the car. She might have been put in the sleeping bag later. Which might suggest that the murder wasn't pre-meditated, otherwise the killer might have had the sleeping bag ready to put her in immediately." Joe rubbed his jaw tiredly. "I suppose I shouldn't be surprised she was in a car, probably not many murders actually happen in Tinicum Marsh—she had to get there somehow."

"Ah, but this *is* more interesting. This particular type of carpeting has been used for the last several years in the Mercedes E-Class which, according to the file, is the kind of car that her husband drives. Did anyone do an analysis on his car?"

Joe grimaced with annoyance. "Turns out he took it to a self-service car wash after driving to the shore, supposedly to look for his wife."

"Those self-service vacuums aren't very effective—I don't bother with them myself—there might still be some evidence in the car, even after all this time—"

"That's not the worst of it—while Firth Senior's lawyers were fighting us about getting a search warrant for the car, some guy backed into Biden Firth's car and the place that did the repairs detailed it."

Roger snorted. "God, what are the chances."

"We even looked into whether Firth somehow arranged for the guy to hit his car or specifically asked for the detailing. The first seems unlikely and the repair place confirms Firth didn't make any special requests, they detail all the cars they work on. If he did kill his wife, it was just a lucky break for him."

"Firth one, dead wife and police zero," said Roger, removing his glasses and polishing them contemplatively with a silk handkerchief.

Chapter 12

The Sunday after Elizabeth's body was identified, Biden used his key to let himself into the offices of Firth Investments. There was none of the bustle that generally filled the offices and hallways, created by ambitious young men and women who were involved in managing his father's real estate holdings. In fact, Biden was counting on the quiet, planning to spend a few hours in his office with the Sunday *Chronicle* and a large Starbucks. His unease at being in his own house had only gotten worse as the weeks went on—he always felt like someone was in the room with him.

On the way down the hall to his office, he saw that the door of his father's office was partially open and a light was on. "Damn," he muttered under his breath. He considered trying to sneak out but it would be humiliating if his father caught him. He dropped the newspaper into the trash can next to the secretary's desk and knocked on the frame of the office door. His father looked up from a fan of papers on his desk, a red pen poised over them. He rarely worked on his computer, preferring to have his secretary print out hardcopies of documents for him.

"What are you doing here today?" asked Morgan Firth.

Biden shrugged. "Thought I'd catch up a little."

Morgan beckoned Biden into the office and then waved him toward one of the chairs in front of his desk. Biden slid into one, wondering if it had been the decorator's idea or his father's to put visitors in a chair that felt like a trap.

Morgan took off his glasses and put down his pen. "You

don't need to be here today of all days."

Biden had barely been to the office at all since Elizabeth had disappeared, despite his father's advice that work was just the thing to take his mind off the waiting. Biden shrugged again and looked out the window behind Morgan's desk.

Morgan sighed and sat back in his chair. He rotated his chair so that he too was looking out the window and then turned back. "The Dormands are arranging the memorial service?"

"Yes. Amelia said she wanted to do it."

"You talked to them?"

"Briefly."

"I don't know why you told the police you hit her," said Morgan irritably.

"Because that's what happened." Morgan didn't say anything. "It was the only time."

"Her parents don't want to hear that there was even one time, Biden." There was a long pause, then Morgan Firth sighed. "You know your mother and I thought the world of Elizabeth," he said. "She was a fine woman. A fine wife and mother. Would have made a fine executive if she had decided to stay with the company."

An executive. Biden couldn't recall that his father had ever suggested that he, Biden, would ever be an executive with the company.

Morgan Firth shook his head. "It's a terrible, terrible thing. You think a place like Rittenhouse Square will be relatively safe but I suppose nowhere is safe these days." He looked closely at Biden. "Sophia, she's doing OK?"

"Yes, she's fine."

"Do you need us to take her for a while?"

"No, I can take care of it," said Biden, bristling a bit.

"You're taking care of Sophie?" asked Morgan skeptically.

"Well, me and Joan."

"Ah, Joan, yes, that's good," said Morgan, sitting back in his chair and examining Biden. "You don't look so good, Biden," he said. "Maybe you should go home and rest. You've been through a lot. No one would fault you for not working today." He picked up his pen, indicating that the conversation was over. "You let me and your mother know if you need anything."

Biden struggled out of the slippery chair and nodded. "Maybe I will go home."

Morgan nodded and put his glasses back on.

Biden turned to leave then stopped at the door. "I'm thinking of selling the house."

Morgan took his glasses off again and looked at Biden, his face impassive. "Bad memories?" he said eventually.

Biden shrugged. "Sophia and I don't need all that room."

"And Joan," said Morgan.

"Why this sudden obsession with Joan?" said Biden peevishly. His wife had just been found dead, he guessed he had the right to be peevish.

Morgan opened his mouth then clamped it shut and scowled at Biden for a few seconds, then said, "Biden, you're a good father but you're not a ... caretaker. Actually, neither was Elizabeth—that's why you have Joan and Esme. I don't think now's the time to decide you're going to let Joan go. It would be disruptive to Sophie. Especially if you're also thinking of selling the house."

"I don't need all that room."

Morgan sat back in his chair and considered Biden for a few moments. "You could move back home," he said eventually, "maybe rent the house out in case you change your mind. Now's not really a good time to sell. Your mother would love having Sophie around. And Joan could have the apartment over the garage."

"I'll think about it. But I'm going to give Mark Pironi a call."

Morgan shrugged. "It's your decision."

Biden nodded and pulled the door closed silently behind him.

Biden didn't go back to the office after that, although his pay checks continued to arrive in the mail.

Chapter 13

Elizabeth Dormand Firth's memorial service was held on a pretty April Saturday at a Presbyterian church just over the border of southern Chester County in Delaware. The ground was still wet from rain during the night but the day was sunny and warming, the trees beginning to show blossoms. The parking lot was full of Mercedes and Porsches and even a Bentley—Joe was glad he had taken his elderly Accord through the car wash on the way to the service. He was wearing his standard funeral suit which he noticed was a little tighter in the waist than it had been the last time he had worn it. He arrived early, having overestimated how long it would take him to get there, and passed the time wandering through the churchyard reading the grave markers.

Once the guests started to arrive he took up position— unobtrusively, he hoped—in the back of the church with Harry Deng. It was standard procedure for the investigating detective to attend any memorial or funeral service for the victim of an open case since it was not unheard of for a murderer to show up to observe, or perhaps even to participate in, the event. It was a sign of Elizabeth's father's influence that two detectives had been assigned to cover the service and the reception to follow but Joe doubted that after this much time they would glean anything useful from the exercise.

The small church was packed with attractive, well-groomed, and expensively dressed people of all ages, most of whom seemed to know each other. Joe couldn't remember a time he had seen so many women in hats. He saw Lydia Levere, dwarfed by a man Joe assumed to be her husband who was built like a linebacker—she likes all her possessions big, he thought.

Amelia Dormand, Elizabeth's mother, sat in the front row, her tanned face a stony mask, her black hair pulled back in a severe bun, her unadorned dress—which even Joe could tell was finely made—as black as her hair. Throughout the service, she sat with her back ramrod straight, staring straight ahead, seemingly unaware of her husband's hand on her back. Bob Dormand wiped his eyes with his handkerchief and periodically patted his wife's back, a gesture that seemed more comforting to him than to her.

Biden Firth and his parents sat in the front row across the aisle from the Dormands. Biden glanced over at his in-laws periodically but neither of them returned his glances.

The service was short and, as far as Joe could tell, right from the prayer book. No one other than the pastor spoke. When it was over, the Dormands and then the Firths passed down the aisle, Joe slipping out after them. The Dormands stepped into a black limousine waiting at the door while the Firths went to a large, older model Mercedes, the elder Firths in front, Biden in back.

The cars streamed out of the church parking lot and down Kennett Pike to the Hotel du Pont where a reception was to be held. They passed private schools sequestered behind brick walls and upscale shopping centers and, nearing the hotel, entered Wilmington's financial district, largely unpopulated on the weekend. Most of the guests used the hotel's valet parking but Joe parked his car in the self-park lot across the street.

The reception was held in a series of rooms off the lobby with richly paneled walls decorated with original paintings by

Andrew, N.C., and Jamie Wyeth. Waiters moved through the crowd taking drink orders and passing hors d'oeuvres. There was murmured conversation and the occasional burst of surprised, but quickly suppressed, laughter.

Harry, who was much more smartly dressed than Joe and seemed to be enjoying the event, swirled his glass of tonic water.

"They've got a couple of private security guards making sure it's invited guests only"—Harry nodded to a couple of equally nattily-dressed men wearing discreet ear pieces with cords running into the back of their jackets—"but it looks like they don't have much to do. I'm surprised that there aren't more crashers."

Joe nodded. "It's not getting much news coverage, I'm guessing that Morgan Firth and Bob Dormand have something to do with that."

"Must be nice to be loaded." Harry put his glass on a table topped with an enormous floral arrangement. "I'm going to take a walk around, see who *is* here," he said, and wandered off through the crowd.

Joe looked at his watch, wondering how much longer they would need to stay, and when he looked up Elizabeth Firth's parents stood in front of him. Bob Dormand, in his early sixties, was thin like his daughter but tall, with a narrow, almost gaunt face, his skin stretched tight over prominent cheekbones, and grey hair cut in a crew cut. He had a sharp beak of a nose and icy blue eyes. Joe had learned he had been on a record-breaking rowing team when he had been at Penn and now spent many of his weekends doing competitive ocean sailing. In other circumstances, even if one had not known of his prominence in the Philadelphia business community, one would have recognized him as a man to be reckoned with but now he was just a grieving father, his eyes shot with red, his face haggard.

Where Elizabeth had inherited her whip thinness from her father, she had inherited her beauty from her mother. Amelia Dormand was of medium height with a softer, more rounded figure than her daughter but with a sense of athleticism one didn't get at a gym—Joe knew she spent most of her days in the barn of the Dormands' Chester County horse farm. She was in her late fifties and up close Joe could see the tiny lines of crow's feet at her eyes and a slight loosening of the skin at her throat, but from a distance—and not a very great distance—one could easily have mistaken Amelia for Elizabeth's taller, shapelier sister. During the entire investigation Joe had never seen her cry, but the tautness of her mouth and her rigid posture reflected a pain as great as did her husband's bloodshot eyes. She carried a seemingly untouched glass of red wine. Bob Dormand released her elbow to extend his hand to Joe.

"Good of you to come," he said. "Official business, I know, but even so ..."

Joe shook his hand and nodded an acknowledgement, then turned to his wife. "Mrs. Dormand."

She nodded back. "Detective."

"Any news from the analysis of the ..." Dormand's voice trailed off. "... of what they found?"

"Nothing yet," said Joe. "These things can take some time."

Dormand sighed and rubbed his eyes. "It's been so long now that she's been gone. I suppose all the trails are cold by now."

"It does get more difficult the more time that goes by but we haven't thrown in the towel yet, there are still leads to follow up on." Joe hoped Dormand wouldn't ask him what those leads were.

Dormand took a sip of his drink—it looked like a

Manhattan—and said, "Yes, I appreciate all the time the police department has put into the case." Joe scanned his face for a sign of sarcasm but the man just looked very, very tired.

Over Dormand's shoulder, Joe saw Biden and Morgan Firth making their way toward them, Biden in the lead and Morgan walking beside him and whispering angrily to his son. As they reached the group, Morgan stepped back, looking tense and aggravated as Biden reached out to touch Amelia Dormand's shoulder.

Amelia turned and, when she saw who stood next to her, her entire body jerked back, sloshing wine onto her dress and onto Biden's shoes. Her expression never changed but the blood drained from her face, leaving her skin looking almost white against the blackness of her dress.

Biden himself stepped back at Amelia's reaction and after a moment stammered, "I'm sorry, I didn't mean to startle you—"

"You didn't startle me," said Amelia, staring into his face. The guests who stood near the group had noticed the incident and there was a pocket of silence around them.

"Come on, Biden," said Morgan Firth, "they're obviously having a conversation with Mr. Booth ..."

One of the waiters had noticed the incident and held out a small stack of cocktail napkins to Amelia. Instead of taking them she handed the waiter her glass. "If you'll excuse me," she said and, turning from the group, left the room.

Biden Firth stood looking after her with his mouth open. The waiter turned to him to offer the napkins but Biden gestured him away. "What did I do?" he asked.

"You startled her, Biden," said Morgan, taking his son's elbow. "We've got to be going anyway." He handed his glass—scotch on the rocks to Joe's eyes—to the waiter who was still hovering nearby with Amelia's abandoned wine glass in his hand then turned to Bob Dormand. "Nice service,

Bob," he said. "Just what Elizabeth would have wanted."

"Thanks," said Dormand, looking after his wife—he seemed to be still processing the incident and Joe realized he had probably had several drinks already.

Morgan Firth nodded to Joe and, still grasping Biden's elbow, steered him toward the door through which Amelia had left.

Bob Dormand shook his head and, evidently having forgotten Joe, made his way to the bar. Joe handed his glass of tonic water to the waiter, who was now having some trouble juggling the glasses he was collecting, and followed Amelia and the Firths into the lobby. He arrived just in time to see Morgan Firth propel his son out the door and raise his hand to flag down one of the valets. He wondered how Scottie Firth was going to be getting home.

Joe assumed that Amelia had gone into the ladies' room off the lobby and stood for a minute so that he could keep an eye on the door. Then, realizing she was hardly likely to turn fugitive, he began wandering around the lobby and down the hallways that led off it. He was passing the restaurant—the Green Room—which had emptied of the lunch crowd and was not yet open for dinner when he caught a glimpse of one black-clothed figure sitting at a table by the windows, her back to him. He stepped into the restaurant. A maître d' who was examining the reservation book looked up from his desk. "I'm sorry, sir, we don't open for dinner until six—"

"I was looking for the lady," said Joe.

"I don't believe she wants company," began the maître d' but Joe flipped open his badge and, after glancing at it, the man shrugged and gestured him into the restaurant.

Amelia sat at a table set for four, her hand resting on the base of a water glass, looking out the window. Joe circled toward her so that he wouldn't come up on her from behind but she still gave a start when she realized she wasn't alone.

"May I?" asked Joe, gesturing to one of the other chairs. She hesitated then nodded. He sat down and looked out the window onto the Wilmington street.

"They said I could sit in here for a few minutes," said Amelia. "They brought me some water."

"That was nice. It's a beautiful room," said Joe.

"Yes," said Amelia, looking around disinterestedly. She lifted the glass of water to take a sip and the ice in the glass chattered loudly in the empty room and she put the glass down and clasped her hands under the table.

"You're cold," said Joe, rising and starting to take off his jacket.

"Oh, no, thank you, I'm fine," said Amelia. "It's just ..." She turned to look out the window again.

Joe waited and, when she didn't continue, said, "Just what?"

"It's nothing," she said. They sat in silence for some time, her shivering not abating, and eventually she said, "Perhaps I will borrow your jacket after all."

Joe stood up, removed his jacket, and draped it over her shoulders.

"Thank you," she said.

"What happened?" said Joe.

Amelia didn't pretend to misunderstand him. "I can't be around him anymore," she said. "I tried to make it clear that I would prefer that he not attend the service and certainly not the reception, but he was her husband ..." She grasped the water glass again and took a sip, the ice cubes chattering again. "I arranged not to have anyone speak at the service because I couldn't very well exclude him, could I?"

"Why can't you be around him anymore?" asked Joe.

Amelia looked at him directly for the first time. "Because he killed her." Joe was silent and in a moment she looked away. "There's no evidence of that. Of course you know that. It's just what I believe."

"Why?"

"They weren't a good match," said Amelia. "I knew there would be trouble eventually."

"Well, there's trouble and then there's murder—" said Joe.

"Yes, I know," said Amelia impatiently, although whether she was impatient with Joe or with herself, he couldn't tell. "As I said, there's no evidence, it's just ..." she paused and a small, sad smile came to her face "... mother's intuition."

"Well, I can't arrest a man based on intuition," said Joe, "but I don't discount it either. Oftentimes what seems like a hunch turns out to have some logic behind it, it's just that the logic is hidden, even from the person with the hunch."

Amelia looked at him again. "Yes. I think that's true," she said. She thought for a time, running her finger across the condensation on the outside of her water glass. Finally she said, "I never loved anyone the way I loved my daughter. She was so beautiful and smart and strong. But no one ever made me as mad as she did." Again the small smile came to her face. "Does every parent say that about their child? But she could be very willful and there were times when it took every ounce of my self-control not to over-react. And I consider myself to be a very self-controlled person. But Biden is not self-controlled. He's ..." she searched for a word, "... outwardly controlled. Controlled by his environment, by the people around him. I think Elizabeth prodded him one too many times and he snapped." She looked over at Joe. "But as you say, it's not exactly grounds for arrest."

"No," said Joe, "but I appreciate you telling me this. Every bit of information—or intuition—helps." They sat in silence for a minute. "Were there times you recall seeing him angry with Elizabeth?" Joe asked. "Especially in the months before she disappeared?"

"There's one time I've thought about a lot," she said immediately. "Biden took us—Elizabeth, me, Bob, Morgan, and Scottie—to the Fountain for dinner." Joe nodded. He had never eaten in the Fountain Restaurant in the Four Seasons Hotel but he had once arrested a suspect in an embezzlement case in the hotel lobby. "I remember it was January, about a month before Elizabeth disappeared, because Biden kept ordering bottles of expensive champagne and telling us how this year was going to be his year. He got pretty drunk and I could tell Elizabeth was getting angry with him. Bob thought it was funny, he kept egging Biden on, getting him to say things that made him sound foolish. Anyhow, the check came and all the men got out their wallets but Biden said it was his dinner and his treat ... but they rejected his credit card. It turned out later that it was just some administrative mix-up with the credit card company but you can imagine how embarrassing it was for him, especially with the way he had been acting." Amelia took a sip of water. "Well, no one knew what to do. I think Bob and Morgan both thought it would look even worse for them to try to pay again after Biden had rejected their initial offers. But then Elizabeth got her purse out and handed her credit card to the waiter and when the waiter was gone she said, 'My God, Biden.' She said it with ... contempt. She wasn't even looking at him, which somehow made it even worse. And she didn't say it loud but everyone at the table heard her. Everyone was very embarrassed. Bob and Morgan started talking about sports and Scottie started sorting through her purse for something but I was looking at Biden and he gave Elizabeth a look ..." She shook her head slowly. "I thought at the time that if he had still had his steak knife he would have stabbed her, he looked that furious."

"Did Elizabeth ever say she had felt threatened by Biden?" Joe had of course asked this question before but he wanted to see if he got the same answer.

Amelia sighed. "No, she never felt threatened."

"Would she have told you if she did?"

"She wouldn't have had to. If she had felt threatened she would have left him. And taken Sophia."

"Do you feel that Sophia is in any danger?"

Amelia laughed bitterly. "Not until she's old enough to talk back to him," she said, then glanced at Joe. "I'm sorry. It's not something to joke about. No, I don't think she's in danger. But at the same time I don't like the idea of him having her. Now that we know Elizabeth is gone I plan to start looking into ways we can have Sophia live with us. It's what Elizabeth wants."

"Wants?" asked Joe.

Amelia blushed. "Would have wanted."

"But you said 'wants,'" pressed Joe.

Amelia for the first time Joe had known her seemed uncertain, her usual composure rattled. "You'll think I'm even more foolish that you must already think," she said.

"There aren't many words that I would be less likely to apply to you than 'foolish,'" said Joe.

She glanced at him with that wan smile then looked back at her water glass. "Sometimes when Biden isn't home, when it's just Joan there, I'll go over to see Sophia. I'll play with her, I'll watch her if Joan needs to run out for something. Sometimes I'll just sit in her room with her when she's napping. A couple of those times, when it's quiet ..."

She was silent so long that finally Joe said, "Yes?"

"I hear her. She tells me to take care of Sophia."

"Elizabeth?"

"Yes. It's not exactly like I can hear her talking. But it seems very clear what she's trying to tell me."

"Always about taking care of Sophia?"

"Yes." Amelia gave a small, self-deprecating laugh. "You'd think she might at least tell me she misses me—" and then she gave a little hiccupping gasp as tears came to her eyes. She picked up one of the napkins from the table and quickly dabbed her eyes. "Good heavens, where did that come from?"

"You miss your daughter," said Joe.

"Yes. Yes, I do," said Amelia, composing herself. After a moment she folded the napkin and placed it next to the water glass then leaned forward and rested her hand, still cold from the glass, on Joe's. "I appreciate you listening," she said. She removed her hand and stood up, shrugging Joe's coat off in a graceful gesture. She smoothed it and handed it to him. "I hope you prove who killed Elizabeth and I hope the bastard goes to jail and dies there."

Amelia Dormand walked to the entrance of the restaurant, acknowledging a small bow from the maître d' and leaving Joe standing with his coat over his arm and the feel of her fingers still on his hand.

Chapter 14

The following Tuesday, Ann was scheduled to fly from her home in the Adirondacks down to West Chester for another engagement for the Van Dykes. Ann would be visiting two locations—one a house near Kennett Square in southern Chester County and the other a townhouse near Rittenhouse Square in Center City Philadelphia. Mavis, who was always solicitous about not overtaxing Ann, had proposed looking at the Kennett Square house on Tuesday and the Center City house on Wednesday. On Tuesday morning at 7:30, Ann pulled into the small parking lot of Adirondack Regional Airport to meet up with Walt Federman.

Walt was a retired welder who did a variety of odd jobs around the Tupper Lake area to fund his obsession with flying, including ferrying Ann to engagements in the Northeast in his 1979 four seat Piper Arrow. Walt especially liked flights to the Brandywine Airport in West Chester—not far from Ann and Mike's childhood home and Mike's current home—because it was within walking distance of Turk's Head Books where, if the stop in West Chester was only a few hours, he could pass the time stocking up on books (mainly history) and reading in the bookstore café. Today, since it was an overnight visit, Walt would be renting a car and staying at the Microtel. Mike and his partner, Scott Pate, always extended an invitation to Walt to stay at Mike's West Chester townhouse but Walt always declined, saying he didn't want to intrude.

Aside from the radio communication required by the

flight, Walt rarely said more than a few dozen words during their excursions. Being a quiet person herself, Ann liked Walt's taciturn nature but hadn't fully appreciated how well she and Walt suited each other until, for one engagement a few months before, Walt had been stricken at the last minute by a virulent stomach virus and Mike had had to arrange alternate transportation for her. That engagement had been unpopular with Mike since the only plane available to charter was considerably more expensive than Walt's and eliminated most of the profit from the engagement; it had been unpopular with Ann because the pilot, who had read an article about her a few weeks before, plied her with questions during the entire trip and Ann arrived at the engagement tired and irritable and knew she had not done her best work for the clients.

The flight from Adirondack Regional to Brandywine Airport took about two hours through cloudless April skies. Mavis Van Dyke was waiting for her in the small passenger terminal, a rental car for Walt waiting in the parking lot.

Normally Mavis would contact Mike when she had located a house she wanted Ann to visit but the Kennett Square house was an exception. Mike had been contacted by the owner, Flora Soderlund, whose children were encouraging her to sell the family home which she had shared with them and her husband, Harold, for almost 50 years until the children had moved away and Harold had died two years ago. Flora had seen a rebroadcast of a History Channel show that had featured Ann and wanted to engage Ann to give her advice on what to do. Her primary concern was that her dead husband would be angry if she sold the house and moved away. Mike had explained that Ann did not converse with spirits but Flora had been sure Ann could help her.

When Mike quoted the standard rate for such a service, Flora let out a quickly suppressed squawk and sheepishly apologized for wasting Mike's time. Mike briefly considered dropping the rate—although he hated to set a precedent—but then came up with an alternative he was quite pleased with. Both Ann and Mavis would visit Flora's house, with Mavis paying half the fee for what Mike thought was a high probability of being able to experience a sensing, although she was sworn to silence throughout the proceedings. Mike himself would sit out the visit since three people descending on Flora's house seemed excessive. Flora quickly accepted the proposal.

For the Kennett Square visit they had dispensed with the usual limo and Mavis drove them to the house in her Jaguar, seeming a bit giddy at the opportunity for a road trip (albeit a very local one). They passed through the rolling horse pastures of southern Chester County, hedgerows intersected by jumping gates, low stone walls that seemed to run for miles.

Mavis's GPS directed them to a modest, century-old, two story clapboard house set by itself near the road—Ann guessed that at one time it might have housed a caretaker of one of the surrounding farms. The yard was a bit overgrown and the paint was peeling in places but the flower beds with their bright patches of daffodils were lovingly tended and the brick walkway was carefully swept. Ann knocked on the door and it was opened so promptly that she suspected that Flora had been watching for them.

Flora was a diminutive woman with wavy white hair pulled back in a bun, wearing a flowered dress under a white cardigan that looked to Ann like a going-to-church outfit.

"Miss Kinnear, please come in, I recognize you from the TV," said Flora, standing aside for them. "And you must be Mrs. Van Dyke," she said, nodding at Mavis. Mavis, who was taking her vow of silence very seriously, nodded back.

They stepped into the central hallway of the house, a tidy living room on one side and a dining room on the other. The furniture was obviously the same that Flora and Harold had acquired as newlyweds. Ann smelled wood polish.

"I'm so glad you agreed to come. Would you like some coffee or tea?" Flora asked.

"What are you having?" asked Ann.

"Tea," said Flora. "But I could have coffee," she added quickly.

"Tea sounds fine, thank you," Ann answered.

Flora looked at Mavis who risked a word by replying, "Splendid!"

Flora led them back through the central hallway to a seventies era kitchen complete with knotty pine cabinets and Harvest Gold appliances. She seated them at the kitchen table with a plate of homemade butter cookies, then busied herself with the kettle and tea pot and tea leaves.

"I talked with your manager, er, your brother—well, your manager *and* your brother, I suppose. Did he tell you what I'm looking for?"

"He told me in general but why don't you tell me yourself."

The kettle whistled and Flora filled the tea pot. "My husband, Harold, died two years ago. Lung cancer."

"He died at home."

"Yes," said Flora, glancing at Ann. "Did your brother tell you that?"

"No," said Ann.

Flora waited for a moment to hear more but when no more was offered she nodded. "Yes, he died at home. In the end he wanted to die in his own house, in his own bed. That's how it should be." She brought the tray of tea things to the table and sat down. "I thought I could keep the house even after he was gone—a neighbor cuts the grass and there are people from church who would help with the handyman-type work if I asked, but it's still a lot to take care of. And the winters are hard, I don't like driving in the snow, so I have to ask people to bring me groceries. Which they do, but I hate to ask. And now both my children are in South Carolina which is very pretty. Also nice and warm. And I'd be able to see my grandchildren more often. I have four grandchildren, all in their teens so it's not like they're babies but still it would be nice to see more of them. Even at that age they change so much in a year! But other than my children and grandchildren I don't know anyone there. Plus, you know, if you live in a place long enough you get everything just the way you want it. I hate to think of starting that all over in a new house. And maybe I wouldn't be able to afford a house, maybe I'd have to rent an apartment. I know people who live in apartments and they say it can be very noisy. I'm not used to having to deal with other people's noise." She stopped for a breath, then smiled sheepishly at Ann. "Heavens, that's probably more than you needed to know." She poured out the tea and nudged the creamer and sugar bowl toward Ann and Mavis.

Ann added sugar to her tea with a delicate demitasse spoon. "Did Harold spend a lot of time in the kitchen?"

"Oh, no," laughed Flora. "He wasn't a kitchen-type man, not like a lot of men these days. My son and son-in-law are both quite good cooks but Harold only knew how to heat up soup."

"He spent most of his time in the living room?"

"Yes."

"Can we have our tea in there?"

"Oh yes, of course!" said Flora starting to pick up the tea tray.

"I can just take my cup," said Ann. Mavis nodded vigorously.

"Of course," said Flora, picking up her cup as well as the plate of cookies.

In the living room Flora put the plate down on the coffee table in front of the couch and cleared some books to the side to make room for their cups.

When they had gotten settled, Ann said, "Tell me about Harold."

Flora smiled fondly. "Oh, we were childhood sweethearts, you know. My family moved to this area when I was in first grade and we knew each other ever since then. Even said we would get married, the way children do. Harold's father owned the hardware store in town and Harold took it over when his father died." She continued, occasionally sipping her tea, but Ann only partially paid attention. Harold had only been gone for two years and his spirit was still strong. Ann could smell the lingering scent of pipe tobacco which she sensed was both a physical residue and a manifestation of Harold's spirit. She thought it was likely a good way to describe Harold's essence—earthy and comfortable.

When Flora finished Ann asked, "Can we walk through the house?"

"Oh yes," said Flora, "wherever you like."

Ann stood—Mavis also popped up—and walked around the living room, examining knickknacks and guessing at their provenance. Followed by Mavis and Flora, she crossed the entrance hall to the dining room where a sideboard held a number of framed photographs. Harold must have been the family photographer because she didn't see any recent pictures of him, but there was a photograph of Harold and Flora on their wedding day, Harold, with bushy brown hair and wire frame glasses, towering over his smiling bride.

They made a cursory tour of the upstairs but Ann already knew that what she needed was in the living room. Flora offered to show them the basement but Ann declined. They returned to the living room and Ann and Flora sat on the couch, Mavis standing to one side.

"My brother explained to you what it is that I do?"

"Oh yes," said Flora, "and I saw you on the TV."

"I don't converse with spirits—I'm not going to be able to convey a message from you to Harold, or from Harold to you. Harold's spirit is very strong here and I can tell you the sense I get from that spirit, for example, if it's contented or confused. Or angry. But that's all I can do."

"Oh, I understand, your brother explained," Flora said eagerly.

"All right," said Ann, standing up and smoothing her slacks.

Flora stood too. "What should I do?"

"You sit where you would normally sit in here," said Ann.

Flora went to sit in a chair near the window that had a knitting basket next to it.

Ann gestured to the armchair on the opposite side of the window. "This is where Harold sat."

"Yes," said Flora.

Ann glanced around the room and, not finding any easily transportable chairs, went into the dining room and came back with one of the dining room chairs which she put down next to the armchair. She sat down and nodded to Mavis to sit on the couch.

"Now I want you to tell me, very slowly, what the decision is that you need to make. Tell me what the alternatives are and what your questions and concerns are about different options. Tell it just like you told me earlier but very slowly." Ann rested her hand on the arm of the armchair and settled back in her chair, looking out the window at the view that Harold Soderlund had no doubt looked at every evening for most of his 77 years.

Flora began her story, telling it slowly as Ann had requested. She ran through the unordered list of pros and cons of moving or staying but always came back to the key question of whether Harold would be angry if she sold the house and moved away.

Ann sensed a press of emotions, now more like colors than scents, drifting around Flora as she spoke. She had expected more of a variation in response as Flora reached different points of her story but the emotions were steady and the color of the spirit—a rich brown—hovered near Flora protectively.

Ann suspected that Flora had not stopped talking to Harold when he died and that he had heard this story many times before. The answer had been right before Flora all the time but she had not seen the answer, or perhaps had seen it but had not trusted herself to understand it.

When Flora stopped talking Ann sat still for so long, looking out the window, that Flora thought perhaps she should start talking again but then Ann stirred.

"There's no anger. But then I don't sense that Harold was a man given to anger." She smiled at Flora.

"Oh no, he wasn't. The only time I saw him really angry was when Bert ran the car into a tree. Bert had been drinking," she added with embarrassment. "But selling the house, I thought it might make him angry. He spent his whole life here."

"No, not angry," said Ann. She sat still for another minute, looking out the window. "Sad, but understanding. I sense he understands that it's time for you to move on." She looked at Flora. "You don't need to stay here for Harold's sake."

Flora, who had been perched in the edge of her chair, slumped a bit in relief. "Oh, that's good, that's what I thought but I wanted to be sure." They sat looking out the window for a minute. Then Flora said, "You sense Harold's spirit in the house?"

"Yes," said Ann. "Very strong."

"If I moved," Flora hesitated. "If I moved, would he come with me?"

"No," said Ann. "He would stay here. This is where he belongs."

Flora pulled a tissue out of her pocket and dabbed at her eyes. "Yes, that's what I thought too." She smiled at Ann. "Thank you."

After they left, Ann acquiesced to Mavis's suggestion that they stop for a glass of wine at a nearby restaurant. Ann figured that she owed Mavis more than the hour with Flora and Harold to make her investment worthwhile, although Mavis seemed perfectly happy with how the visit had turned out.

They took stools at the nouveau rustic bar and Mavis asked for a wine list. "What are you in the mood for?"

"Something red."

Mavis scanned the list and then handed it back to the bartender. "A bottle of the 2008 Beaulieu Cab. And the cheese plate."

Ann might have been alarmed that the person who was her ride home had ordered a bottle of wine but from experience she knew that Mavis's practice was to pour herself one glass which she nursed for the duration. She resigned herself to the task.

"So," said Mavis, leaning in conspiratorially, "what could you sense about him?"

Ann recounted what she had experienced—the solid

earthiness of the essence, the protective aura surrounding Flora.

"You didn't tell the wife about all that," said Mavis reprovingly.

"It wasn't what she had hired me for. I've found it's best to stick to answering the questions they ask to have answered—you never know when you might describe a spirit as having a smoky scent and then you find out that his pipe smoking was a major issue between them and now you have an upset client."

"Is there anything you're not telling me?" asked Mavis, alarmed.

"No, I tell you everything because that's what you've hired me for." She took a sip of wine. "Plus, you're not personally involved. It makes it easier."

Mavis took a minuscule sip from her glass. "No, I suppose I'm not," she said wistfully, then added hopefully, "This Harold Soderlund sounds like a nice man."

"Yes," said Ann, "I think he was."

After the wine, cheese, and analysis of the Soderlund visit had been exhausted, Mavis dropped Ann off at Mike and Scott's townhouse. It was located in an upscale development outside of West Chester, just a few miles from where Mike and Ann had grown up. The house was sleek and sophisticated, geared to entertaining, with a layout designed for mingling, a high-end sound system, and a well-stocked basement wine cellar.

Ann found that recently built homes generally did not have spirits since spirits often existed in the location where a person had died, and with each generation fewer and fewer people died at home. However, Mike and Scott's townhouse was inhabited by a small, gray, fuzzy presence that Ann took to be their cat Scooter who had chewed through an electrical wire and electrocuted himself in the living room a few years before. Scott especially took great glee in Ann's reports of what Scooter's spirit was doing; tonight Ann reported that Scooter was sitting on the kitchen window ledge.

"She loved the window ledge," said Scott wistfully. Mike poured three glasses of Pinot noir and delivered two of the glasses and a small bowl of nuts to the kitchen table where Ann and Scott were sitting. Ann groaned.

"What?"

"I just 'shared' a bottle with Mavis."

"I could get you some orange juice—"

"No, I'll tough it out," said Ann, taking a sip.

"So it sounds like the arrangement worked out?" Scott asked.

"I think so. Flora didn't seem to mind Mavis being there and Mavis likes any sensing event. I keep expecting her to get bored ..."

"Why would she get bored? It's exciting!" Scott gave a little shiver of appreciation. "Plus there's the human interest angle—you were able to set Mrs. Soderlund's mind at rest about moving."

Ann shrugged and swirled her wine. "I didn't tell her anything that anyone else couldn't have told her. In fact, I'm guessing it's exactly what a lot of people probably already *have* told her. Why does she think that I can tell what Harold would want better than all the people who actually knew him when he was alive?"

Mike sat down at the table. "Because they could tell her what they think Harold would have wanted but only you can tell her what Harold feels right now."

"That's right," said Scott, looking at her with concern.

Ann gestured with her chin to the slightly ajar basement door. "Scooter's going downstairs."

"You see? It's a gift!" said Scott, patting her arm.

Chapter 15

Wednesday morning, another beautiful April day, the limo picked up Ann and Mike at Mike's townhouse. They drove to Collegeville to pick up the Van Dykes and then headed into Philadelphia to the second house on the itinerary.

The limo let out its passengers across the street from a handsome old townhouse just off Rittenhouse Square. The brick building was three stories, with a short flight of marble steps leading from the brick sidewalk to a dark green door topped by an arched marble surround enclosing a semi-circular fanlight. Wrought iron grates covered the windows at the basement level. Through the large windows on the first floor they could see what appeared to be a library. The door of the house opened and Joyce Grigson, the Van Dyke's long-suffering realtor, waved to them from the doorway.

"Beautiful house," said Mike.

"Nice work on the inside, too," said Lawrence. He and Mavis usually visited prospective houses themselves before involving Ann and Mike so they could eliminate ones that were unacceptable for reasons other than the lack of a spirit.

"Let's go in," said Mavis, and started across the street.

"No!" said Ann, and they turned to her in surprise.

Her face had gone pasty and her arms were crossed as if she were cold despite the warmth of the morning.

Usually the nausea she felt after sensing a spirit was similar to what she imagined must sometimes overcome long-distance runners—a rebelling of the self against too great a demand being placed on it. In the case of the runner, it was a physical demand; in the case of the sensing, it was a psychic demand.

This, however, was totally different. The clench she felt in her stomach was what she might have experienced if she opened a jar of food from her kitchen cupboard to find it filled with blood. The impact first struck her as an odor but then she realized it was less a smell than it was a physical assault, a force pushing her away from whatever was in the house.

At the same time, she felt something call to her, like a cry for help from the occupant of a burning house.

She staggered back a step, then turned back to the limo but the space was empty, the driver having glided around the corner to look for a parking space.

"What's wrong?" asked Mike.

"You don't want this one," said Ann tightly.

"Why not?" asked Mavis eagerly.

"It's not what you want," said Ann. "It's … unhealthy."

"What does that mean?" said Lawrence.

"It's unfriendly," said Ann. "Bad karma. We don't need to go in, I can tell from here."

"But we have to go in," said Mavis. "I'd like to hear more about what this 'bad karma' is."

"You wanted to know if you should buy a particular house," said Ann loudly, her agitation was increasing. "I'm telling you, you don't want this one."

Mavis crossed her arms. "We paid for you to go through these houses and that's what I expect you to do."

"I'm not going into that house," said Ann. "Doesn't that tell you what you need to know?"

Mike touched Ann's arm. "Should we go get a cup of coffee first?" He gave her elbow a squeeze but she jerked her arm out of his hand.

"I'm not going in! Why should I have to go in if I can tell from here that they shouldn't buy it?" And Ann turned and strode down the street toward Rittenhouse Square.

Her breath was short and her face was now flushed but the nausea was fading the further she got from the house. In a few minutes she saw a taxi and flagged it down and told the driver to take her to King of Prussia. She got out her phone and, her hand shaking, dialed Walt's cell number. When he answered she could hear what was likely The Weather Channel in the background.

"Walt, can you pick me up at the King of Prussia Mall?"

"Sure," said Walt, sounding baffled. "When?"

"If you leave now we'll probably get there at the same time."

"OK."

Ann named an entrance to one of the anchor stores as their meeting place, ended the call, then sat back staring out the window and running the strap of her handbag through her fingers again and again. Her phone buzzed periodically, showing her brother's number, but she ignored it. Two hours later she and Walt were in the air and on their way back to the Adirondacks.

Chapter 16

The day after the abortive attempt to show the Rittenhouse Square house to the Van Dykes, Joyce dialed the number for Mark Pironi, the seller's agent.

"Pironi here."

"Hi, Mark, it's Joyce Grigson."

"Hey, Joyce, how did the showing go yesterday?"

"Well ... interesting, to say the least." She patted her hair self-consciously. She wished Mark Pironi would ask her out on a date. "We didn't even get to go in—"

"Wasn't the key in the lock box? Man, I *told* my assistant it had to be there first thing in the morning—"

"No, it wasn't that. The clients wouldn't go in. One of my clients is very interested in the occult and she had brought along a ... well, I don't know what you'd call her but she claims to be able to 'sense spirits,'" she said, warming to her story. "My client is looking for a house that's, well, haunted, but in a friendly way, I suppose you'd say. But when we got to the Rittenhouse Square house this psychic woman completely freaked out, wouldn't go in, just ran off. I guess she must have taken a taxi because she didn't take the limo they had come in—"

"Weird," said Pironi. "And the actual buyers wouldn't go in either?"

"They already saw it a couple of weeks ago—the Van Dykes, remember?—and liked it, but now they want to know if it's haunted so they didn't care about looking at it again without this woman."

"Oh, right, Van Dyke," said Pironi, having no memory of that conversation with Joyce. "Well, it takes all kinds. Listen, if your buyers are interested in a townhouse, I have a nice one in Old City, can't say if it's haunted but same period as the Rittenhouse Square place but a little bigger with a chef-grade kitchen ..."

Pironi and Joyce chatted in realtorese for a bit, Pironi deflecting any suggestions of discussing the state of the market over drinks. As soon as seemed reasonably polite, he ended the call.

He briefly thought about calling Biden Firth with an update but he was actually supposed to be accompanying anyone looking at the townhouse and he didn't feel like extending the deception quite so far as pretending he had witnessed the event in person, with all the potential pitfalls that entailed. He did, however, relate the story to a hot agent from Wayne between puffs of a post-coital cigar who repeated it, without attribution, to her husband. Her husband passed it on to his squash partner who mentioned it to his accountant who the next day was paired with Morgan Firth for an early-morning round of golf and who erroneously thought the anecdote would amuse his partner. So it was that less than a week after Ann's visit to Rittenhouse Square that Joe Booth got a call at work from an angry Morgan Firth.

"What the hell are you people doing to find out who killed my daughter-in-law? I'm having to listen to morons tell me stories about how she's haunting my son's house! It's been two months since she disappeared, it's been more than two weeks since they found her body—don't you have *anything*?"

Joe made soothing noises about continued investigation, following up leads, something bound to surface soon, and Morgan Firth, not at all soothed, said, "I'm not above calling the Commissioner and telling him what a sorry cluster this investigation is—" Joe heard a woman's voice in the background. "Pardon my French," grumbled Firth, then continued, wearily, "just find out what happened to my daughter-in-law. I'm just sick and goddamned tired of this hanging over my family," and the line went dead.

Joe hung up and ran his fingers through his hair. "Fantastic," he said gloomily.

He sat back and drummed his pencil vigorously on the desk blotter until someone yelled, "Hey, Booth, knock it off!" He sighed, rolled back from his desk, and took his Flyers mug to the break room for a coffee refill. Back at his desk he turned to his computer. He had very little to show for his work over the last two months besides his suspicions—any lead was worth following up on, he thought.

A read through the file, a couple of phone calls, and an internet search gained him the phone number of the real estate agent who had attempted to show the Firth house to her spooky clients and their paranormal advisor.

After identifying himself—Joyce Grigson sounded quite excited to be receiving a call from a police detective—and hearing her version of the event, Joe asked, "Do you know what that woman's name was?"

"Ann Kinnear," said Joyce promptly. "I've spoken with her brother, Mike Kinnear, who is also her business manager. I have his number here somewhere ..." After a few moments she read it out. "May I ask why you're interested?"

"A woman who lived there disappeared." Joe chose not to add that she had recently reappeared in Tinicum Marsh.

"Really?" said Joan. "How awful! Did something happen to her in the house?"

"We have no reason to think that," replied Joe.

"How interesting. What was her name?"

"I really can't share any more details," he said, regretting that he had shared any details at all. "And I'd just like to reiterate that there's no evidence that the house had anything to do with the woman's disappearance." All he needed was for Morgan Firth somehow to hear that the police were interfering with the sale of his son's townhouse.

"Yes, of course," said Joyce conspiratorially. "Well, maybe that woman does have some supernatural powers. Or," she continued, "she just did a little homework ahead of time."

Joe thanked Joyce Grigson for her time and hung up. He ran a search on "ann kinnear" then sat back to read what his search had brought back.

Joe clicked on the first link, for annkinnear.com. The web site's design was conservative and the colors muted.

Ann Kinnear is a spirit senser whose skills have been reported on and documented in the national media. Miss Kinnear is able to perceive manifestations of spirits in color, sound, and scent and, based on those perceptions, can provide advice regarding the demeanor of the spirit— for example, if it is welcoming or otherwise. Miss Kinnear's skills can be of value to people considering purchase of a home who wish to ensure that their ownership experience will not be marred by a malign spirit. She has also been able to put the minds of many homeowners to rest by confirming whether or not phenomena they are experiencing in their homes are the result of a resident spirit.

Miss Kinnear's skills have been documented by the History Channel in *The Sense of Death*.

Links provided access to a trailer of the History Channel show and a video excerpt of Ann's interview. Joe clicked on the link and saw Ann Kinnear speaking to an off-camera interviewer.

"When a person dies," she said, "it's like a door opens and lets some essence of them out. Sometimes it's like a color, sometimes it's like a sound, sometimes it's like a scent. You might go into a house and know right away that someone is baking bread or has burned something on the stove, or you might go into a house where no one has cooked for years but know that the family that used to live there used a lot of garlic. It's the same with people, they leave an essence when they die and it's good or bad, it's recent or old."

Joe returned to the web site and continued reading:

> Miss Kinnear also works with law enforcement officials on recovery missions in missing persons cases, helping to bring a sense of closure to families in distress. Please click the links below for coverage of two of Miss Kinnear's most celebrated such cases.

The links displayed news coverage of a young woman who had died while caving in Pennsylvania and another who had died on a hike in Wyoming, along with references to Ann's involvement in locating the women's bodies. Joe read through the linked material. The site continued …

> Please note that Miss Kinnear does not engage spirits in two-way conversations as some others claim to be able to do.
>
> Ann Kinnear grew up outside Philadelphia, Pennsylvania, and currently lives in New York's Adirondack Park.

A Contact page provided a phone number and e-mail address for those "interested in discussing the possibility of engaging Ann Kinnear."

He sat back, drumming his pencil on the blotter, thinking about what Amelia Dormand had said about hearing her daughter speak to her in the Firth house. After sipping his coffee for a minute, he sat forward at the keyboard again and did a few searches that gave him the name of the person on the Lewistown, Pennsylvania, police force—Adrian Brunauer—who had been in charge of the Pennsylvania caver case and another search that provided him with the police department number.

Joe dialed the number and asked for Brunauer, not expecting the person in charge of a fourteen-year-old investigation to still be with the department, but the person who took his call put him through. To Joe's surprise, Brunauer turned out to be a man. Joe introduced himself.

"I'm investigating the disappearance of a woman named Elizabeth Firth. It's possible she was killed in her home in Philadelphia. The house is for sale now and I understand that some potential buyers brought in a psychic to check it out and she had a very negative reaction to the place. Her name is Ann Kinnear. Do you remember her?"

"Sure," rasped Brunauer. "The Barboza case."

"Yes. I understand she helped find the body?"

"Yup, just an hour or so after the girl died."

"Was there anything, I don't know, *fishy* about her finding the body?"

Brunauer cleared his throat a few times. "I never got the idea she was scamming us. In fact, I got the impression she would just as soon not have been there. I was suspicious of the brother for a while, he seemed like the ringleader, but there wasn't anything to suggest he had any inside scoop or had set anything up. There sure wasn't anything to suggest that the Barboza girl's death was anything but an accident."

"So how do you think Ann Kinnear knew where the girl had died?" asked Joe.

Brunauer cleared his throat a few more times and finally said, "I honestly don't know. I tried to figure out a logical explanation for a while and then I gave up. I figured the

Kinnear girl found the body, I don't know how, and saved us and the Barboza family a bunch of heartache. It ended up not being worth trying to figure out."

"You think she really has some kind of ability to sense dead people?" said Joe.

"You got me," said Brunauer. "She found the Barboza girl and I decided not to ask why."

Joe thanked Brunauer, gave him his phone number out of habit, and disconnected.

Joe refilled his coffee mug again and, returning to his desk, placed a call to the number on annkinnear.com. The call was answered after a few rings.

"Hello, this is Mike Kinnear."

"This is Detective Joe Booth from the Philadelphia Police Department. I was calling with a question about the services described on the Ann Kinnear web site."

"Certainly, Detective, how can I help you?"

"Miss Kinnear is your sister?"

"Yes."

"I spoke to a realtor, Joyce Grigson, who said that her clients had engaged Miss Kinnear to check out a house they were thinking of buying, a house off Rittenhouse Square, and that she had a very negative reaction to it."

"Yes, that's true."

"Did she say why she had such a negative reaction?"

"Only that something bad had happened there. Did something bad happen there?"

"I don't know. We're investigating a disappearance."

"Did someone disappear from the house? Or at the house?"

"I'm afraid I can't discuss the case, but I'd be interested in speaking with your sister."

"I'd be happy to set up a conference call for us," said

Mike.

"I'd prefer to talk to her one-on-one, at least initially," said Joe, thinking of Brunauer's description of Mike Kinnear at the "ringleader."

"Certainly. You said your name was Joe Booth?"

"Yes."

"What precinct do you work out of?"

Joe told him.

"Could you hold for a minute?"

"Sure."

Joe was on hold for more like three minutes, then Mike came back on the line. "Sorry about that," he said. "If it's all right I'd like to give her a call first to let her know you'll be contacting her, she's a very private person and doesn't like unsolicited phone calls. She probably wouldn't even answer if she didn't recognize the number."

"Yes, that's fine," said Joe.

Mike gave him Ann's number.

"Could I have the address too?" said Joe.

Mike gave him the address. "Just give me half an hour or so to give her a call before you try her," he said.

"Actually I was planning on driving up there," said Joe.

"Really?" said Mike. "She lives in the Adirondacks. It's about eight hours away."

"I know. Tomorrow's my day off, I don't mind a drive. I hear it's a nice area."

"Oh, it's beautiful," said Mike. "Pretty time of year, too. What time do you think you'd be arriving?"

Joe had typed the address into an online map site and did a quick calculation. "I'd say between three and four," he said.

"I'll let her know. Can I get your mobile number?"

Joe gave it to him.

Mike jotted the number down. "If Ann is able to help out with a police investigation, I assume we would be able to post information to that effect on her web site?"

"I'm not sure how that works, you'd probably need to work with the PR department, but let's cross that bridge when we come to it."

"Of course," said Mike.

A few minutes after they hung up, the internal line on Joe's phone rang. "It's Stu," said The Mouse. "A guy called a couple of minutes ago asking if you worked here. Name was McAneer or something like that. I tried to put him through but your line was busy."

"Thanks, Stu," said Joe. "I think I was on hold with him when he called you."

"Ah. Checking to see if you were who you said you were, eh? OK." The Mouse disconnected.

Joe hung up. If you were in the psychic business it probably paid to be cautious, he thought, you never knew what kind of person was going to take an interest.

Chapter 17

Ann, Mike, and their parents had vacationed in the Adirondacks when Ann and Mike were children. They had first gone there when Ann was seven, stretching the eight hour drive to twelve with stops at various historic sites and scenic overlooks along the way. Her mother had wisely reserved a motel room for the first night in anticipation of a late arrival but they had spent the next few nights camping, her parents' latest interest. She remembered on that first trip her parents consulting a camping book borrowed from the library for nearly everything, from pitching the tent to building the fire. And she especially remembered sitting around the fire that first night, her father poking the logs proprietarily with a stick, and her mother saying, "Annie, see the fireflies?"

Of course she had seen the fireflies, but she had thought they were spirits, rising from the ground and drifting up into the high branches—in the woods and with the firelight flickering they somehow had looked more otherworldly than fireflies in her own backyard.

She had learned not to talk about seeing spirits because such declarations were inevitably met with worry (her mother), amusement (her father), or taunts (her classmates). Only Mike always believed her.

That week in the Adirondacks, as they drove through the park or hiked the trails, she began to notice with surprise how few spirits she sensed. The hiking paths could be so dark and the woods so primeval-looking that it seemed like a place that should have ghosts. But already Ann sensed that "ghosts" was not the right word, implying as it did something malevolent, the husk of a whole person returned from the dead. She believed that what she sensed was the inner essence left behind by a person now gone.

But she felt that "haunted" was not a bad term to describe what the spirits did. The ones she had encountered were haunting a place, not a person. Susan, the spirit in the house in West Chester, wasn't there because of Ann or anyone else living there now—and Ann was quite sure that Susan wasn't there because of anyone who had lived there when she herself was alive. Susan's spirit haunted the house because she was tied to the house itself and wasn't ready to leave it. But Ann had discovered that using the word "haunted" had even less desirable consequences than talking about seeing spirits and so she had learned not to talk about that either.

She began to think of the Adirondacks as "clean"—she came to apply this term to anywhere free of spirits—and she returned there again and again, on more trips with her family, on trips with Mike when she was old enough to drive and her parents' interests switched to island vacations, and later on, when Mike was occupied with his own circle of friends, on trips by herself. She was able to relax in the Adirondacks in a way she couldn't relax in places where spirits were more prevalent. It wasn't so much that she objected to the spirits themselves as that she felt more normal when she wasn't dealing with them, when she was relieved of the need to pretend they weren't there when they were.

When Ann and Mike were in college, their parents were killed in a car accident. They received a considerable inheritance, one that, had they been willing to live quite modestly (which they weren't), could have relieved them of the need to work. They sold the house they had grown up in and for several years after they graduated from college had shared a much smaller rented house in West Chester. But when Mike, who by this time had established his credentials as a financial planner, bought the townhouse he now shared with Scott, Ann had started looking for properties in the Adirondacks and soon found exactly what she was looking for—a two story log cabin on seven acres on the shore of Loon Pond.

One of the many things that had attracted Ann to the cabin was that it appeared to be "clean." But over time she began to think that there was a spirit, not in the house itself but in the woods surrounding the house. When she was walking in the woods or chopping wood or throwing a toy into the pond for her dog, Beau, to fetch, she would sometimes get a sense of being not alone, of being observed, but there was never any other manifestation accompanying this sense—not the colors, sounds, or scents she was used to experiencing. Sometimes she thought it could be the spirit of a person who was so long dead that only the faintest whisper of their essence remained. Sometimes she thought she was just imagining things.

In casting about for a way to occupy her time, Ann began working on developing her skills in oil painting, an interest that had begun in high school with a gift of painting supplies from her father. Now she mainly painted Adirondack wildflowers and other vegetation. A few mornings a week, usually weekdays when the Adirondack Park trails were less busy, she would load Beau and her camera into her car to scout subjects for her paintings. When she found what she was looking for and had gotten a digital image that pleased her, she would spend the next few days capturing the image in oil. As her skills grew, and with Mike's encouragement, she started shopping the paintings around to local galleries, using the name Kay Near. The paintings sold well and Mike had expanded the business by having note cards of the paintings printed. Ann was starting to experiment with small landscape paintings as well; one she had done of a Chester County barn had sold recently at a gallery in West Chester.

Ann's cabin, being surrounded by trees, was too dark to serve as a studio and the Adirondack Park regulations prevented her from building on the one reliably sunny part of the property—on the shore of the pond—so several years before she had bought a twenty acre lot a few miles from her cabin that had a cleared area at the height of the land giving excellent views of the surrounding mountains. She had a studio built—a twenty by thirty foot space surrounded on three sides by large windows, with a small kitchen and bathroom tucked into the fourth side.

Mike loved the studio and when he visited they would often spend the day there with a cooler of beer, cooking burgers on the grill and playing horseshoes while Scott fished in the river that bordered the property.

But Ann's favorite location, after the dock, was the fire pit near the cabin, created with rocks she had collected from the woods and surrounded by three worn Adirondack chairs. In the evenings, she and Mike and Scott would sit—fanning themselves with newspaper pages from the kindling supplies or huddling in their coats, depending on the season—roasting hot dogs or marshmallows. Beau especially enjoyed the hot dog roasts and would scooch closer and closer to the fire, drooling copiously, until Ann gave him a hot dog which, rather than wolfing down immediately, he would take to a sheltered area under the screen porch where he would settle into a smooth-packed, Beau-shaped depression in the dirt and nibble on delicately. Mike enjoyed teaching Beau music-themed tricks, such as touching his paw to his muzzle in a canine salute when Mike whistled "Reveille" and playing dead to "Taps." He had tried, with the help of some peanut butter, to teach Beau to lick Ann's cheek when he whistled a bar of "Kiss Me" by The Cranberries but the closest Beau got was to snuffle Ann's ear.

Chapter 18

Joe Booth left Philadelphia for the Adirondacks early the next morning and reached his destination a little before 4:00. He followed his GPS's instructions from the two lane state highway to a gravel turnoff and began skirting the large "pond" that was one of the hundreds of bodies of water in Adirondack Park. He followed the road to its end and then continued on past a small "Private Drive" sign. About fifty yards further on, up a gradual incline, was a dirt parking area, one of its two spaces occupied by a Subaru Forester, its edges marked by birch logs. From here Joe could see the sparkle of water down a steep, tree-covered slope while the view in the other direction, up the hill, was blocked by a bank of fluffy, bright green ferns. About twenty yards diagonally down the hill and joined to the parking area by a series of log steps stood a two story log house.

Joe stepped out of the car and as he slammed the door a large, shaggy German Shepherd-like dog appeared from behind the ferns and came trotting toward him. He opened the car door, ready to retreat into the car, but the dog stopped about ten yards from him and gave a sharp bark, then stood motionless, eyes fixed on Joe.

"Good boy," said Joe experimentally. "Are you a good boy?"

"Usually," said a voice from beyond where the dog stood and now Joe noticed a woman leaning on the axe, a pile of split firewood at her feet. Her stance seemed relaxed at first glance but Joe noted the tightness of her grip on the axe handle and a tautness in her jaw. She was wearing an old Rush concert t-shirt, cargo pants, and heavy hiking boots. Her reddish blonde hair was held back in a ponytail, wispy tendrils curling at the nape of her neck.

"Friendly?" said Joe.

"It depends."

Joe reached into his pocket and held up his badge. "Joe Booth, Philadelphia police."

There was a long pause and then the woman gave a short, sharp whistle and the dog sat down.

"Thanks." Joe put his badge away. "Are you Ann Kinnear?"

"Yes."

"I'd like to speak with you if you don't mind."

There was another long pause. Finally she said, "OK," and started down the slight hill from where the chopping block stood, carrying the axe.

"Would you mind leaving that up there?" said Joe.

She shrugged and sank the axe into the chopping block. She came down to the parking area, pulling off leather gloves. When she reached Joe she said, "Yes?"

"Could we sit down somewhere?"

"Could I see your badge again?"

Joe pulled out his badge and handed it to her; she examined it for a moment and handed it back.

"We can go in the house." Ann gave a long ascending whistle and the dog trotted over to her side as they walked down the hill to the house. Ann unlocked the door with a key on a string around her neck.

"I'm surprised you bother to lock up way out here," said Joe.

"Better safe than sorry," she replied.

They walked into the tidy-looking kitchen of the cabin. Straight ahead, a counter-height breakfast bar separated the kitchen from the dining area which was walled with windows giving on to a screened-in porch through which Joe could see the water at the bottom of the hill. To the right a short hallway led from the kitchen to what looked like a living room, a section of floor-to-ceiling bookshelves visible from the kitchen. Off the hallway were doors that Joe guessed led to a bathroom on the right and the basement on the left. A flight of stairs at the center of the house led to the second floor.

The dog sat down on a rag rug in the kitchen, still watching Joe attentively.

"Nice looking dog," said Joe.

"Thanks."

"Shepherd?"

"Mostly."

"What's his name?"

"Beau. Have a seat." She motioned to the table in the eating area. Joe took a seat but she remained standing in the kitchen on the other side of the breakfast bar, her arms crossed.

Joe took a small notepad and a pen out of his shirt pocket. "I understand you were in Philadelphia recently."

"Yes."

"Could you tell me what you were doing there?"

"It would help me if you told me why you're asking me these questions."

"I'd rather get the answers to my questions first."

"How did you know where I live?"

"Your brother told me."

Ann raised her eyebrows. "My brother would hardly give directions to my house to someone without letting me know."

"He said he was going to call you."

Ann pulled her cell phone out of a holster clipped to the waistband of her pants and glanced at the display. "No messages."

"Check your voicemail. Or, better yet, call your brother."

Ann arched her eyebrows skeptically then speed dialed voicemail and heard the voice intone, "You have two unplayed messages."

"Shit," she muttered.

The first message was from the morning of the previous day. "Hey, I got a call from a guy named Joe Booth, he's a detective with the Philly police. I checked him out and he's legit. He heard about what happened at the Rittenhouse Square house and wanted to talk with you about it. He asked for your address and I didn't realize until after I had given it to him that he was actually planning on driving up there. He wouldn't give me any details because it's part of an active investigation. I'm thinking the house was a crime scene. Might be a PR opportunity in this. Anyway, I'll try you back again later."

The second message was from the afternoon. "Hey, A., it's me. Do you have your phone turned off? Anyhow, hopefully you got my earlier message, I'll try you again later."

According to the incoming message log, Mike had called again in the evening but had not left a message. Ann hit redial on the last message. The phone rang then went to Mike's voicemail. "Hey, it's me. I got your messages, didn't want you to worry, everything's fine, my phone's been acting up per usual. I'll call you back later." Ann replaced the phone in the holster and turned to Joe. "OK, what do you want to know?"

"Tell me what happened at the house near Rittenhouse Square."

"My brother and I were there with clients. Did he tell you what we do?"

"I read your web site and a couple of other articles about you."

"OK. Well, these clients were considering buying the

house and they wanted to know if it was … haunted. I could tell without even going in the house that there was something wrong with it and I told them that. I told them I wasn't going to go in but they were insistent so I left."

"What was it that was wrong?"

"I don't know, I just knew it was bad."

"But you couldn't tell what had caused it?"

"No."

"Do you think you could if you went in the house?"

Ann sighed. "I don't know. Maybe. But it's not like I see things happening like a movie playing."

"But your web site says that this sense you get," Joe glanced down at his notebook, "the colors or the sounds or the smells, comes from when a person dies."

"Yes."

"So if you had that reaction to that house, it probably means someone died there, and since it was so strong that it was probably recently, right?"

Another pause. "Probably."

Joe tapped his pen vigorously on the notepad then stopped himself. "Do you know what happened there?"

"No, I told you, I don't see details."

"But you could find out details if you wanted to," he said cautiously.

"What do you mean?"

"I mean a couple of internet searches and you could probably find out what happened there. Or at least get an idea of what might have happened there."

"If it's so easy, why don't you just do that?" she said testily.

"Because I already know what *might* have happened there, my problem is that I have to prove it."

Ann blew out her breath. "Sorry. To answer your

question, both my brother and I have a policy not to read any news that might end up having a bearing on a current or potential engagement. Which means I know a lot about international news but practically nothing about anything going on in the eastern half of the United States." Joe raised his eyebrows and she shrugged. "It's a strange profession."

Joe sat back in his chair to look at her. She looked small and forlorn, barricaded behind the breakfast bar, her arms crossed. He realized she was telling him these things without any expectation that he would believe her.

"I have a favor to ask you," he said.

"What's that?"

"I'd like you to come back to Philly and go through the house and tell me what you sense."

"You'd *like* me to do that? It's not an order?"

"No, it's not an order, I don't think the department would look kindly on issuing a warrant to bring a ..." He stopped.

"Psychic?"

"Is that what you call what you do?"

"No, but that's what a lot of people call it."

"Well, anyhow ... it's a request, not an order. I also can't reimburse you for the trip, but your brother seemed to think it might be good publicity if something comes of your participation in the investigation."

Ann looked out the dining room windows toward the water. "What do *you* think happened at that house?" asked Ann.

"I'd rather not say until you've been through it."

"So do you often go to 'psychics' for help with your investigations?"

"Well, I did try more traditional methods first but I keep coming up on dead ends."

"So you're desperate."

Joe shrugged. "I'm willing to try less traditional

methods."

"How do you propose I get in the house?" asked Ann.

"You had a deal with your clients to go through the house. Tell them you're willing to do it now."

After Joe left, with a recommendation from Ann for where he could get dinner before starting back to Philadelphia (Ann wondered if he was planning on making the round trip in one day), she called Mike.

"Hey, you need a new phone," said Mike.

"I know, I'll look into it. Joe Booth was just here."

"Did he ask about the Rittenhouse Square house?"

"Yes. He seemed interested in the fact that I got the sense of something bad having happened there recently."

"He told me he was investigating a disappearance," said Mike.

"He wants me to go back, to go through the house and let him know what I think."

"Well, you'd get no argument from me there," said Mike. "We still owe the Van Dykes a visit, and if we can help the police with an investigation and get some PR out of that, that's icing on the cake."

Chapter 19

Some years before, Mike had been contacted by a producer from the History Channel named Corey Duff who was producing a show called *Talking with the Dead* about people who have claimed to be able to communicate with the departed and how they have been accepted or rejected by society. Duff had read about the Barboza incident, as well as a similar event that had taken place a few years later involving a lost hiker in Wyoming whose body Ann had found, and wanted to interview Ann. Mike explained that Ann did not "talk with the dead" in the sense of engaging in a conversation with them but Duff was still interested and they arranged an interview in a conference room in a Lake Placid hotel. Ann rarely gave interviews, leaving the public side of the business to Mike, but to Mike's surprise she agreed to appear on camera.

Duff was a skilled and encouraging interviewer and Ann talked at some length about the Barboza tragedy—talked more, in fact, than she ever had before, even to Mike—and discussed some of her other engagements in what had become a sort of consulting practice after she and Mike had graduated from college.

Ann's interview ended up on the cutting room floor during editing for *Talking with the Dead* but the following year Duff produced a follow-up show called *The Sense of Death* and not only used Ann's interview but also arranged for an additional segment featuring Ann. Without providing her with any information in advance, he arranged visits to three locations where someone had died within the previous few months—one a home where an old man had choked to death on a piece of pizza, one the roadside site of a car accident that had killed a teenage girl, and one a convenience store where the middle aged male owner had been shot and killed during a robbery.

At the first location Ann correctly identified the kitchen as the place where someone had died, specifically in the area by the sink, a fact Duff himself had not known until he investigated further after Ann's visit. Ann guessed at a choking death because the sense was one of surprise and then panic—the spirit seemed to be inhabiting the house out of a sense that "it wasn't his time yet." The home's current owner said that late at night—the time the old man was thought to have died—they sometimes heard banging coming from the kitchen which they had always attributed to the plumbing.

Ann got nothing at the site of the car accident. When Duff explained the circumstances of the death to her, she speculated that it was because there was nothing that tied the girl to that location; when she died she had probably passed on immediately to whatever lay beyond the dimension Ann could sense. And what was that? Duff has asked. Ann said she had no idea, her sense of the dead did not extend that far.

At the convenience store, Ann sensed anger—a bright red aura and a bitter, skunky smell. She told Duff she sensed someone whose spirit was waiting to even a score, to get revenge. In fact, the brothers of the dead man, co-owners of the store, sold the store not long after Ann's visit, saying that they too could sense the anger—although its manifestation was not as physical for them as it was for Ann—and that being in the store was too upsetting for them.

The show featured two other "sensers" as Duff called them. One was a woman in New Mexico who could summon up visualizations of the dead by holding objects that had been important to them—usually wedding rings or other pieces of often-worn jewelry. The other was a man from Maine named Garrick Masser who had been featured in Duff's first show and who saw and heard the dead as they had been in their lives. Based on viewer response, there was some skepticism over the claims of the other two sensers—despite Duff staging similar tests for them and the apparent accuracy of their results in those tests—but it seemed that the relative modesty of Ann's claims convinced many in the audience of her legitimacy.

Mike was pleased that after the show aired the number of calls he received for Ann's services increased markedly—he was able to be more selective about the work they accepted, and was able to charge significantly more for those engagements.

For Ann, the increased attention was a mixed blessing—when Mike informed her that an infatuated teenager had set up an internet fan site, she was more alarmed than flattered. In many ways she regretted trading her anonymity for the public validation she realized had been her impetus for accepting Corey Duff's invitation to participate in his project.

But in addition to the validation was the opportunity to get to know other people who shared her ability—and just as her internet fan doubtless scoured the web for the infrequent mentions of Ann Kinnear, so did Ann begin surreptitiously tracking the activities of Garrick Masser.

Chapter 20

A little over a week after the visit from Joe, Walt flew Ann back to West Chester. Mike and Mavis met them at the passenger terminal; Lawrence had evidently decided to sit this one out.

"Sorry about before," said Ann.

"I'm curious to learn more about what you sensed that made you beat such a hasty retreat," said Mavis stiffly.

As before, Joyce was waiting at the door when they arrived although this time the limo didn't pull away after dropping them off across the street, Mike having whispered to the driver that they might not be very long.

Ann steeled herself as she crossed the street and mounted the marble steps. The sense of horrible foreboding had not been as immediately apparent upon stepping out of the car as it had been on the first visit but the sense reasserted itself as she neared the door. Again she felt the force of whatever terrible thing had happened in this house making her want to turn away. And again she felt something summoning her to the house, this time with less frenzy but no less urgency. She crossed her arms and a shiver ran through her body despite the warmth of the May morning.

Reaching the steps, she nodded to Joyce and was introduced, along with Mike and Mavis, to a new addition to the party—Mark Pironi, the seller's agent. Then the party entered the house.

The house, although not large by Rittenhouse Square standards, was, as Lawrence had said, beautifully finished, with the entrance hall floored in black and white marble in a diamond pattern, expensive-looking oil paintings on the walls, and a staircase with an elaborately carved newel post along the right-hand wall.

Ann glanced around the foyer, her lips tight and her face pale. "Let's start at the top," said Ann, and they climbed the steps after her.

The third floor included the gym, outfitted with professional grade equipment. "The seller might be willing to include the equipment if you're interested—" began Pironi but stopped when Mike gave him a slight shake of the head.

Ann circled the room quickly and then made an equally cursory tour of the small two-bedroom apartment that Joan and Esme used when they stayed overnight. "Nothing," she said shortly and descended to the second floor.

There were four bedrooms on this floor. The front room had large windows overlooking the street and was outfitted as a study—likely a woman's study based on the delicate furniture and light, airy decor. Ann walked behind the desk and sat down, gazing around the room then glancing across the mostly bare desk top. She picked up a silver-framed photograph—it showed a couple seated on a rustic wooden bench and, on the woman's lap, a little girl. The man, strikingly handsome with very short gray hair and startlingly blue eyes, had his arm draped over the woman's shoulders. The woman, with black hair pulled back from an elegantly beautiful face, was waving the little girl's hand at the photographer, the little girl looking curiously at her own, waving hand. The man and woman were laughing—Ann could almost hear the photographer laughing with them. Behind them a green field rolled away to distant trees. No doubt the owners of the house, she thought—they looked a bit old to be the parents of such a young child but such things were getting less surprising with each generation. What did surprise her was the contrast between the obvious happiness of the people in the photographs and the distress that the house exuded. She shook her head. She wasn't expert in understanding people when they were alive, only in understanding what they left behind once they had died.

She glanced toward the door where the group stood, looking at her expectantly. She shook her head. "Nothing." She replaced the photograph on the desk, its place marked by a dust-free area, and crossed to the group which parted to let her pass.

The next room was obviously a guest room—as beautifully decorated as the other rooms but lacking the comfortable clutter that marked rooms used regularly. She barely stuck her head into the room before shaking her head and continuing down the hallway to what turned out to be a nursery decorated in a Beatrix Potter theme. She glanced briefly at a grouping of small photos on the dresser—mostly of the little girl alone with one or two also including the dark-haired woman—but she knew there was nothing for her to sense in this room either.

The last room on the second floor was the master bedroom. She passed fairly quickly through the bedroom itself but lingered in the walk-in closet, lightly touching the boxes and suitcases on the upper shelves and running her hands over the clothes.

"Uh, the clothes aren't included in the sale," said Pironi.

"Yes, we know that," said Mavis dismissively, not taking her eyes off Ann. "Ann, are you sensing anything?"

"Not clearly. It's not a happy place," said Ann.

"What do you mean?" asked Mavis.

"Not happy. Sad," said Ann shortly and moved into the hallway.

She descended the stairs slowly, almost unwillingly, to the

first floor. She started to cross the foyer to the living room and then, near an antique sideboard, abruptly sidestepped and stopped. After a moment she took another step toward the living room, then jerked her head back to the center of the foyer. Mavis looked questioningly at Mike who raised his eyebrows and shrugged.

After another moment Ann shook herself, scanned the foyer, then moved into the living room. She circled the room, running her fingers over the furniture and knick-knacks then shook her head; she passed through the dining room with the same result. They returned to the foyer and crossed to the library, Ann skirting the area near the sideboard.

In the library Ann took her time, touching the furniture, sitting on the leather couch, running her hands over the book cases. At one point she squatted down and ran her hands over the rug. She also began displaying what looked to the others in the party like a nervous tic, periodically jerking her head slightly to the left or right. Then she walked to the window and looked out at the street.

"This room has a lot of anger in it. Hurtful words were spoken here and infected the space. Those feelings will color anything that happens here for a long time."

"How can you tell about what words were spoken?" asked Mavis. "I don't recall you sensing anything like that before."

"No, I don't either," said Ann. "But an argument definitely happened here, there's a sort of ... buzzing in the air. Like a wasp. If wasps buzz."

"Bees buzz," said Pironi helpfully.

"More like a wasp," said Ann.

"Well, bee or wasp, I suppose this one is off the list," said Mavis with an air of satisfaction. Experiencing a house with an unfriendly spirit was only slightly less gratifying than finding one with a friendly one. "I suppose we can go now," she said to Ann solicitously.

"No, we haven't seen everything," said Ann and, leaving the library with the group following her, turned left toward the back of the house. She passed the kitchen with scarcely a glance and in the back hallway, off the kitchen, opened a door and descended a short flight of steps to the garage. One bay held a pristinely clean Porsche Carrera, the other was empty.

"Very unusual to have a garage as part of the house in Center City," Pironi said gamely and then lapsed back into silence when Mike glared at him.

Ann became more animated as she walked around the garage, first circling the garage bays and then beginning to pat her way around the room, along the walls, across a workbench, until she came to a metal cabinet, secured with a combination lock, where she paused for a moment and then continued around the wall back to the stairway. She continued exhibiting the tic that had developed in the library. She turned and surveyed the room, then crossed to a door in the opposite corner and fiddled with the lock. "Mike, I can't get this," she said.

Mike crossed to the door and as he flipped the lock, which opened easily, Ann whispered, "Get Pironi out of the garage for a few minutes."

Ann and Mike stepped out of the garage into the alley behind the house, Mike looking up at the back of the house in an appraising manner as the others joined them.

"Nicely maintained," he said.

"Yes, no fixing up needed on this one," said Pironi.

Mike was now walking down the alley as if to get a view of the house from the side. "Now how much of this is original and how much has been added? Because," he said to Mavis, "oftentimes the presence of spirits is more strongly concentrated in the older parts of a building ..."

She slipped back into the garage unnoticed and crossed to the metal cabinet and stood with her hands resting on top of it. She was sure this was where the spirit was directing her. She had felt it throughout the house—not just the usual sense of the person, sometimes as they were throughout their lives and sometimes as they were in the moments of their death, but rather a communication directed specifically at her. It was largely a physical sense of being lightly pushed in a certain direction—to the garage—but light not because of a lack of urgency on the part of the pusher but because of her own inability to fully absorb the sensation.

Along with this physical sensation was a visual aspect that was different from the amorphous manifestations she was used to. She had a clear sense of a person—a woman—glimpsed just at the periphery of her vision but gone when she turned her head. It reminded her of an episode when she was little when Mike had thrown a ball to her when she wasn't looking and it had hit her eye and torn the retina, creating a myriad of "floaters" that had taken months to settle out of her vision. She had spent a lot of time in her darkened bedroom during those months because the floaters were less noticeable in the dark—it had made her crazy to try to look at one and have it track just outside her point of focus, disappearing from sight just as she thought she would catch up to it.

She removed her hands from the cabinet and pressed them to her eyes, trying to block out the onslaught of unfamiliar sensations, when she felt a hand on her shoulder.

She dropped her hands and, whirling around, again caught that infuriating glimpse of someone, but the garage was empty.

"What do you want?" she whispered hoarsely and very faintly she heard a response ...

In there.

Ann turned back to the cabinet. "In here?"

Yes.

Ann knelt in front of the cabinet and tugged on the combination lock. "What's the combination?" she said, only half joking.

This time there was no auditory response but Ann sensed anger and frustration. She shook her head and dropped the lock which clattered on the metal cabinet. "I can't. It's locked." And she heard the voice again, growing ever more faint ...

Get it ... blue ...

Ann shook her head, "I don't understand. Get something from the cabinet that's blue?"

She didn't hear the voice again but suddenly something grabbed her wrist and her hand was pulled toward the lock. She gasped and jerked her hand back, falling from her kneeling position onto the cement floor of the garage and as she did she heard the voices of the rest of the party drifting in from the alley. They mustn't see her by the cabinet, she thought. Especially Pironi. She scrambled unsteadily to her feet and backed away from the cabinet, then, scanning the garage one more time, made her way to the door to the alley.

The voices were coming from around the corner of the building and she came up behind the group as Mike was saying, "... then during the Victorian era there was an increased interest in the occult. Consider Sir Arthur Conan Doyle—" Pironi was staring pointedly at his watch and even Mavis seemed only politely interested. Mike saw Ann who gave him a quick nod and, with obvious relief, Mike said, "Well, perhaps we should be going—" just as Ann sank to a sitting position on the ground.

"Hey, A.," said Mike, startled, as he pushed through the group to Ann and knelt down beside her. "You OK?"

Ann shook her head to clear it. "Yes, I just got dizzy."

"What happened?" asked Mavis.

"I don't know," said Ann, then, realizing that didn't sound too believable after her earlier pronouncements about the house, added, "It's not healthy here, we should go."

Mike helped her to her feet while Joyce went in to get Ann a drink of water. Mike kept his hand on Ann's arm and as they re-entered the garage he noticed her surreptitious glance around the space before they climbed the stairs to the kitchen.

Joyce had a glass of water ready for Ann and was in the process of wringing out a dish towel in the sink.

"If you feel faint it sometimes helps to put a cool cloth on your face," she said, handing the towel to Ann but Ann shook her head.

"Thanks, I feel better now."

"Maybe it's the house that's healthy and the outside that's unhealthy," muttered Pironi peevishly.

Mavis replied with an irritated "Hmph."

When Mike was convinced that Ann was recovered, the group left the kitchen and headed toward the front door but turned when they realized that Ann had stopped in the entrance hall. She had squatted down and, as in the library, was running her hands across the floor. Her face was screwed up, as if she were being confronted with a foul odor. When she stood up she seemed unsteady once again, and leaned against the sideboard for a few seconds before following the rest of the party to the door. Before leaving the house she made a full turn, scanning the entrance hall, and then they stepped out into the May sunshine, Pironi locking the door behind them.

After seeing off the party, Mark Pironi walked to his car which was parked on the street a couple of blocks from the Firth house. Leaning against it he pushed a speed dial on his mobile phone. The call was answered on the second ring.

"Pironi here. They just left."

"What happened?" Pironi could hear traffic noises in the background.

"They had the psychic woman with them again, just like

Joyce described, except she went into the house this time. She kept talking about which rooms were happy and which rooms were sad. I think we can safely assume that the Van Dykes won't be making an offer."

"What did she say specifically?"

"Hardly spent any time on the third floor. I told them you might be willing to include the gym equipment …?"

"Maybe. What else?"

"She spent a little more time on the second floor, especially in the master bedroom. Most of the time she spent on the first floor. She said the library had bad karma—she didn't use those words exactly, but that was the sense of it. She had some kind of attack out back, had to sit down and have a glass of water. She spent a lot of time in the foyer running her hands over the floor."

"Where in the foyer?"

"Near the sideboard."

There was a pause on the other end of the line. "What did you think of her?"

Pironi hesitated. "She didn't seem strange when she first showed up but it got a little freakish by the time she was done. I don't think the Van Dykes would have bought anyway but she certainly put the nail in the coffin of that deal."

"Did you get her name?"

"Ann Kinnear. Her brother was there too—Mike Kinnear."

"OK. I appreciate you going, I like to know what people are saying about the house even if it's crazy stuff."

"No problem. Give my best to your dad, Biden, I haven't seen him for a while."

"Sure," Biden said and disconnected.

"Asshole," said Pironi and flipped his phone shut.

After the excitement of the visit to the Rittenhouse Square house, lunch was evidently an option again and Mavis suggested meeting up with Lawrence for a meal at her favorite Main Line restaurant.

"I want to hear all about it," she said, "it seemed so much more *vivid* than our other sensings have been!"

Before Ann had a chance to object to Mavis using the word "our," Mike said, "What do you think, A., feel up to lunch or would you like to call it a day?" Before Ann had a chance to reply, Mike turned to Mavis, saying, "I imagine that was quite exhausting for Ann."

Ann opened her mouth to weigh in but Mavis was nodding vigorously. "Oh, I'm sure that's true," she said, "we could certainly do lunch another day, but this morning's experience, it was quite extraordinary—"

Ann cleared her throat pointedly and they both looked at her expectantly. When she realized she didn't have anything to say, she sighed and turned to look out the window.

After a few uncomfortable moments had passed, Mike began, "Why don't we plan to have lunch with Lawrence next time—" when Ann turned back from the window in some excitement.

"I know, I'll paint it!" she said.

"What?" said Mike and Mavis at the same time.

Ann sat up straighter in the seat. "The visual part of the sensing was much more ... vivid than usual, like you said, Mavis. I think the spirit I was sensing was trying to show herself to me, not just as some kind of colored light but as she actually was. I think maybe if I could paint it for you it would be a better representation of what I experienced than if I tried to describe it."

"A painting of it," said Mavis, excited. "Yes, that might be very interesting. Plus it would provide a memento of our experience, wouldn't it?"

"A memento mori, one might say," said Mike as Ann rolled her eyes at both of them.

They dropped Mavis off at her home in Collegeville and Mike called Walt to let him know they were wrapping up. Then he turned to Ann. "So what *did* happen in the house?"

"Let's wait until we get to the airport, then I'll only have to tell it once."

Mike drummed his fingers on the arm rest impatiently, then said, "Hey, the painting idea is a good one, I should have thought of it before now."

"I don't think it would have worked before now, it would have been just spots of color—I'm not even sure I'm going to be able to come up with anything recognizable from today but it seems worth a try." She paused. "Plus it seemed like a good excuse to jettison Mavis."

"I hope that wasn't the primary reason," said Mike sternly. After a moment he added, "We should stay off the internet on this one, it wouldn't be good to happen on a photograph or other information that might subconsciously influence your painting."

"Yeah, I never surf the web anyway," replied Ann.

When they got to the airport they found Walt, a copy of *Aviation Safety* tucked under his arm, chatting with a tall, heavy-set man near the windows overlooking the ramp area. Ann and Mike approached them.

"Mike, this is Joe Booth," said Ann. They shook hands.

"I appreciate you coming back," said Joe to Ann.

"Lucky for us Walt was available," said Mike, nodding to Walt.

"No problem," said Walt. He turned to Ann. "Ready to go?"

"I will be in a few minutes," she said.

"I'll just get her checked out then," he said and, tipping his baseball cap to the two men, headed outside.

The three of them sat down. "How did it go?" Joe asked.

"It wasn't as bad as last time, not as strong. But still bad," she said.

"What happened?"

Ann looked out the window. "The whole house is filled with bad feeling. All except for the nursery and the kitchen and I figure the owners didn't spend much time there. But the two rooms that had the worst feeling were the library and the entrance hall. In the library I got anger and … disdain. But in the entrance hall I got fear. Terror. I think there was an argument in the library and someone died in the entrance hall. Is that what you were expecting?"

"Yes, that's what I think happened but I can't prove anything."

"Tell him about the garage," said Mike.

"I got the strangest sensation in the garage," said Ann. "The sensations in the rest of the house were very emotional but in the garage it was more …" she searched for a word, "… directive. Like someone was trying to tell me something." She didn't mention the sensation of a hand grabbing her wrist—that sort of physicality in a spirit was not something she had ever sensed before and she was still somewhat flustered by it. Best to consider and plan for the possible responses to such a revelation before she shared that fact with anyone.

"What was it they were trying to tell you?" asked Joe.

"It was directing me to this metal cabinet in the garage, it wanted me to look there. For something blue."

"And you had me get rid of Pironi," interjected Mike. "Why was that?"

"Who's Pironi?" asked Joe.

"He was the seller's realtor. He wasn't there for the first

visit," said Mike.

"I felt like I'd get a clearer message if I was alone," said Ann. "But I also sensed the spirit especially didn't want to show me whatever it had to show me with Pironi there."

"Did you find what you were looking for?" asked Joe.

"No, there was a lock on the cabinet."

"But *you* could look," said Mike.

"I can't," said Joe, running his fingers through his hair, "not anymore, it's been too long."

"Too long since what?" asked Mike.

Joe looked out the windows toward where Walt was peering into the wing fuel tanks. "The house was owned by Biden and Elizabeth Firth. Mrs. Firth disappeared back in February and her body was found in April in Tinicum Marsh near the Philadelphia Airport. The husband is always a suspect in these types of situations and I question his story, especially since it sounds like the relationship between them was strained, but I haven't found anything to prove he's not telling the truth."

"What did the husband say happened?" asked Ann.

Joe related Firth's description of his activities over the day of his wife's disappearance and the following day.

"We confirmed that he had just lost a lot of money in an investment he had made and also confirmed with the housekeeper that she had washed a shirt and sweater of Firth's that smelled like scotch. The credit card company has a record of his call and someone at one of the hotels remembers talking to him. The timing of when he left for the shore house and when he returned generally jibes with his story, and the friends of his wife who he said he called confirm it."

"Maybe he is telling the truth," said Ann.

Joe scratched his chin. "You know, I think in general he *is* telling the truth. A lot of criminals get caught because they come up with elaborate stories and can't keep the details straight. I think that with the exception of a couple of key omissions he is telling us what he did those two days. It's a smart strategy. Plus, he was lucky."

"Why lucky?" asked Mike.

"Because there's no definitive evidence to tie him or the house to the crime. No blood, no witnesses, nothing that he doesn't have a viable explanation for."

"So what do you think happened?"

"I think he accidentally killed his wife when they argued, maybe in the entrance hall. Maybe she fell and hit her head on something. I could ask the forensic guys to re-do the entrance hall but it's probably too late now. The housekeeper confirms that he was at home that night so I think he hid the body somewhere until the next morning and then he disposed of it at Tinicum, probably on his way back from the shore house. I think he ate lunch as late as he did on that day because he had to kill time so it would be dark when he dumped the body."

"But why would I have an especially strong reaction to some storage box in the garage?" she said.

"Maybe he hid the murder weapon in there," said Mike.

Ann shrugged. "Or maybe she really did leave the house and got attacked by some stranger and that person dumped the body."

Joe nodded. "It's certainly possible. When her body was found all her expensive jewelry was missing which makes it look like it could have been a mugging."

"There must be something in the cabinet," said Mike, with increasing excitement. He turned to Joe. "Can't you get a search warrant?"

"I don't have any valid reason for getting one now," Joe said and held up his hands as Mike opened his mouth, "despite what Ann experienced. We searched the house shortly after Mrs. Firth disappeared and I don't have anything that would justify searching it again now. His father would probably have me up on harassment charges."

"I don't think *anything* I told you is going to help you," said Ann. "I doubt I would be considered a viable witness for the prosecution, let alone providing a reason to search the house again."

Joe sighed. "I know, but at least I feel like I'm not crazy for continuing to look at the husband as a suspect." Joe didn't want to add fuel to Mike's enthusiasm by mentioning that Amelia Dormand had also felt that her daughter was trying to communicate with her.

"This is going to sound terrible," said Ann, "but ... why do you care? Couldn't you just close the case?"

Joe looked out the window and shrugged. "It's never a good feeling to leave a case unsolved. It's not only a professional failure, but you also leave a lot of people wondering what happened. It can eat people up." He thought of Amelia's expression when she had asked him to find the bastard who killed her daughter.

A few minutes later Walt waved from the plane and Ann kissed Mike on the cheek and shook hands with Joe who promised to be in touch after he had had a chance to mull over this latest development. Ann walked out to the plane as Joe and Mike watched from the waiting area.

"It would be huge if we could see what's in that cabinet," said Mike presently, as Walt and Ann got settled in the plane.

"Seems like you're more curious about it than she is," said Joe.

Mike began to bristle, then sighed. "She's sometimes conflicted about her skills. But if she could use them to help in some concrete way—like bringing a murderer to justice—I think it would be good for her. Not to mention good for business," he added with a grin.

The plane's engine fired up and they turned from the windows and made their way down the steps to the parking lot, Joe stopping at a rack of brochures to pick up one for the Helicopter Museum next door. He was always looking for ideas for the days he babysat his niece and nephew.

Chapter 21

As the Kinnears' limo had pulled into the parking lot of Brandywine Airport, a black Mercedes, following at a discreet distance, pulled into a spot on the opposite side of the small parking lot from the equally small passenger terminal. In the Mercedes, Biden watched Ann Kinnear and a man he assumed was her brother get out of the limo, the brother tip the driver, and the two of them climb the stairs to the terminal as the limo pulled away.

The hill into which the terminal was built kept Biden from seeing the planes on the ramp behind the building. He noticed a stairway leading up the hill on the right side of the building and took that, using the bushes along the stairway to screen himself as he got near the top. For a minute or two nothing happened and then a tall, thin older man wearing a baseball hat and aviator glasses emerged from the building, crossed to a white four-seater plane with orange, gold, and red stripes along the fuselage, and began doing what Biden assumed was a pre-flight check. Biden noted the plane's tail number.

After some time the man waved toward the terminal building and shortly Ann Kinnear came out of the terminal and crossed to the plane. The older man removed the chocks from the plane's wheels and climbed in, followed by the woman. Beginning to feel exposed in his observation point, Biden started down the stairs, hearing the plane's prop rev as he descended.

He reached the bottom of the stairs just as Mike Kinnear came through the door of the terminal, stopping on the pavement outside the door and, hands in his pockets, looking idly at the sky.

"Damn," said Biden. He had expected the man to stay in the terminal until the plane took off. He thought for a split second about stepping back behind the bushes but if the man saw him out of the corner of his eye that would certainly look suspicious. The man was turned slightly away from Biden and, besides, even if he did glance his way, it's not as if he would be likely to recognize Biden—as far as Biden knew, no photographs of himself had been published in connection with coverage of Elizabeth's disappearance or even of the murder investigation (even photographs of Elizabeth herself had been rare after the initial push for leads from the public after her disappearance). He suspected he had his father and father-in-law to thank for that.

Biden stepped out from behind the bushes and started for his car just as a second man left the terminal. This man stepped up to Kinnear and they shook hands and had started toward the parking lot when Biden realized with a jolt that the other man was Joe Booth. His heart pounding, he changed his direction from his car to the pavement the men had just vacated and, beyond it, the door of the terminal. He struggled against the urge to pick up his pace, not wanting to do anything that might attract the attention of Booth who had now reached his car which was, Biden noticed, parked quite close to his own. Biden reached the glass entrance door and slipped in and, with an exhalation of relief, climbed the stairs to the passenger waiting area.

A man stood behind a desk reading a magazine but otherwise the waiting area was empty. Firth stood by a display of tourist brochures near the windows overlooking the parking lot, picking ones up at random as he watched Booth drive away. When both Booth and Kinnear were safely on their way, Biden headed back to the parking lot, dumping the brochures into the trash can near the front door as he left.

On his way home, Biden stopped at a public library and used one of their workstations to do a search on the tail number of the plane Ann Kinnear had boarded and found that it was based in Lake Clear, New York.

He also did a search on "ann kinnear" and found the web site, reading through it and the linked material as Joe had done. And, also as Joe had done, he looked up the contact information for the police department that had handled the Barboza case. From a public phone outside the library he placed a call to the department and asked if there was anyone there who had been around fourteen years ago when the Beth Barboza disappearance occurred.

"Sure, hold on," said the person who answered the phone and in a minute a man with a deep, gravelly voice picked up. "Brunauer."

"Hello, my name is Jim Smith and I'm calling from *Sports Illustrated*. I'm doing a story about spelunking safety ..."

"What safety?" interrupted Brunauer.

"Spelunking. Caving."

"Oh."

"I understand that some years ago a young woman died when exploring an undocumented cave near Lewistown. Were you around for that case?"

"Sure. Beth Barboza. What magazine did you say you're from?"

"*Sports Illustrated*," said Firth. "I understand that the circumstances surrounding the recovery of her body were quite unusual."

"You could say that. A woman named Ann Kinnear located the body—I'm getting a lot of calls about her lately."

"Who else is calling about Ann Kinnear?"

"Detective from Philly. What did you say your name

was?"

"Smith." Biden couldn't remember what first name he had given. His hand was suddenly slippery on the phone. "Why was a detective from Philadelphia interested in Ann Kinnear?"

"Can't recall off-hand. Hold on a minute, I probably have some notes here somewhere ..."

Biden didn't hear any telltale rattling of papers or clicking of computer keys. He felt his breath getting short. He pushed his thumbnail under the nail of his index finger, into the quick. "I have a call coming in from my editor, I have to take this—"

"Sure, just give me a phone number and I'll call you back."

There wasn't a number on the phone. Biden rattled off a random series of numbers.

"You going to be there for a while?" said Brunauer.

"Sure," said Biden and hung up. What was going on? Was it possible that Joe Booth was actually taking Ann Kinnear's skills seriously? Biden wiped his hands down the sides of his pants, his gouged finger leaving a small smear of blood. Taking a deep breath, he started down the street, sidestepping to avoid a teenager in an Alice in Chains t-shirt from whose earbuds the strains of heavy metal were clearly audible. Biden was about to hit the key fob button to unlock the Mercedes when he heard the phone ringing.

Alice had just reached the pay phone and stopped—how could he possibly hear anything with that music blasting in his ears? He looked around, shrugged, and, pulling out one of the earbuds, picked up the phone. Biden unlocked the Mercedes with his key—he wanted to avoid even the chirp of the key fob-activated unlock—and slipped into the car just as the teenager looked up and down the street and, shaking his head, said something into the phone. After another minute of conversation he hung up the phone, replaced his earbud, and continued down the street, Biden feeling as if he could still hear the sound of discordant strings and drums in his head.

An hour later, Biden was seated behind his desk with a scotch, staring at his dormant computer monitor. If he could just spend some time online on his own computer, not hunched over a PC in some fucking library or internet cafe—he was always sure that the person next to him was looking over his shoulder—he could save himself a lot of trouble.

Why had he followed the Kinnears? It had been a way to kill some time—he had been vaguely curious about what a psychic would look like (more normal than he had expected, actually fairly attractive) and he had expected to be able to follow her back to her home or office, but it looked like her services were more high end than he had thought if she flew in from, as it turned out, upstate New York.

But it had turned into something more serious if Joe Booth was taking an interest in her. What would a Philadelphia detective want with some "spirit senser," as her web site called her? Booth didn't take her seriously ... did he?

Well, if the man investigating his wife's murder was taking Ann Kinnear seriously, Biden would too.

Chapter 22

When they landed at Adirondack Regional, Ann left Walt to wash down the Arrow while she drove to his house, only a few miles from the airport, to pick up Beau who stayed with Helen Federman when Ann was away. Beau enjoyed playing with the Federman's Jack Russell terrier, Fizz, and, Ann suspected, enjoyed eating people food that he didn't get at home.

When she had first moved to the Adirondacks her companion had been her black lab Kali but a few years previously Kali had died and when Ann started her search for a new dog Mike had suggested a guard dog. Ann's talents earned her some unsolicited attention and from time to time an unwanted — although so far friendly — fan had appeared at her door.

A few months later Ann reported to Mike that she had obtained a guard dog; curious, Mike got a ride from Walt up to the Adirondacks to check it out.

Beau was a big, shaggy Shepherd mix whose pant-y geniality, and the fact that Beau made not a sound when Walt drove up Ann's gravel driveway, made Mike skeptical of his ability to guard. Ann produced what she called a "dog bite sleeve" and invited Mike to put it on which Mike, beginning to regret his skepticism, did. They went out to the clearing near the fire pit.

"Hold your arm out as if you're fending off an attacker," said Ann.

"'As if'?" muttered Mike, pulling on the protective arm

cover and striking the pose. Beau instantly became very interested.

Ann gave a fast ascending whistle followed by five quick high whistles and Beau galloped over to Mike, grabbing his encased arm and knocking him down.

"Whoops," said Ann.

"Holy crap!" said Mike. He was less worried than he might have been because it seemed as if the knocking down had been accidental and, unlike attack dogs Mike had seen on TV, Beau didn't worry his arm, he just held it in his mouth as he stood over Mike. Then he sat down on Mike's legs.

"Uh, Ann…" said Mike.

Ann gave the recall whistle and Beau released Mike's arm, trotted over to Ann, sat by her side, and received a treat.

Mike sat up and pulled the sleeve off.

"Where did you say you got him?"

"I didn't," said Ann cheerfully. "I got him from Walt's brother-in-law."

"Is every person in this entire area related to Walt?" Mike asked irritably, standing up and brushing himself off.

"It does seem that way," said Ann, stroking Beau's big head.

"Walt happens to have a brother-in-law who trains attack dogs?"

"Well, no, he raises basset hounds. But he *is* a dog trainer. He helped me pick Beau out and we decided this was a sufficient amount of attack training."

"Aren't they supposed to be, I don't know, *fiercer*?"

"I didn't want fierce. But I think the grabbing-the-arm trick could be a pretty effective deterrent."

"Not to mention the knocking-people-down trick."

"He's not supposed to do that," said Ann apologetically.

Beau snapped at an invisible bug near his head and

panted at Mike in a friendly manner.

"Doesn't he even bark?"

"I came here for the quiet," said Ann. "I don't want barking."

When Ann and Beau got back to the cabin after a cup of coffee with Helen Federman (and surreptitiously offered cookies for Fizz and Beau) she changed into jeans and a sweatshirt, poured herself a glass of Pinot noir, and took it and a dog toy down to the dock. She tossed the toy into the water for Beau who, she believed, fetched only as an excuse to go rocketing off the end of the dock and into the water with a dramatic splash then scramble out of the water onto the small, stony beach and create a spray of water with an enthusiastic shake. When Ann got bored with the game she told Beau "That's enough" and he flopped down on the dock to gnaw the toy while Ann walked up the log stairway that led from the water to the cabin.

Most of her painting supplies were at the studio but she did have some sketch paper and pencils at the cabin. She collected her materials and settled down at the dining room table. She tried mentally to put herself back in the Rittenhouse Square house, to see now what she had seen, or at least glimpsed, then. The person she had seen was female, she was quite sure of that, and petite, but definitely an adult. She sketched in some limbs but the figure needed context.

She began drawing in the garage behind the figure from the perspective of someone standing in front of the metal cabinet—garage doors on the opposite side of the garage, the Porsche in the bay to the right, the door to the alley just beyond it. She began adding other parts of the room—the workbench to the viewer's right, the stairway to the kitchen to the left—warping the perspective to get them into the view. She added more detail—some tools hanging on a peg board over the workbench, a plastic garbage can between the garage doors—and sat back to examine her work.

Wonderful, a picture of a garage—Mavis would be so pleased. She tossed her pencil down in frustration and went to the kitchen to refill her wine glass and to let in Beau who had been peering at her patiently through the screen door. She closed the inside door against the chill of the May night and locked it, then went back to the dining room table.

She tentatively drew in some locks of long dark hair falling to behind the woman's shoulders and sat back again. Another minute passed and she added a few lines suggesting a blouse with a low V neckline. She had intentionally pushed the image of the woman in the photographs at the Rittenhouse Square house out of her mind in an attempt not to let it influence her but now she thought back to the photograph and compared it with the drawing and realized to her surprise it was not the same person. Similar in the dark hair but dissimilar in some other, impossible-to-define way. She had hoped that the act of drawing might bring the figure she had glimpsed into focus for her but if anything it became more elusive the more she concentrated on it.

She went into the kitchen, opened a can of New England clam chowder, dumped it into a small pot, put it on the stove to heat, and returned to the dining room. She began gathering up the materials, meaning to throw out the drawing, then sat down again. At the bottom of the drawing she sketched in the metal cabinet and then added to the figure an outstretched arm, its finger pointing to the cabinet. It wasn't true to what she had seen but it was true to what she had felt—the woman she had seen wanted her to get something out of the cabinet. Something blue.

She knew it would drive Mike crazy not to know what was in the cabinet but she was just as happy not knowing. Whatever had happened in that house was something she would just as soon not be a part of.

But the drawing was an interesting souvenir of a new experience of sensing—whether she was pleased by this development or not she wasn't sure. She tore the drawing out of the sketch pad, went to the kitchen, and stuck it to the front of the refrigerator with a couple of magnets. She poured herself another glass of wine.

Chapter 23

The day after Ann's second visit to the Firth house, Joe was typing up a report when his direct line rang. "Booth here," he answered.

"Hey there, Joe, this is Adrian Brunauer of the Lewistown police, how you doing?"

"Pretty good, Adrian, how are you?"

"Fielding lots of phone calls about ancient history lately," he said. "I got a call yesterday about Beth Barboza and Ann Kinnear."

"Who called?"

"Some guy named Jim Smith who claimed to be with *Sports Illustrated* but they don't have anyone by that name working for them and they don't know anything about any caving safety article. I tried the number he gave me before he hung up but it didn't work. Then I auto-called back the number the call had come in on. Turned out to be a public phone—I thought it was, I could hear street noises in the background when he called—and a guy answered but he claimed he was just walking by. Sounded like a different voice too. I asked him if he had seen anyone on the phone, or saw anyone hanging around, but he didn't. We did get a location, it's a public phone at a library in the Philly area." Brunauer paused. "Probably shouldn't have called back, might have been able to lift some prints if that other guy hadn't picked up the phone. Not as quick-thinking as I used to be."

"No problem, it would have been a long shot," said Joe, "by the time we got a print tech out there, there probably would have been a bunch more people who had used the phone. What was he asking?"

"Not much, he rang off in a hurry when I told him he wasn't the only one interested. Realized I probably shouldn't have said that either. About time for me to retire and leave the business to the sharper tacks," said Brunauer despondently.

"No problem," said Joe, somewhat less convincingly this time. It looked like luck had been with Biden Firth once again.

Chapter 24

Mike got a call Wednesday morning on the number listed on annkinnear.com.

"Hello. I'm calling for Ann Kinnear," the man said.

"This is Mike Kinnear, I coordinate Ms. Kinnear's engagements. How may I help you?"

"I think I might have a need for Ms. Kinnear's services. I have a house at the shore that I think is …" The person on the other end of the line cleared his throat. "… haunted. I saw your sister on the show on the History Channel a while ago and it seems like she might be able to tell me if I'm imagining things or if it's true."

"Certainly," said Mike. "Have you eliminated other possible causes of the symptoms that lead you to think the house may be haunted? For example, sometimes old houses have plumbing or heating problems that can explain odd noises such as banging and thumping."

"The house isn't that old."

"What symptoms are you experiencing?"

There was a pause. "I can hear people talking."

"Really?" said Mike. "That's quite unusual. You hear people talking when you have reason to believe you are the only person in the house?"

"Yes."

"It's not an apartment building, is it?"

"No, it's a single house. It's a whispery sound, I can't hear exactly what they're saying."

"If you saw the History Channel show you'll know that

my sister doesn't actually speak with spirits, but she could certainly tell you whether or not there is a spirit in the house. Then if she senses a spirit you might further pursue it with ... someone who does that sort of thing."

"That's fine, I don't need to know what it's saying."

"Very good," said Mike. There was a pause and a shuffling as of someone collecting pen and paper. "Does this happen more at certain times of the day?"

"Usually during the daytime."

"Continuously or occasionally?"

"Fairly continuously."

"When you're alone in the house or when other people are there?"

There was silence on the line for a moment. "I definitely hear it when I'm alone in the house. I can't remember if I've heard it when there have been other people there."

"Think about that," said Mike. "If you think of a time when you heard the sound when other people were around, let me know, it might be helpful."

"Sure. So, could your sister come and check it out?"

"Very likely," said Mike. "If it's continuous she may not need to stay too long to hear it and get a sense of what is causing it. If neither of you hear anything then she may have to stay longer to get a sense, or may not be able to get a sense at all. That's why I asked about whether you've heard it in the past when other people are there. If you hear it and she doesn't, there might be another factor at work."

"Like what?" said the caller irritably.

"Tinnitus, for example," said Mike. "Ringing in the ears. But it could certainly manifest as a whispery sound. Perhaps you'd like to eliminate that as cause before you bring us in?"

"No," said the caller. "If it were that, I'd hear it other places too, right?"

"That's true," said Mike. "Well, why don't we plan on a

visit of a couple of hours and if Ms. Kinnear hasn't perceived a spirit we can discuss alternatives—extending that visit or coming back on another day."

"That sounds good," said the caller. "There's another house that I'm thinking of buying and I'd like for her to check that one out too. I wouldn't want to move and find out there's the same problem in the new place."

This request made Mike suspect that the problem was with the caller and not with the house. "Certainly. What timeframe were you looking for?"

"As soon as possible."

Mike paged through his calendar. "I would have to confirm with Ms. Kinnear but I believe she would be available this coming Monday. We do require payment of half the agreed-upon amount of the engagement in advance."

"That would work for me but I would need to do the visit to the current house on Monday afternoon and visit the other house the next morning."

"We could do that, we would just need to factor in overnight accommodations for me, my sister, and her pilot for that night."

"Do you always accompany your sister when she's … uh …"

"Consulting," prompted Mike.

"… consulting?"

"Yes, I take care of all the logistical details so she can focus completely on the matter at hand."

"How much will the fee be?"

"I'll need to get some more information from you and then I can send you a quote and a contract."

The man on the phone hesitated. "Um, listen, my wife doesn't know I'm doing this, she wouldn't be happy if she knew, so I'd like to do everything over the phone or in person,

I don't want to have anything mailed to me and I'd like to pay cash."

This was not an unusual request from Ann and Mike's clients. "Certainly, I understand. All our engagements are strictly confidential with the client who engages us. However, I *would* need a signed contract and half the payment in advance. I could e-mail the contract to you and you could use a money order for the payment."

After a moment the man said, "That sounds OK."

"Very good." Mike said. "Could I have your name?"

"Bob Dormand."

"And where are the houses you'd like us to look at?"

"Harvey Cedars, New Jersey."

Biden Firth hung up the phone in the business center of a hotel near the airport. He wanted to see this psychic at work himself, see what it was that had caused Joe Booth to have formed such a collegial relationship with Ann and Mike Kinnear. Although he couldn't imagine how it could be possible, he would see if she really had this skill she was claiming. And he would find out where she lived. Then he would decide what to do.

Chapter 25

Amelia sat in Sophia's room, looking at, but not actually reading, a book in her lap. The house was quiet, the faint hum of traffic and an occasional dimly heard honk from a car horn being the only accompaniment to the tiny snores coming from Sophia's crib. But Amelia was listening for another sound, one even fainter than the sounds of the traffic. And then it came to her, not so much a sound as a sense. It was her daughter, telling her to take care of Sophia.

She looked around the room, turning her head, trying to locate where the sound was coming from, but it seemed to come from everywhere and nowhere at the same time.

"Elizabeth?" she whispered.

There was no response to her question, just the directive, hanging in the air.

"Honey, I will, I promise. But can you hear me?"

Her daughter was fading, fading back into the background noise of the house.

"I'll take care of her, I promise. Can you hear me?"

"She's asleep," said a voice from the door.

Amelia shot to her feet, the book falling from her lap. "I didn't know you were home."

"No," said Biden, "I doubt you'd be here if you knew I was going to be home. I notice you never come by when you think I'll be home."

He's drunk, thought Amelia, even though it was barely five o'clock.

Biden walked to the crib and looked down at Sophia. She

was fussing a bit in her sleep. "She's asleep. Why were you asking her if she could hear you?"

"I don't know," said Amelia. "It's about time for her to be getting up. I'll be going." She bent down to pick up her purse which was on the floor next to the rocking chair. When she straightened up Biden was standing only a foot or so away from her.

"Why won't you stay?" he asked, now sounding wounded rather than angry. She could smell alcohol on his breath. "Why won't you talk to me anymore? You used to like me."

"I do like you, Biden," she said stiffly, "but I have to go. I've actually stayed later than I intended." She tried to pass him but he blocked her way.

"You think I did it, don't you?" said Biden.

It felt to Amelia like everything became still—no traffic noise, no honking horns, no mutters from Sophia in the crib.

"Why do you say that?" she said eventually, her voice sounding steadier than she felt.

"Because of how you treat me. Avoiding me. Leaving when I get home. Jumping like I was a ghost at the reception."

"Biden, you're drunk," she said coldly. "I'm not going to speak to you when you're like this." She tried again to go past him.

"That's what she said," said Biden.

"Who?" said Amelia, her heart going cold.

"Elizabeth. She told me not to drink too much."

"When?"

"The night she died."

Amelia stared into his eyes and they were glazed and listless. "How do you know when she died?" she asked, the tremble in her voice finally beyond her control.

"She must have died that night, right?" said Biden. "She walked outside and someone hit her over the head and took her jewelry and dumped her body. Let's hope she died that night, because if whoever it was had her for a while before they killed her—"

"Biden, stop it," said Amelia in a ragged whisper. "She was my daughter."

"She was my wife," said Biden, and took a step even closer to her.

"Mrs. Dormand?" said a voice over Biden's shoulder and they both turned to see Joan standing in the doorway with a basket of laundry. "Mr. Firth? Is everything all right?"

Amelia stepped around Biden, tripping on the book that still lay on the floor. "Yes, thank you, Joan, everything is fine. I think that Sophia is just about done with her nap." She nodded in Biden's direction without looking at him. "Biden." And she hurried out of the room, down the stairs, and out the front door with her heart hammering against her rib cage. "Oh, honey," she said, tears springing to her eyes. "What did he do?"

When Amelia got to her car she pulled out her cell phone and pressed the speed dial for her husband but before it even rang she disconnected. She sat staring out the windshield with her phone in her lap until she jumped at the honk of a car horn right outside her window. She looked over to see that a man in a battered sedan had pulled up beside her and had leaned over to roll down the passenger window.

"Hey, lady, are you leaving?" he yelled.

"No, I'm waiting for someone," she said loudly, through her closed window.

The man sighed disconsolately and pulled away. Amelia realized she had been pressing the brake pedal and she removed her foot so at least her brake lights weren't on.

She put her cell phone aside, got her wallet out of her purse, and rifled through insurance cards and dry cleaning receipts until she found what she was looking for. She dialed the number on the business card, her heart still beating hard.

"Sergeant Little."

"Yes, I'm calling for Detective Booth. This is Amelia Dormand."

"Detective Booth isn't available right now, can I take a message?"

"Do you know when he'll be available?"

"No, sorry. Want me to have him give you a call?"

Another car honked its horn outside her window and she waved it away.

"No, thank you, I'll call back," she said, and disconnected. She started the car and backed up, bumping hard into the car in back of her which resulted in the wail of a car alarm. Her hands white-knuckled on the wheel, she pulled out of the space and headed for home.

Chapter 26

When Joe walked into the precinct building the next morning, sipping his Wawa coffee, The Mouse waved a pink slip of paper at him.

"Hey, Joe, that Dormand lady called you yesterday."

Joe took the slip which read *dormand lady called for joe* with the date and time.

"Did she leave a message?"

"Nope, said she'd call back."

"OK, thanks, Mouse."

"Don't call me that," said The Mouse peevishly.

Joe went to his desk, looked up the Dormands' number, and placed the call.

"Dormand residence." He recognized their housekeeper, Ruby.

"Hello, Ruby, this is Joe Booth. I was wondering if Mrs. Dormand was available."

"Let me check, Mr. Booth, hold on." He could hear the click of Ruby's steps on marble—she must have been walking through the foyer of the Dormands' home—then heard her voice, muffled by a hand over the receiver, "It's Mr. Booth."

There was a brief pause and then Joe heard Amelia's voice. "Detective Booth?"

"Hello, Mrs. Dormand. I understand you called yesterday?"

"Oh, yes. How are you?"

"I'm fine, thanks. You?"

"Just fine." There was a long pause.

"Is there anything I can help you with?" said Joe.

"Um," said Amelia, followed by another long pause. Then she said, in an unnaturally loud voice, "I think that's in my office, let me get it."

Joe could hear more footsteps through the phone, then what sounded like a door clicking shut. He imagined her in the room in her home she used as an office, large windows opening out onto a view of the horse pastures.

"Hello," she said.

"Mrs. Dormand, are you OK?" asked Joe.

She laughed shakily. "Yes, I'm fine. I wouldn't make a very good spy, would I?" There was another pause. "I'm sorry to bother you, Detective, I'm sure it's nothing, but I had a very strange conversation with Biden yesterday."

"Yes?" said Joe, pulling his notepad and a pen out of his pocket.

"I was at Elizabeth's, watching Sophia while Joan was out, and I was listening for ..." She paused again. "For Elizabeth. Like I mentioned when we talked."

"Yes."

"Well, I did hear her, and I said that I would take care of Sophia and then I said, 'Can you hear me?' and then I realized Biden was in the room. He thought I was talking to Sophia. I told him I had to go and he got angry, he said I didn't like him anymore and wanted to know why." She laughed bitterly. "He had been drinking—it was still the afternoon—and I told him I wasn't going to talk to him in that condition and he said, 'That's what she said the night she died.'" Amelia stopped.

Joe sat forward. "Did you ask him what he meant by that?"

"I asked him how he knew when she died and he said we better hope she had died the night she disappeared, otherwise who knows what the person who killed her might have done to her." Amelia's voice cracked.

"Then what happened?"

"He came up close to me, he was very angry. I tried to get away from him but he blocked me but then Joan showed up. I don't think he knew she was there."

"Did he threaten you?"

"No, not explicitly, otherwise I definitely would have gotten in touch with you right away. It was just his whole demeanor. And the comment about when Elizabeth died."

Joe tapped his pen on the notepad. "He never says or does anything that's quite enough to bring him in ..." he said with frustration.

"I'm probably being foolish, I'm imagining things—"

"No, you were right to call," said Joe.

"It's just that ..." and now Joe could tell she was crying, "... I told my daughter I'd take care of Sophia and my son-in-law is drunk and rude to me and what do I do? I run away and leave him there with Sophia and Joan."

"I'll go check on them," said Joe. "I'm going to be near there anyway." Joe was mentally reviewing his to do list for the day, trying to figure out how he could juggle things so that he could fit in a visit to Rittenhouse Square.

"Please don't let him know that I talked with you," she said, suddenly worried.

"No, I won't."

"Well, it would make me feel better. I'd appreciate it."

"I'll call you back after I've been to the house."

"Thank you, Detective."

"My pleasure, Mrs. Dormand."

Joe knocked on the door of Biden Firth's house later that day, a thin drizzle soaking into his light jacket. In a moment the door was opened by Joan, Sophia on her hip.

"Detective Booth, I wasn't expecting you. Come in." She stepped aside. "Mr. Firth just stepped out but he should be back in a few minutes. I was just going to have some tea, would you like some?"

Joe hated tea. "Yes, thanks, that would be great." His initial irritation at finding Firth not at home was moderating—he might actually have better luck accomplishing his mission talking with Joan.

"If you'd like to have a seat in the parlor I'll bring it."

"Actually I'd rather have it in the kitchen with you if you don't mind," he said. "All these antiques, I'm always afraid I'm going to break something."

"Certainly," said Joan with a smile. "Right this way." She led him to the back of the house to the comfortable, somewhat old-fashioned, kitchen, and gestured for him to sit at the table. Joe draped his damp jacket over the back of his chair. Joan put Sophia on the floor while she got out mugs and tea bags. Sophia made a bee-line for Joe.

"Don't bother Detective Booth, Sophie," said Joan.

Sophia hung onto Joe's pant leg and said what sounded like "Tango."

Joe raised his eyebrows toward Joan for a translation. Joan sighed. "I have no idea what she means by that," she said as Joe swung Sophia up on his lap. "I can hold her if you like—"

"No, we're doing fine, aren't we, Sophie?"

"Tango!" exclaimed Sophia, investigating Joe's shirt pocket and removing his pen.

Joe removed the pen from her grip which threatened momentarily to bring on tears but then she discovered the notepad. Joe figured she couldn't do too much harm to herself with the notepad. Sophia experimentally put the corner of the notepad in her mouth, found that not to be satisfying, then discovered that the pages were rip-able. Joe retrieved the few that had notes on them and surrendered the rest to Sophia.

"Oh, dear, Detective, let me—" said Joan, coming toward them just as the tea kettle whistled.

"It's OK," he said, "plenty more where that came from, right Soph?"

"Do you have children of your own, Detective?" asked Joan, watching Sophia disassemble the notepad.

"None of my own, but a lot of nieces and nephews," he said. "She seems like a nice little girl."

"Oh, she is, a very good girl," said Joan with a smile, then assumed a more stern expression. "But very destructive." She put a tea cup and small plate for the used tea bag down in front of Joe. "Milk or sugar?"

"Both, please," said Joe, hoping some dosing would mask the bitter taste he disliked. He poured and spooned from a delicate creamer and sugar bowl Joan provided and took a sip, suppressing a shudder. "Are you pretty much full time here now?"

"Yes, I have two days a week off—Esme, the nanny, takes those days—but I'm here the rest of the time."

"How is that working out for you?"

"Oh, very well. I was able to give up my apartment and I stay at my sister's house on my days off so I've been able to save a lot of money."

"But it must be hard to work in a house where a tragedy has occurred."

"Yes, but I feel I can help Mr. Firth by making sure he knows Sophia is well taken care of. This has been very hard on him."

"How is he dealing with his wife's death?"

"It certainly hasn't been easy for him, as you can imagine," said Joan.

"Does he get out much? It's important for people who

have had a loss to get out and about, not lock themselves away."

"Oh, he gets out and about," said Joan, a bit stiffly, Joe thought.

"I understand Mrs. Dormand comes by to visit with Sophia."

Suddenly Joan seemed less enthusiastic about the discussion. "Yes, Mrs. Dormand does like visiting with Sophia."

"Does she spend time with Mr. Firth when she's here?"

"No, she usually comes when I'm here by myself. That way she can watch Sophia while I take care of the housekeeping."

"Maybe it's a little awkward for Mrs. Dormand to be coming here when her daughter isn't here anymore—"

"Oh, not at all," said Joan. "Mrs. Dormand loves spending time with Sophia, and I think it's so good that Sophia can form a special relationship with her mother's mother." She looked down at her hands. "I think the world of Mrs. Dormand."

"What does Mr. Firth think of Mrs. Dormand's visits?"

There was a long pause, then Joan said wanly, "He's usually not here when she visits."

"But when he is here, there's some tension?"

Joan paused again. "I think they had an argument."

"What were they arguing about?"

"I don't know, I didn't hear any of it but the other day I was walking by the nursery with some laundry and I heard them talking—they weren't yelling but it sounded ... strained. When I looked in, it looked like Mrs. Dormand wanted to leave but Mr. Firth was blocking her way. But she did leave then," said Joan hastily. "That's the only time I saw them in what might have been a disagreement."

Joe leaned forward. "Joan, sometimes when someone has experienced a terrible loss, like Mr. Firth has, it can make them kind of crazy, make them do things they would never do in normal circumstances. Did you feel he was threatening Mrs. Dormand?"

"I really didn't see anything," said Joan. "I can't imagine ..." and her voice trailed off.

"Have you ever felt threatened by Mr. Firth?"

"Oh, no," said Joan, her eyes wide.

"Have you ever felt that Mr. Firth could be a danger to Sophia?"

"Good heavens, no!" exclaimed Joan, obviously shocked at the thought.

Joe sat back. "That's good. I have no reason to think you have anything to worry about, but it's standard operating procedure to check on these things."

"Yes, well ..." said Joan, and took a distracted sip of her tea.

"But I know this is a very hard time for Mr. Firth and I think it would be best if you didn't share our conversation with him."

"Yes, I think that would be best," said Joan, putting the cup down with a rattle.

Joe glanced at his watch. "You know, I should probably get going, I was just going to let Mr. Firth know we're still working the case but really haven't uncovered anything new. If we do I'll certainly let him know right away." He stood up and stood Sophia up on the floor. "Thanks so much for the tea, Joan."

"You hardly drank any of it," said Joan, peering into his mug. "There's probably a travel mug I could put it into— "

"Oh, no need," said Joe hastily. "Let me just get this," he said, gathering remnants of his notepad off the table.

"Oh, heavens, I can get that," said Joan. "Really, Sophia," she tutted.

Joan saw Joe to the door then, returning to the kitchen poured his virtually untouched tea down the drain with a shake of her head.

When Joe got to his car, he called Amelia Dormand's home number; she answered it herself after only two rings.

"Mrs. Dormand, it's Detective Booth. I just stopped by the house—Biden wasn't there but I talked with Joan."

"How does she seem?" asked Amelia. "Does she seem all right?"

"Yes, she seems fine. I told her it was just a standard visit to see how everyone was doing—"

"Yes, Joan would believe that a Philadelphia detective would have time to play social worker," said Amelia with a smile in her voice.

"I asked her if there was any tension between you and Mr. Firth and she brought up the argument herself, she was obviously troubled by it. I asked if she felt Mr. Firth posed any danger to her and she seemed surprised I would ask that, and when I asked if Mr. Firth posed any danger to Sophia she seemed positively shocked. I don't think she was hiding anything, I think those ideas really hadn't occurred to her." Joe paused. "And I get the impression Mr. Firth might not be spending a lot of time at home anyway."

"Yes, we hear Biden has been sowing some wild oats," said Amelia tightly.

"Still, I wonder if it might be best if you could look into having Sophia—and Joan as well—spend some time with you and Mr. Dormand. It might be more ... well, a more stable environment for Sophia."

"Do *you* think they are in danger?"

Joe sighed and contemplated the wavering images beyond

his drizzle-misted windshield. "I honestly don't know, Mrs. Dormand. At a minimum, Biden Firth seems like a man under a great deal of stress—he might welcome having some time to himself." Joe didn't believe this for a minute, but he knew he'd feel better knowing Sophia and Joan were not living in the same house as the man he believed had killed Sophia's mother.

"Yes, I believe you're right, Detective, I'll speak with my husband about it right away." Joe heard a note of relief in Amelia Dormand's voice—he suspected she was glad to have a course of action to pursue. "I very much appreciate your help with this."

"It's my pleasure, Mrs. Dormand. Good luck."

Chapter 27

On Monday morning Mike drove from West Chester to the Atlantic City Airport to pick up Ann and Walt, then dropped Walt off at the AC boardwalk before driving with Ann up to Harvey Cedars for their 1:00 appointment with Bob Dormand.

After crossing the bridge over Manahawkin Bay and turning north up Long Beach Island, they made a left off Long Beach Boulevard, toward the bay. The short street was lined with expansive, expensive houses on lots noticeably larger than was usually the case at the shore, where the most common view was often of the neighbor's house a dozen feet away.

"This should be it," said Mike, checking the address on his cell phone.

They pulled in behind a black Mercedes parked in the driveway. The street was quiet, the May weather not being quite warm enough to lure the owners to their vacation homes. They mounted the steps to the front door and Mike tapped a brass door knocker in the shape of a starfish.

Mike's internet search had shown that Dormand had owned the house for almost 30 years so Mike was surprised when a relatively young man, in his mid-thirties, opened the door. He was tall and athletically built, with longish dark, wavy hair and rather pale skin beneath several days' worth of dark stubble. He was wearing khakis, a white polo shirt, a navy blue windbreaker, and boat shoes.

"Mr. Dormand?" asked Mike.

"Yes." The man stood aside to admit them.

The house was dark, the only light coming from chinks in the storm shutters, the open front door, and a light coming from what Mike surmised was the kitchen. They were standing in an entrance area floored in cream-colored tile which gave way to light hardwood in the large combination living and dining room. The decor was done in various shades of cream, sand, beige, and white, with pops of tropical color provided by throw pillows, a bright rug, and a large abstract oil painting hanging over a gas fireplace.

Mike put out his hand. "Mike Kinnear. And this is Ann Kinnear."

Dormand shook their hands wordlessly then swung the front door shut behind them, leaving them in near darkness. Mike reached out and flipped on the entrance hall light. "Little murky in here with the shutters closed," he said pleasantly.

"Yes," said Dormand, examining Ann.

"So," said Mike, "have you had the place long?"

"My parents bought it when I was little."

Ah, thought Mike, that explained the age discrepancy.

"Do you spend much time here?"

"Mainly in the summer."

"Is it all right if Ms. Kinnear starts by looking around?"

"Yes. I'd like to watch," said Dormand.

"Of course. We'll stay in the same room with her, we just don't want to crowd her."

"Does that make it harder to ... sense things?" asked Dormand.

"No, I just generally don't like being crowded," answered Ann. She gestured toward the living room. "May I?"

Dormand nodded.

As Ann wandered around the large room, sitting in chairs

and running her hand along the mantel above the fireplace, Mike leaned toward Dormand. "I didn't tell Ms. Kinnear any of the details you gave me about why you wanted us to look at the house. We find it's often better to let her experience the location without any preconceived ideas."

Dormand nodded, his eyes following Ann.

"Have you ever encountered the situation you described to me when you're outside?" asked Mike.

"No, only inside."

"Recently?"

"Fairly recently."

"In the last few days?"

"No, not that recently."

Mike gave up. Getting information from clients about what they were experiencing that led them to call on Ann sometimes helped provide direction for their investigation and allowed Ann to get a sense sooner, if there was a sense to be gotten. But just as often a client didn't want to share any information, wanting to test Ann, to see her demonstrate her skill without assistance. Mike was often both appreciative of and perplexed by the people who hired Ann—they paid considerable money to have her bring her skills to bear on an issue that troubled or intrigued them but at the same time were suspicious of the results. They wanted to believe and yet were unwilling to believe fully.

While they watched from the entrance area, Ann walked through the dining area and the adjoining kitchen, and popped her head into a mud room, a half bath, and a utility closet. Then she wandered back to where Mike and Dormand stood and shrugged. "It seems clean," she said.

"'Clean' meaning free of spirits," said Mike to Dormand. "Let's go upstairs just to get the lay of the land and then we can decide on our plan of attack."

There were four large bedrooms upstairs, darkened like

the rest of the house by storm shutters. The master suite, complete with its own sitting area and gas burning fireplace, was decorated in light blues and greens, set off by white trim and accessories. The second and third bedrooms carried forward some of the tropical colors of the living and dining room accessories. The fourth bedroom was outfitted with a crib and a small bed. Mike turned on an overhead light and a ceiling fan began a slow rotation. The walls were decorated with a hand-painted underwater scene complete with sea horses, mermaids with billowing hair, cheerful looking dolphins, and fantastical fish. Ann glanced around and then wandered down the hall.

"This is charming!" said Mike, examining the painting with obvious enjoyment.

"My mother-in-law," said Dormand.

"She commissioned this?" asked Mike.

"She painted it." said Dormand.

Mike shook his head. "Quite a talent. For her grandchildren?"

"Listen," said Dormand, "I don't usually hear the voices up here. Maybe we should go back downstairs."

"Certainly," said Mike. "Let's find Ann."

Ann was in the master bedroom, sitting on the bed.

"Anything?" asked Mike.

She shook her head. "I'm not getting anything. Have we seen all the rooms?"

"Yes, this is it," said Dormand.

"I saw a garage when we came in," she said.

"I never hear the voices in the garage," said Dormand.

"You hear voices?" said Ann, with raised eyebrows.

"I can hear someone talking," said Dormand.

Ann shot Mike a look then turned back to Dormand. "Can you hear what they're saying?"

"Almost, but not quite."

"Well, we might as well check out the garage just to be thorough," said Mike, "then we can decide how we want to proceed."

They descended to the first floor and Dormand opened a door off the kitchen that revealed a flight of steps leading to the garage. He flipped the light switch and stood aside to let Ann and Mike descend.

The garage was empty of cars. Ann wandered around the perimeter, absently touching a few gardening implements hanging on the wall, the empty trash and recycling cans under the stairs, and some swimming pool paraphernalia stacked in a corner. She began crossing back to where Mike and Dormand stood, then stopped in the middle of the garage, cocking her head. She bent down, still turning her head, then sat down on the concrete floor.

"Ann?" said Mike, surprised.

Ann made a shushing motion.

"What's she doing?" said Dormand, and Mike shook his head.

There was something near the floor—a sound so faint she could barely hear it. At first she had thought it was the creak and whisper that even modern houses make, but it was coming from the concrete floor—no, not from the floor itself but from just above it. When she sat the sound was microscopically louder but no more distinct. She turned her head, trying to locate the source of the sound, and when she scooted toward it she encountered a pocket of barely cooler air. Then the cooler air dissipated and the faint sound faded to silence. Ann stretched out her arms and strained her ears, searching, but they were gone. She climbed to her feet, stiffer than she would have expected to be.

"What was it?" asked Mike.

Ann shook her head. "I don't know. I thought there was something but it's gone. A sound—but not a voice as far as I could tell," she said to Dormand. "Do you hear anything?"

Dormand's already pale skin appeared to have paled further. He shook his head.

"Why did you sit on the floor?" asked Mike.

"I thought I'd be closer to it there."

"Closer to what?" asked Mike.

"I. Don't. Know," said Ann. "Just a faint sound. And a coolness. It was probably nothing. Sorry for the false alarm." Glancing around the garage one more time, she climbed the stairs back to the main floor, followed by Mike and Dormand.

They congregated in the living room. Ann turned to Dormand who seemed to have regained some color. "The voices, do you hear them during the day?"

"Yes, during the day, but always when I'm alone," he said.

"Well, we haven't been here that long," said Mike, "these things sometimes take some time to manifest themselves." He turned to Dormand. "Maybe if Ann sat in the house by herself for a bit …?"

"I'm very interested in the process," said Dormand. "I'd like to stay, too. After all, they might be speaking directly to me."

Mike looked at Ann who shrugged. "It's all right with me."

"OK," said Mike, looking at his watch. "Why don't I go wait in the car and I'll come back in, what do you think, one hour?"

"Maybe they'll be scared away even if you're in the driveway," said Dormand.

"I'm sure it will be fine," said Mike, scrutinizing Dormand. "Can you open these shutters?" Mike asked, gesturing to the window that would overlook the front yard.

"Why do you want me to open them?"

"So I can see in from the driveway. Is that a problem, Mr. Dormand?" said Mike, raising his eyebrows.

Dormand picked a glass paperweight off a table and tossed it from hand to hand as he looked at the shuttered window. After a few moments he said, "No, I suppose not. I just thought darker might be better."

"You'd be surprised how few spirits have a preference for darkness over natural light," said Mike, "based on what Ms. Kinnear has told me."

Dormand looked at Ann who nodded. He sighed, put the paperweight back on the table, and, opening the windows, pushed back the storm shutters. He closed the window and turned back to Mike and Ann. "OK?"

Mike went to the window, looked out, and adjusted one of a pair of nearby chairs. "Ann, you sit here. I'll plan to come in in an hour but if either of you want me to come in sooner just wave." Ann nodded and sat down in the chair. Dormand sat down on a stool at the breakfast bar, turning it so he could see Ann. Mike left by the front door and Ann watched him walk down the driveway, look back at the window and give a wave, glance at his watch, and then lean against the car, his hands in his pockets.

Ann settled back in the chair, looked around the room, smiled politely at Dormand, then turned her gaze out the window again, not focused on anything in particular. They sat that way for some time before Dormand cleared his throat. "Still seems like it might be better if it were darker," he said, gesturing toward the window blinds.

"I'm sure this is fine," said Ann. They sat in silence again for some time.

"Maybe I'm the only one who can hear it," said Dormand.

"Maybe," said Ann. "Do you hear it now?"

"No."

Again they sat in silence.

"Maybe it's my late wife," said Dormand eventually.

"I thought Mike said your wife wouldn't approve of this," said Ann sharply.

"My current wife," replied Dormand. "My first wife died."

"I'm sorry," said Ann.

"It was a car crash."

"How long ago was it?" said Ann.

Dormand hesitated. "Years ago."

"And you never heard anything in the house until recently?"

"No."

"Has anything happened in your life recently that your first wife would want to communicate with you about?"

Dormand shifted in his chair. "Not that I can think of."

"From what I understand, it would be unusual for a spirit to wait this long to communicate with someone unless there was a precipitating event. Oftentimes in the case of a spouse it's their spouse's remarriage."

"'From what you understand'?" asked Dormand.

"I don't speak with spirits," said Ann. "I'm sure my brother explained that to you."

"Yes."

"I can only sense a spirit, and sometimes give an idea as to what kind of spirit it is—friendly or unfriendly, for example."

Dormand nodded.

"But there are people who do claim to be able to converse with spirits, maybe you need someone like that," she continued.

"Maybe," said Dormand, then continued after a pause, "Actually I'm not sure I *do* want to 'converse' with her, I just want to know if she, or someone else, is here in the house."

"Did she spend a lot of time here? Was it somewhere that

was special to her?"

Dormand hesitated. "Yes."

"Well, let's give it some more time," said Ann.

Dormand and Ann were silent for a while, then Dormand said, "Do you do this often?"

"It varies," said Ann. "It's been busy lately."

"What's the usual reason people call you?"

"Usually one of three reasons. They are experiencing unexplainable events in their homes and want to find out the cause. Or they are thinking of buying a new home—or establishing an office, whatever—and want to confirm if it's inhabited by spirits."

"Are they hoping you find spirits or don't find spirits?" asked Dormand.

"It depends on the person," said Ann.

"And the third reason?" Dormand asked.

"When people go missing and families want to find them."

"Like Beth Barboza."

"Yes," said Ann, glancing sharply at Dormand. "Although in that case the request didn't come from her family." She paused then said, "How do you know about that?"

"When I decided I wanted to hire someone to check out the house I did some research," said Dormand. "Do you ever find them alive?"

"No."

Dormand waited for Ann to continue but she sat silent, her gaze turned out the window again.

The minutes stretched out. Dormand began jingling the keys in his pocket then stopped. He crossed his arms, trapping his hands under his biceps but after a moment released them to rest his hand on top of the breakfast bar. After a moment he began drumming his fingers on the countertop, then reached out to snatch up an object from the bar—a brass letter opener in the shape of an elongated mermaid with a sharp tail. He drew his finger along the edge, then pressed his finger onto the tip.

"How do you get business? Do you find clients by what's going on in the news?"

Ann roused herself from her reverie and sighed. "No, we let the people who are interested come to us. In fact, the less we know about a client's situation the better. Then there's no question about where any information we can provide came from." She paused. "No question for us, at least."

Again they sat in silence. Then, mermaid in hand, Dormand stood, crossed the room, and sat in the chair next to Ann's. He leaned forward in the chair. "Do you ever investigate crimes?"

A flicker off distaste crossed Ann's face. "Not very often. Nothing I sensed would be admissible in court so there's not much incentive for people to pay for my services."

"Have you ever discovered a crime by accident? When someone asked you to investigate a house, for example? Or an office?"

Ann looked more closely at Dormand. The silence stretched out.

Finally Ann said, looking down at her hands, "One time a man in Wisconsin who had bought an old hunting camp asked us to check it out because he thought it was haunted. He was right. It was …" she cast about for the right word, "… *soaked* in this violent aura, it was almost physical, almost a vibration. It was clearly a murder. And I could tell where the murders had taken place—one in the kitchen and one in the bedroom. I hated being in that house." Ann turned to look out the window again. "I couldn't tell more than that but we did some research afterwards and it turns out that back in the 1800s a woman killed her child and husband with a meat cleaver one winter."

"Were you sensing the ghosts of the child and the husband?"

"No, it was the ghost of the woman. She killed herself after she killed them."

"How did she kill herself?"

"With the meat cleaver. She chopped her arm off."

"Jesus," said Dormand, sitting back.

"Anyhow, the guy tried to sell it but by then the story had gotten out and no one was interested in buying it. I think he ended up just boarding it up and abandoning it." Ann turned back to Dormand. "I think our time is up."

Oftentimes such engagements were quickly completed. With the exception of those like the visit to the Maryland house with the Van Dykes, where the manifestation was reported to occur only at a particular time, the spirits Ann sensed were usually always present in their location, or the location was perceptibly free of spirits.

However, these things were unpredictable and Mike didn't want to leave a client dissatisfied so, while Ann examined a quite fine shell collection on one of the living room bookcase shelves, he suggested some alternatives to Dormand—Ann coming back later that day or spending more time in the garage—but Dormand, fidgeting with his car keys, suddenly seemed anxious to end the meeting.

"We can always come back again tomorrow after our visit to the other house," said Mike.

"Yes, that's fine," said Dormand.

"At that time we'll need the second half of the payment."

"Yes, I said I'd have that," said Dormand irritably.

After Dormand had closed the storm shutters they went

out into the fading May afternoon, Dormand seeming not to notice Mike's outstretched hand. As soon as Mike's Audi was clear of the driveway, Dormand backed out and sped away, barely stopping at the corner before turning onto Long Beach Boulevard.

"Mr. Congeniality," muttered Ann.

"Takes all kinds," replied Mike cheerfully.

Chapter 28

That evening Ann and Mike sat in the restaurant of their hotel in Atlantic City at a table by the windows. Walt, unexpectedly fascinated with Atlantic City, had decided to walk the boardwalk to see the sights. Mike had ordered gin martinis, up and dirty, for himself and Ann.

"So, what did you think of Dormand?" asked Mike.

"I don't think he was hearing voices. I think he was just one of those people who get interested in the idea of sensing spirits and want to see it for themselves."

"It would be an expensive way to satisfy his curiosity if that's all it was."

Ann shrugged. "Bored son of parents with enough money to own a shore house."

"What did he do while I was outside?"

"He told me he thought the voice might be his late wife. He's remarried. Then he wanted to hear about crime scenes."

"What did you tell him?"

"About the hunting cabin in Wisconsin."

"Ugh," said Mike. He had been pleased when he got the call about the Wisconsin job because it had represented an expansion from their usually East Coast-based business. But he had seen what that experience had done to Ann—both the sensing itself and the further shock of learning what event had precipitated it—and he was sorry he had taken it. He was also sorry this Dormand guy had stirred up those memories for Ann. He shouldn't leave her alone with clients—if he had been there he could have fielded those questions himself. In this business it was never a good idea to let the client call the shots.

Mike shook himself. "Weird," he said, taking another sip. "After the job is over, maybe I'll do a little research on him and his late wife." Mike also observed the boycott on internet research on clients and prospective clients beyond what was needed to screen out cranks—for example, checking to make sure the house they were visiting was in fact owned by someone named Robert Dormand.

After dinner they walked down the boardwalk to one of the casinos. It was a warm evening for May and Ann walked with her arm hooked under Mike's elbow. Passersby might have thought they were a couple because they looked very little like each other—Ann being slender and fair skinned with reddish blonde hair like their mother and Mike, like their father, being stockier with dark hair and a darker complexion.

Mike enjoyed playing blackjack when he had the opportunity—he had learned the rules about when to split and double down and was reasonably good at remembering what cards had been played so he rarely lost much money and occasionally won some. They found a table and Mike took a seat, Ann standing behind him with a gin and tonic. She watched the cards being dealt out and the bets being placed but didn't pay much attention to the game itself except to note in general how Mike was doing.

After twenty minutes or so she leaned over his shoulder and said, "I'm going to get another drink. Do you want one?"

"They'll bring you one," said Mike, looking around for a waitress.

"No, that's OK, I'll get it," said Ann. "Want anything?"

Mike glanced at his drink. "I'm OK for now."

Ann wandered over to the bar and ordered another G&T and a glass of Perrier for Mike. She was on her way back to the table when she saw a young man approaching her whom she had noticed earlier as another observer at Mike's table. He blocked her path.

"I know you," he said squinting at her.

"I don't think so," said Ann. She tried to pass him but he stepped to block her.

"I saw you on a show about people who speak with the dead."

Shit, thought Ann. "No, that must have been someone else."

"No, it was you," the man said, becoming excited. "And you found that hiker in Montana."

"It wasn't me and it was Wyoming," said Ann irritably.

He laughed. "I knew it! This is perfect! I was looking at your web site not …" he thought "… three weeks ago."

Ann smiled grimly at him and tried again to get past him but he stepped in front of her again. Over his shoulder she saw that Mike had noticed the dance they were conducting.

"Listen, here's why it's perfect," he said, lowering his voice and leaning toward her conspiratorially. "My brother died earlier this year. Right after the holidays." He looked down into the drink he was holding and spun the ice cubes, then looked back up at her, any trace of excitement gone from his face. "He killed himself. And no one knows why. No note, no nothing. One day he seems fine and the next," he put his index finger to his temple and cocked his trigger thumb, "bang!"

Over the young man's shoulder Ann could see Mike gathering up his chips.

"You could find out why he did it!" the young man said, his face regaining its excitement. "It would mean so much to my parents to know." He bent down to put his drink on the floor and Ann tried again to pass him but he lurched back up and blocked her again. He reached into his pocket and pulled out a roll of bills. "Look, I've been really lucky, and it's all so I can hire you to find out why he killed himself!" He held the roll out to Ann. Ann saw Mike heading toward them.

She shook her head. "I don't do what you want me to do. I'm sorry."

Mike reached the two of them. "Everything OK?" he asked, eyeing the young man.

"I'm talking to this lady," the young man said. "Bug off."

"I'm thinking this lady would like *you* to bug off," said Mike.

"Get lost," said the young man and reached out for Ann's arm as if to lead her away from this man intruding on their discussion.

Mike's hand flashed out and grabbed the young man's wrist. "Leave her alone," he said quietly.

The young man jerked his hand out of Mike's grasp and stepped back, whether to improve his angle for taking a swing or to retreat was unclear since he tripped on his glass and fell backwards. Beneath the Musak, the area round them had gotten quiet as people turned to watch the commotion. Ann saw a security guard, a beefy older man with a placid face, approaching.

"Everything all right here?" he asked, looking down at the young man who was still sitting on the floor.

"This gentleman was bothering my sister," said Mike. "He tripped on his drink."

"You OK there, buddy?" the guard said to the young man.

"I was just talking to her," the young man said truculently.

"Well, maybe she doesn't want to talk to you," said the guard. "You OK to stand up?"

"Yeah," said the young man, watching Ann but making no move to rise.

The guard hooked his hand under the young man's arm. "Up we go," he said, hoisting him to his feet. The man swayed for a second and then regained his balance. The security guard picked up the overturned glass and turned to Ann. "You OK, ma'am?"

"Yes, thanks."

"Is it OK if we go?" asked Mike, his hand on Ann's elbow.

"Yup, we're just going to go have a little sit-down," he said, turning the young man away.

"Here, can I give this to him?" said Ann, who had removed a fragment of paper and a pen from her purse and had written something on it.

"You're giving him your number?" said the guard disapprovingly.

"No, he had me confused with another person, this is who he needs to talk to." She passed the piece of paper to the young man. "He might be able to help you," she said to him.

The young man looked at the slip of paper, looked back at Ann, and then let the guard lead him away. The people near them began turning back to their own pursuits.

"What did you give him?" said Mike.

"Garrick's web site."

Mike snorted. "That fraud?"

"How do you know?" said Ann sharply.

Mike shrugged. "Want to go back?"

Ann nodded.

After Mike had cashed in his chips, they walked back along the boardwalk to their hotel but Ann didn't hook her arm into Mike's; she walked a little apart, her arms crossed against the evening chill, and this time passersby might not have even realized that the two of them knew each other.

❖

Back at their hotel they saw Walt in the nearly empty bar indulging in another one of his favorite pastimes—getting the bartender to tell him stories.

"I'm going to get a nightcap," said Ann.

Mike opened his mouth to say something and thought better of it but not before Ann had noticed.

"What?" she said belligerently.

"Nothing," he said, holding up his hands in a defensive gesture. "What do you want?"

They crossed to the bar and Mike ordered a martini for Ann and a glass of ginger ale for himself and they chatted with Walt while the bartender got their drinks.

"Gino here was just telling me about the Atlantic City mafia," said Walt. "I figured with a name like Gino he must have the inside scoop."

Gino rolled his eyes.

When they had their drinks, plus a bowl of nuts from Gino, Mike and Ann retired to a table in the corner.

"So what did that guy want?" asked Mike.

"He wanted me to ask his dead brother why he had killed himself."

"Jesus," said Mike, shaking his head.

"How come people always want more from me than I can give them?" burst out Ann, causing Gino and Walt, in addition to another couple at the bar, to turn and look. "Or they want less from me than I have," she added, taking a hefty drink from her martini.

Mike had heard the first complaint before; for those who believed Ann's claim to be able to sense spirits, many assumed she could also communicate with them and were disappointed—or, in some cases, disbelieving—when she said she could not. The young man at the casino was not the first person Ann had directed to Garrick Masser and Mike sensed that to do so was both a relief for Ann—a way to disengage herself from a fruitless conversation—but also in some way an admission of failure.

Mike and Ann had met Masser at a screening party for *The Sense of Death* and for all Mike had never doubted Ann's abilities for a moment, he never for a moment believed Masser's. Masser was extremely tall and painfully thin, with deep set black eyes and bushy eyebrows set over prominently jutting cheekbones; he tended to stand with his hands clasped together at chest height. Mike had had too much to drink and suggested to Masser that he should wear a cape and Ann had had to smooth things over.

In fact, Ann was deferential to Masser in a way Mike could not remember her being to anyone else, not even their parents—the novice deferring to the expert. For his part, Masser was patronizing to Ann—as he was to everyone—but in Ann's case it was tempered by something else. Masser's attitude conveyed that he felt everyone in the room to be unworthy of his attention but Ann to be the least unworthy. There was some unspoken acknowledgement from Masser of their common *area* of expertise if not of a common *level* of expertise.

The second complaint Mike had heard Ann voice only once before, many years ago. She was twenty-four and he was twenty-three and she had sat in his kitchen, drinking beer, crying silently while he stroked her hair or patted her back, the only things he could think to do.

Ann had met Dan Kaminsky when he took over her retiring vet's practice and she brought her black lab, Kali, in to have a cut on her paw seen to. Kali padded happily around the exam room, leaving a trail of bloody paw prints in her wake.

"If I could just keep her off it for a few days, I'm sure it would heal on its own," said Ann, exasperated.

"Not a likely scenario—right, darlin'?" Ann was momentarily taken aback until she realized he was talking to the dog. "They gotta run and play. Lots of playing—am I right, punkin?" Dan talked to the dog in the same conversational tone he would have used if he had been talking with Ann. Kali leaned adoringly into his leg. "I'll bet you do that to all the guys," said Dan as he wrote out care instructions on a prescription pad.

Ann ran into Dan again a few weeks later at a wine tasting fundraiser for the local animal shelter, which they followed up with an impromptu meatloaf-and-mashed potatoes dinner at a West Chester diner. Ann found that Dan had the same patient, low key approach to his interactions with people as he did with animals, although without the corny terms of endearment ... until the first time he called her "darlin'," which gave her a school girl flutter and which brought a smile to her face when she thought about it days later.

When Dan's parents visited from Washington state a few months later, Dan took the three of them out to dinner. His father was a research chemist and his mother taught high school physics and they were charming and funny and Dan obviously enjoyed spending time with them. Ann felt a pang as memories bubbled up of her own parents who had died just a few years before, but by the end of their visit Ann felt she had found a wonderful surrogate in the Kaminskys. Dan had even received the seal of approval from Mike, especially when they discovered a mutual interest in biking.

In fact, the only thing that cast a shadow over their relationship was that Ann had not told Dan about her sensing abilities. It was something that seemed ill-advised to share early in the relationship and then as time went on Ann tried to convince herself it was immaterial. She had spent a couple of distracted hours over dinner with Dan at an old Chester County inn trying to ignore a spirit that hung—playfully, she sensed—behind Dan's chair.

"What are you looking at?" he asked curiously, turning in his chair, his nose inches from where the spirit shimmered.

"Nothing. Just admiring the decor," she said brightly. "Do you want a piece of my popover?"

"He's going to find out some day," Mike counseled her, "it's better to tell him sooner than later."

"Why should he have to find out?" said Ann.

But of course he did find out.

It was right before the holidays and Dan, Ann, Mike, and Scott were at a party at the house of one of Mike's friends from high school. Mike and Scott were mingling and Dan was trying to talk Ann into joining them.

"I thought these were your high school buddies?" he said, scanning the convivial crowd.

"More Mike's friends than mine," she said, settling into the couch.

"I know—you're afraid I'm going to run into your childhood sweetheart!"

Ann snorted. "Not likely."

"Why not? Did you break his heart and he ran off and joined the Foreign Legion?"

"Let's just say I wasn't much of a social butterfly."

"Well, the loss of all those non-discerning boys at West Chester High is my gain," he said, and leaned over and kissed her on the nose.

They sat companionably on the couch, Dan's arm draped around Ann's shoulders, Ann snuggled into his side, watching the party swirl around them, Dan poking gentle fun at the other party-goers—he was a wonderful mimic and entertained her by providing cartoon-character dialog for some of the conversations taking place around the room.

After a bit he jiggled his empty beer cup. "Need a refill. Want to come?"

"No, that's OK, I don't want to lose our seats."

"Suit yourself, Miss Garbo," he said cheerfully. "Do you need a top-off?"

She swallowed the last bit of wine in her glass and handed it to him. "Sure. Whatever the red is."

Dan made his way through the crowd to the makeshift bar, meeting up with Mike and Scott and a third person to whom Mike introduced Dan. Ann was idly trying to place him when she realized who it was and sat up in alarm—Rob Barboza, Beth's brother.

Why had she thought she could keep Dan from finding out about her ability? She glanced around the room— practically everyone at the party knew the Barboza family ... the man standing near the television had been the boy Mike punched on the playground in her defense ... Melanie of the brownie-baking episode was in the basement smoking a joint.

Maybe Beth Barboza wouldn't come up—she knew Mike wouldn't mention it—but the casualness of the introductions of the four men had given way to some more serious conversation and she felt sure Rob had brought up Beth. When they turned to glance at her, she knew for sure. She tried to read Dan's expression but she could only catch glimpses of his face through the crowd.

After what seemed like an eternity, the group broke up and Dan made his way back to the couch. He handed her her refilled glass. "I got to meet someone from your past after all," he said, his tone carefully neutral.

"Yes, I saw," she said, sipping her wine and avoiding his gaze.

"Quite a story." Ann didn't reply. "He said you found his sister after she died. He was grateful. Wanted to tell me how much my girlfriend had helped out his family."

Ann glanced at him, saw the confusion and, under that, hurt on his face and turned away.

"Why didn't you ever tell me about that?" asked Dan.

"It was a long time ago. Who knows what really happened. Mike was there too. We really just stumbled on the cave she was in."

"That's not how her brother tells it, he says they would never have found her if it weren't for you."

Ann shrugged and looked around the room. She caught Mike's eye from across the room. He made a motion— "Should I come over?"—and she shook her head and turned back to Dan.

"I don't know how it happened, if it helped them then I'm glad. That's all."

"You could sense her ... spirit?"

"Yes."

"And this sensing—you still feel you can do it?"

"What do you mean, 'feel I can do it'?" she asked, an edge in her voice.

"I just mean ..." Dan paused, considering. "It's just that it's an unusual thing."

"You're right about that," said Ann tightly.

There followed a period of time when each thought the other would have more to say, but when it became apparent that neither would, they eventually, by unspoken mutual consent, left the party. If Ann had looked back she would have seen Mike standing at the door looking after them, but she didn't look back.

Dan drove to Ann's house in uncharacteristic silence. When they got there he pulled up to the curb and killed the engine.

"So, *do* you still see spirits?"

"Sense them."

"OK, sorry—sense them."

"Yes."

Dan nodded. "That's ... very ... unexpected," he finished with a wan smile.

Over the following weeks, Dan continued to ask her questions—how often the sensings happened, what the experiences were like, what the spirits themselves were like. Ann had never had someone demonstrate such an intellectual interest in her sensings and as time went on she began to enjoy these discussions, to enjoy sharing this odd part of her life in such depth with someone other than Mike.

Then one evening over a pizza at Dan's place, when Ann was describing the sensation of Beth Barboza's bat coming alive in her hand at exactly the time Ann knew Beth had died, Dan said, "Did your parents ever have you talk with anyone about your sensing?"

"Talk with anyone?" said Ann, a little miffed that the rhythm of her story had been interrupted.

"Yes, you know, like a ... psychiatrist. Or a psychologist."

Ann stopped with a slice of pizza half way to her mouth. After a moment she put it carefully back on her plate. "What are you suggesting?"

"I'm just saying that, if a child has an imaginary friend, and the parents don't make it a point to help the child distinguish the real friends from the imaginary ones ... and then if that child grows up and has experiences that seem to confirm a supernatural ability—"

Ann stood abruptly. "You don't believe me."

"I don't blame you, everything around you was encouraging you to—"

"You've never believed me!" said Ann, her voice rising.

"You weren't asking me all those questions so you could understand what a sensing is like, you were asking questions because you were building a case against me. You were building a case against my parents for not breaking me of a 'bad habit' when I was young!"

"That's not what I was doing!" protested Dan. "It's just that ..." he groped for words.

Ann stood with her face red and her arms crossed. "Just what?"

Dan rose to stand next to her and he took her hand as best he could. "My whole life has been built on understanding the world through science. On believing that each thing has an explainable trigger and an explainable consequence. It's what helped me understand what was happening when my sister got cancer, it's what enabled the doctors to help her fight it, and it's what made dealing with the consequences, when we couldn't fight it anymore and she died, bearable." He hesitated. "And when she was gone, she was gone. I'm sure of it."

Ann jerked her hand away from his. "So if you don't have the ability, it stands to reason no one else can have it."

"That's not what I mean. I only mean there are other explanations for what you've experienced and you've never had the opportunity to explore them."

Ann was fumbling into the coat she had draped across the back of the kitchen chair. "I don't need to *explore* anything. I'm living it. And I don't need to spend my life with someone who thinks I'm crazy and is trying to fix me!" She snatched up her purse. "Don't follow me. I want to be alone now." What should have been a dramatic exit line was undermined somewhat by the hiccup of tears threatening to erupt.

She walked the several miles to Mike's house, her hands thrust into her coat pockets, her head down. When she got there, the tears came.

"He thinks I'm crazy," she sobbed, a beer bottle gripped in her hands.

"Well, you're not. He's just being closed-minded."

"And he acts like he thinks I'm proud of what I can do."

"Well, aren't you?" asked Mike, surprised.

"Of course not," said Ann. "I'm a freak. Do you think I would be this way if I had a choice?"

Ann never forgave Dan for what, Mike believed, she saw as a betrayal. And she rarely talked about her sensing abilities, even with Mike, but Mike now knew there were two warring forces at work in her—one wishing that her skill was greater than it was and one wishing she didn't have the skill at all.

At 9:00 the next morning, about an hour before Ann and Mike were scheduled to meet Bob Dormand at the second shore house, Mike got a call on his cell phone as they were finishing breakfast in the hotel restaurant.

"Hello, this is Bob Dormand. Listen, I'm sorry to change the plans at the last minute but based on what your sister was able to tell me yesterday, I don't really think it will be necessary for us to visit the second house. I'll still pay the whole amount, I'll get the payment in the mail."

"You're sure?" said Mike. "If you're paying the full amount anyway you might as well get Ann's assessment of the property, you might find it useful in the future." He wasn't thrilled about having to wait for a money order to be mailed, assuming it ever was.

"It was turning out to be inconvenient to arrange the second visit with the realtor anyway so I'd just as soon avoid that. But I'll have your payment in the mail in the next few days."

"OK," said Mike, shrugging at Ann who was looking at him quizzically. "Please let us know if you change your mind."

"Yes, I will." And the line went dead.

Mike sighed. "Says he doesn't need you to look at the second place after all."

"Why not?" asked Ann.

"I think the second house was an alternative if he got a bad report on the first house. Or maybe, like you said, he got his curiosity satisfied. Anyhow, he claims he's still going to pay the full amount."

"Hmmm," said Ann.

"If he actually does," replied Mike skeptically.

Ann stood up. "Well, I guess Walt and I can head back."

"Yup. Poor Walt, I think he was enjoying Atlantic City."

Chapter 29

Biden ended the call to Mike Kinnear and looked out his motel room window at the small parking lot and, beyond that, the hulking profile of the Adirondacks. He had left Harvey Cedars right after his meeting with the Kinnears and driven to Lake Clear which, he had learned, was about 20 miles west-northwest of Lake Placid. It had taken him about nine hours to get to Lake Clear—avoiding toll roads which he suspected would be more likely to have traffic cameras—and that night he had checked in to a vintage 1950s motel sporting a faux Alpine exterior and a dingy interior.

Biden had had a bad moment when the psychic had her spell in the garage—she had sat down in exactly the place where Biden had put Elizabeth's body in the sleeping bag. She had said she heard something. And that it was cold. Wasn't that the popular wisdom—that where ghosts were, the air was cold?

But even the psychic herself hadn't taken it seriously, had called it a false alarm, so how much did he have to worry about from a person who didn't even trust her own instincts—instincts that anyone else would reject out of hand as a fraud.

Biden felt better today than he had yesterday. He had nothing to fear from this faker and her officious brother. But as long as he had driven all the way to upstate New York he might as well satisfy his curiosity about where Ann Kinnear holed up when she wasn't on one of her "engagements."

Biden left the key in the room—he had paid cash—and found a diner for breakfast. Then he drove to Adirondack

Regional Airport.

Ann and Mike found that Walt was, in fact, enjoying himself—he had grown the $50 he had set aside to play the slots to $130 and was hoping for $150—and so they decided to have lunch before leaving to give Walt a little more time to play.

Ann and Walt arrived at Lake Clear in late afternoon. When Ann got to the parking lot she found that her car wouldn't start. Ann fetched Walt who peered under the hood.

"Not the battery," he muttered. "I could ask Casey to take a look at it tomorrow." Casey, Walt's nephew, was a mechanic in Tupper Lake. "I can give you a ride home tonight."

Ann waited in the passenger terminal while Walt got the Arrow cleaned up, then they stopped at Walt and Helen's house to pick up Beau. Fizz decided to come along for the ride so it was a tight fit in Walt's pick-up, especially with Fizz trying to climb on Ann's lap to get to the window.

Walt dropped Ann and Beau at the cabin, never noticing the black Mercedes that had followed them out of the airport parking lot.

Chapter 30

Biden gnawed his thumbnail. He was beginning to think his plan had gone awry. He had calculated the time it was likely to take for Ann Kinnear and her pilot to get to the Atlantic City airport and fly back to Lake Clear and that time had long since come and gone. Would she have gone somewhere else? It seemed unlikely ... although maybe they had flown to West Chester, which seemed to be the base of operations for their business. With each hour he waited, knowing where Ann Kinnear lived had become increasingly vital. Not only did he want to know where to find her if circumstances demanded, but he wanted to rectify his earlier unsuccessful attempt to find her home, when he thought he could just follow her by car from the "engagement" at his house.

He continued to vacillate between dismissing Kinnear as a charlatan and fearing her as a threat, the latter feeling bolstered by Joe Booth's evident interest in her. Maybe Booth was baiting him, maybe Booth had counted on Biden following Ann when she left his house ... he shook his head. He couldn't let himself get paranoid. But Pironi had said she had had a reaction in all the locations in the house tied to Elizabeth's death—the library and the foyer and the garage. How could she have known that? Had he left any evidence behind that a normal person could perceive? No, he had been too careful ... maybe she really could do what she claimed to be able to do.

He had to piss. He had gone into the small terminal

building to use the restroom once, he didn't want to go in again—someone was more likely to remember him if they saw him more than once. He briefly contemplated using the large styrofoam cup that had held the take-out coffee he had bought at the diner, the remnants just an oily puddle in the bottom of the cup. Jesus, he could be home—or maybe in some nice Old City bar with a Glenfiddich on the rocks—if it weren't for Ann Kinnear.

She needed to mind her own goddamn business. She needed someone to teach her a lesson. She needed a pair of hands—*his* hands—around her neck, and he'd *twist*—

He swam back to the present as he tasted blood and there was a moment of muddled confusion until he saw his torn thumbnail.

Biden was dabbing at the oozing wound when he saw the Arrow coming into Lake Clear.

Even after they landed there was more delay while they investigated some problem with the psychic's car and, after more work on the plane, they left together in the old man's pick-up truck. Once they were on the road there was a stop at a tidy ranch house a few miles from the airport that Biden initially took to be Ann's house but after a time Ann and Walt came out of the house with two dogs—Biden had not counted on dogs—and drove away in the pick-up.

Biden tried to follow at a discreet distance but when the pick-up turned off the two-lane state road onto a gravel road he knew there was no way he could follow them unobserved. He pulled the Mercedes over and confirmed on a map he had purchased at one of the local gas stations that the road was a dead end. Keeping the map out as a prop for the benefit of passing motorists, he waited about fifteen minutes then saw the pick-up heading back; as far as he could tell there was only the older man inside, with the small dog leaning out the passenger window.

When the pick-up was out of sight, Biden turned into the gravel road and began driving slowly along it. For a time it skirted a large pond or small lake on the right but then the road turned away from the lake to accommodate the waterfront properties that lined it and Biden caught only an occasional glimpse of water through the trees. Biden counted nine driveways on the lake side of the road before it dead ended, the houses themselves generally out of sight among the pine trees, the lots rather large based on the spacing of the driveways. Some of the houses had names on the mailboxes—none of which was Kinnear—and Firth thought he could probably, but not definitely, eliminate these as Ann's home. The other side of the road must have been Park land because there was no sign of habitation.

One driveway had a For Sale sign next to it and, on the way back, Biden pulled into it. It wound through the pine woods and ended at a large, modern vacation home. The house itself looked well maintained but a drift of leaves against the front door suggested that it hadn't been visited in some time. Biden walked down to the water and looked up and down the shoreline; the houses were set back from the water so they weren't easily visible from where he stood, although he could see where the houses must be based on the docks dotting the shoreline. The dock of the For Sale house had two kayaks and a rowboat chained to it.

Biden spent a few minutes standing on the dock looking out across the expanse of water then returned to his car and drove to Tupper Lake, the nearest town of any size. He located a hardware store, purchased a pair of bolt cutters and a couple of locks and then returned to what he had learned was Loon Pond. (It figured that a crazy woman would live on a body of water called Loon Pond.) He drove to the For Sale house and, using the bolt cutters, cut free the rowboat and opened the dock box where he found the oars.

The For Sale house was about halfway along Loon Pond Road and, based on the time it had taken the old man to reappear after dropping Ann off, Biden decided to explore the houses toward the end of the road first. He saw lights on in one house but Biden calculated that it was one of the ones that had shown a name on the mailbox so he passed it by for the time being. He was nearing where he estimated the road to end when he saw a movement on one of the docks that dotted the shoreline; at first he began to row away from the dock but then he saw that it was not a person and rowed closer. It was a large dog, like the one that had gotten in the pick-up truck with Ann Kinnear. He had found where she lived.

Chapter 31

Ann sat curled in an overstuffed chair in front of a small fire in the sitting room of the cabin. In her lap was the first book of Shelby Foote's massive history of the Civil War—Mike had gotten her the set for Christmas after they had enjoyed the Ken Burns documentary together. This was Ann's third start on it and she suspected that once again she would get no further than Fort Sumter.

Tonight, though, she was distracted less by the density of the information and intimidating heft of the book itself than by memories stirred up by the trip to Atlantic City. She was thinking back to her first meeting with Garrick Masser.

Corey Duff, the producer and director of *The Sense of Death*, had invited the documentary's subjects, key crew members, a few History Channel bigwigs, his parents and siblings, and their guests to his hometown—Pittsburgh—for a premiere of sorts. Ann's first instinct was to decline the invitation but she liked Corey and he was so obviously excited by the prospect of having all his subjects together that she couldn't bring herself to disappoint him. Plus, she was curious to meet Garrick Masser.

In the afternoon they did an interview with a reporter from WESA—to Ann's relief, Corey and the visualizer from New Mexico did most of the talking. The evening started out with a screening at a historic old movie theater in the center of town (Corey had even rented a red carpet for the occasion). Then they were taken by a quite luxurious private bus to an inn and restaurant several miles outside the city that was reputed to be haunted. The owner, a short, portly man with a ridiculous mustache and a dramatic comb-over, met them at the door accompanied by servers with trays of champagne glasses.

Garrick swept up the stairs but waved away the proffered glass, requesting sparkling water which the owner dispatched one of the servers to fetch. The owner himself handed a glass to the New Mexico visualizer and, after a brief consultation with Corey, who gestured toward Ann, hurried over to where she stood and grandly offered a glass to Mike.

"So pleased to welcome you to our humble inn," he said.

Mike jerked his head toward Ann.

"Of course," said the owner, swinging toward Ann, some of the champagne sloshing onto the pebbled driveway. Ann took the glass from him wordlessly.

The inn's owner turned to the group and clapped his hands. "If I could have your attention ... I thought that before we started dinner we might take a tour of some of the locations in the inn rumored to be haunted and see if our esteemed guests might shed some light—or perhaps I should say some darkness!—on the situation!"

Ann noticed Corey trying to get the innkeeper's attention and shaking his head vigorously but the owner was already heading into the inn, one of the servers holding the door for the guests, Masser the first through the door.

"Oh for God's sake," Ann muttered.

"Come on, it might be fun," said Mike, taking her arm. "Maybe Carnac the Magnificent will drop a quote that the Mayor of Munchkinland can dine off for the next year."

"That's a terrible combination of references," Ann said, draining her glass and swapping it for a full one from one of the servers' trays.

They trailed the group as the owner, casting hopeful looks at Masser and the visualizer, escorted them from room to room. Masser, with barely a glance around, intoned "Nothing" in each room. The visualizer, with no mementos of the dead to work with, just shrugged. When they had visited all the rooms, the owner took them to the private room where dinner was to be held and after bowing them into the room turned away with a muttered "Freaks," which only Ann and Mike, as the last ones in, heard.

After dinner, which was quite good—although as far as Ann could see, Masser ate only rolls—the group moved into one of the inn's sitting rooms for coffee and after dinner drinks. Ann left to use the ladies' room and when she came out Masser was standing in the hallway.

"Did you sense anything?" he asked.

"No. You?"

"Come with me." And he turned and strode down the hall toward a door to a patio, not bothering to check to see if Ann would follow.

Ann briefly considered ignoring him and returning to the party but curiosity got the better of her and she followed him outside.

He was standing on the stone patio gazing out into the dark back yard. Ann looked at him for a moment expecting him to say something but when he didn't she also turned her gaze to the yard.

The moonlit night revealed an expanse of carefully manicured grass bordered by a low stone wall on the other side of which was a grove of short, gnarled, evenly spaced trees—a fruit orchard of some type. Between the trees Ann could see a flickering light. She crossed her arms against the chill of an evening breeze.

"Someone's having a bonfire," she said, nodding toward the light.

"I don't think so," said Masser.

Ann looked curiously at him and then back toward the light. He was right, it wasn't a bonfire—she could see now that it was actually a number of separate, faint lights moving among the trees, only taking on a bonfire brightness when they came together and then fading as they moved apart. "What is it?"

"Let's find out," he said, and descended a few stone steps to the grass, then turned to look at her. She hesitated a moment and then followed him.

They crossed the lawn and stepped over the stone wall into the orchard. Masser strode purposefully forward but she found she had to pick her way along, the heels of her shoes sinking into the soft ground and twigs scratching at her legs. She had gone about fifty yards, glancing up occasionally to make sure she was still headed toward the light, when she came into a clearing next to Masser and could see the source of the light up close.

"What do you see?" he asked.

"What do *you* see?" she replied.

"Asked you first," he said with the ghost of a smile.

She scanned the clearing. "Faint lights, maybe twenty of them, about five or six feet off the ground, moving slowly back and forth, sort of like a wave. Sometimes coming together in the middle of the clearing and sometimes moving apart." They continued watching in silence for a few minutes. Finally Ann said, "What *do* you see?"

"Soldiers. Soldiers in a battle."

"Soldiers? How can you tell?"

"Because they don't look like lights to me. They look like men. Men in uniform."

Ann looked at Masser and then back at the lights. She had thought of them originally as beautiful, even calming, but the way they moved, coming together and breaking apart, swaying first one way then the other—they were the movements of men locked in combat. And now she sensed a faint crimson tint to the lights, like a few drops of red paint added to white, like killing anger dimmed by many, many years.

"How did you know they were here?" she said, her voice dropping to a whisper.

"In the parlor, before dinner, on that interminable tour, one of them came in and said, 'Hurry, they're here!' and ran out."

Ann smiled despite herself. "You told the owner you didn't sense anything."

"I certainly was not going to give that officious little twit the satisfaction of knowing that his inn is haunted."

Ann looked back to the clearing where the lights were beginning to fade, sinking into the ground like fireflies in reverse. "Why did you tell *me*?"

"I was curious if you would see it." Ann watched the last light flicker out as Masser turned back to the inn. "Plus, they weren't lights to me. I could follow their sound but it was faint. I thought since you are sensitive to the light essence you would be able to locate them more quickly and we didn't have much time. Let's get back before your tedious brother notices we're missing." And he strode off through the orchard, leaving Ann to struggle back in his wake.

When Ann got back to the inn, Masser was nowhere to be seen—she assumed he had gone back to the sitting room. She returned to the ladies' room to tend to the damage done by her walk through the orchard. She used some paper towels to clean the mud from her shoes and, finding that a branch had torn a hole in her panty hose, removed them, and, after stuffing them into a feminine hygiene disposal bag, threw them into the trash can. She wasn't sure why, but she wanted to keep her visit to the orchard with Garrick Masser a secret.

When she got back to the sitting room the party was breaking up, Mike had made his cape comment, and Masser was sulking on the front porch waiting for the bus to be brought around. When they boarded, Masser took a seat in the back while Mike chose one toward the front for himself and Ann.

"Window?" he said, standing aside for her.

"Thanks." She scooted in and tried looking out the window but it was opaque in the darkness, revealing only a hazy reflection of the interior.

"What happened to your stockings?" he asked, dropping into the seat next to her.

"Only a gay guy would notice something like that. I got a runner and threw them away. Why do you still have a drink?"

Mike swirled what looked and smelled like the remains of a scotch on the rocks. "I figured he owed me one to go after mistaking me for the famous Ann Kinnear." He took a sip and said contemplatively, "I would have thought straight guys would be more likely to notice missing stockings."

Ann was vaguely irritated that Mike was willing to take her explanation at face value—it took her adventure in the orchard and turned it into a sartorial inconvenience. She turned back to the window.

Then she realized why she wanted to keep her experience with Masser a secret—it was the first time in her life that she had shared the experience of sensing spirits with another person, even if the way they had experienced it had been quite different. Masser had sought her out to share the experience—had, in fact, required her assistance. It had involved a kind of intimacy.

Before now, outside of her consulting engagements, Ann

had only spoken about her sensings with Mike—and, of course, briefly with Dan. She was eternally grateful to Mike just for believing her—having him as a salve to the wounds inflicted by all those who thought she was unbalanced or an attention-monger or a liar had saved her sanity, she felt sure. When she did talk with him about her sensings, Mike responded just as she would have hoped—seriously interested but not agog. But speaking with him about her experiences was like an explorer of the North Pole trying to explain his experience to the armchair traveler—as attentive and appreciative an audience as the armchair traveler might be, he would never truly understand the arctic explorer's experience.

But Masser did understand—in fact, he understood even more than she did. He had seen and heard the spirits as they had been in life—she had no doubt of that. And she had no doubt either he could communicate with them if he wanted to—the test Corey Duff had posed for Masser in the documentary had convinced her. In comparison to Masser's talents, her own were puny, like a parlor trick. But far from making her feel inadequate or jealous, it gave her a feeling of comfort—that she was not alone in her abilities, and that there was someone she might look to for guidance in how to navigate the "normal" world from her abnormal perspective.

Then she heard a murmured query from the back of the bus and Masser's response—"Don't be an imbecile!"—and, smiling slightly, decided that perhaps Garrick Masser should not be her sole model for managing her relationships with her fellow mortals.

Chapter 32

Biden pushed the door of the Trenton pawn shop open and jumped as a bell on the door jingled. Despite the "disguise" he had obtained at the Swarthmore Goodwill store—tan work pants, a denim shirt, a Phillies baseball cap, and sneakers—he felt ridiculously out of place. The shop was dark and as Biden waited for his eyes to adjust he heard a voice from the back of the store.

"Help you?"

Biden made his way down a narrow cleared space between old television sets, kerosene heaters, and ancient bikes on one side and a grimy glass-topped case containing jewelry on the other, his eyes gradually acclimating to the dim light but his sight clouded now by the fug of cigarette smoke hanging in the air.

The man behind the counter at the back of the store was just what Biden would have expected in a place like this—cheap western-style shirt with fake mother-of-pearl buttons, a greasy comb-over, rheumy eyes.

Biden spoke with what he hoped would pass for an Eastern European accent. "I need some protection—" he began.

"They got machines in the men's room for that," said the man with what could have been a laugh or a cough.

"Uh, not that kind of protection," said Biden. "I drive a cab. I need protection in case someone tries to rob me."

"Oh, *that* kind of protection," said the man. "Anything particular in mind?"

"No. Something inexpensive." Biden thought he should probably have said "cheap."

"Inexpensive, eh?" The man looked down into the glass case he was leaning on where rows of handguns were laid out on display. The man unclipped a ring of keys from his belt, sorted through them, and opened the case. "What did you have in mind spending?"

"I don't know," said Biden, hating the situation more with each passing moment. "I can pay cash. Up to five hundred dollars."

The man scanned the case. "Five hundred, eh?" He reached for one of the guns on the top shelf.

"And it has to be off the record," added Biden quickly.

"Off the record?" said the man, his hand wavering. "I don't do off the record."

"I'm afraid they'll take my cab license away if they knew," said Biden.

The man snorted. "Who's going to find out? Your boss?"

"I don't know. I'm afraid they'll find out," repeated Biden.

The man looked at him, Biden struggling to meet his gaze. After a time the man picked up a cigarette from someplace behind the counter, took a drag, and replaced it. Biden waited.

"Five hundred dollars, you said," said the man, smoke coming from his mouth and nose as he spoke.

Biden nodded, trying not to cough.

The man reached down to the bottom shelf and pulled out a gun. It looked like a toy in comparison to the other guns in the case.

"It's ... small," Biden said feebly.

"It's perfect for you," said the man. "Enclosed space like that—if you're going to be shooting someone in the back seat of your cab you don't want to make a big mess, right?"

"Right." Biden picked up the gun and turned it over in his

hand.

"Easy to conceal, too," added the man, taking another puff of his cigarette and blowing the smoke into Biden's face. "Listen, you're that close—from you to me—you don't need a big gun. You just stick that baby into the robber's face," the man pushed two fingers, held out like a gun barrel, up to Biden's face, "and BANG, problem solved."

Between the churning of his stomach and the smoke in his face, Biden began to be afraid he would throw up. "Sure, that's good," he said, "I'll take it."

"Five hundred cash," said the man. "Want it wrapped?" And he gave the hacking laugh again.

"No," said Biden. He took an envelope out of his pocket with five hundred dollars in it—a second envelope in his other pocket contained $1,000 since he had had no idea how much a gun would cost—and handed the cash to the man who counted it and then slid the gun across the counter to Biden.

"Anything else?"

"No, that's it."

"Want ammo for it?"

Biden swore to himself. "Yes, ammo too."

The man disappeared behind the counter and after some shuffling and muttering reappeared with a small box.

"Twenty bucks."

Biden considered arguing—after all, he had already told the man he only had $500—but he wanted to get out of there. He took out his wallet and, opening it as little as possible, pulled out a twenty and placed it on the counter. Biden was unsure what to do next. The man took a drag on his cigarette and exhaled smoke out his nose. After a moment he said, cigarette still dangling from his mouth, "Bag?"

"No." Biden slipped the gun into his pants pocket—he hoped it wasn't loaded—and turned toward the door.

"Hey, buddy," said the man, taking the cigarette out of his

mouth.

Biden turned back to him.

"It's called a hack license."

The trip to the pawn shop had not gone well—he had made it too complicated. "Hack license," not "cab license"—he should have thought of that, but he couldn't even do research on the fucking internet at home. He shouldn't have made up a story to tell that *scum*, he should have just put on a pair of sunglasses and told him he wanted a gun. The idiot had been laughing at him—that was clear. Biden's face burned to think of it.

He had changed out of his pawn shop clothes at the visitors' center at Valley Forge Park and disposed of them in a dumpster. It had been a ridiculously long detour but Biden figured that the less logical his movements were, the more difficult is would be for someone to follow his tracks.

He was home now, in the master bathroom with the door locked, like a randy teenager. He had sent Joan out to pick up some Chinese take-out and, as she always did these days, she had taken Sophia with her. He was going to have to spend more time with Sophia—he had happened upon her in the kitchen the other day holding onto Joan's pants leg and peering up at the counter where Joan was stirring something and Biden had ruffled her hair in what he considered to be an appropriately paternal display of affection. She had cried and Joan said it was just because she was startled but Biden suspected it was because for a moment Sophia hadn't known who he was. He would spend more time with her when things were settled.

He pulled the gun out of the bag he had used to smuggle

it into the house. As a boy he had gone skeet shooting with his father during a trip to Scotland but he hadn't held a gun since then. In the pawn shop it had looked small but now, resting in his hand, it looked deadly enough. He had initially been alarmed when he realized that the pawn shop owner had sold him a revolver, not a pistol, but as he examined it he realized its simplicity was an advantage—no need to sneak off to the library to research how to use a more complicated gun. He spent some time seeing how quickly he could load and unload the gun and soon he found himself liking the small size, the idea that he could go anywhere with it and no one would know. And if he had to use it he planned to use it up close.

He caught a glimpse of himself in the mirror and he liked what he saw—powerful, not a man to be trifled with. He raised the gun and pointed it at his reflection. "I'm not going to let you fuck me up, you bitch. I'm going to do this right." He slowly squeezed the trigger—the click of the empty chamber was loud in the tiled room and he jumped. "Fuck," he muttered. His hands shaking, he put the gun and the ammunition in an old leather toiletries bag of his grandfather's and, stowing it under some towels in the linen closet, snapped off the light as he heard Joan's steps on the marble floor of the foyer below.

Chapter 33

A little over a month after his first Elizabeth Firth-related visit to the Delaware County Medical Examiner's office, Joe was back, showing his badge to the gate guard and making his way to Roger Stanislas's office. Today Roger was casual in a salmon cashmere sweater and grey slacks.

"Cheerio, Detective, how goes the hunt?" he said cheerfully from behind his desk when Joe appeared at the door.

"Not so good, Roger, I'm hoping you have something for me."

"I do, I do," said Roger, waving Joe into a chair. He sat back and tossed his glasses on the desk. "I ran into your favorite Firth this weekend."

"Do tell," said Joe tiredly.

"Yes, indeed. Not looking like his usual patrician self these days. Looks to me like something is wearing on him."

Joe raised his eyebrows. "And what do you suppose that could be?"

"I may have an idea." Roger slid a manila folder out of the top drawer of his desk, set it on the blotter, and laid his hands on top of it, suddenly serious. "He's been untouchable up until now, yes? Rich parents, expensive lawyers. But if you had something that even they couldn't ignore ..."

Joe sat forward. "And what might that be?"

"We just got the report on the analysis of scrapings from the fingernails. God only knows what took them so long—maybe you have Firth Senior to thank. I just got it yesterday

...” Roger stood and gestured Joe to join him behind the desk. "More automobile carpet fibers, but different from the ones on the body and the sleeping bag." Roger pulled a paper from the folder, a print out of what looked like a page from a car sales web site showing the open trunk of a car. "Not Biden Firth's car but the same make and model, same year, same exterior color." Roger pointed at the picture. "There were black fibers on the body and the sleeping bag but the fibers under her fingernails were gray." Roger's finger moved on the picture and he glanced up at Joe to see if he understood. By the tightening of Joe's mouth and the narrowing of his eyes, Roger could that see he did.

Joe sat in his car in the parking lot outside the ME's office, contemplating a stormy gray sky that mirrored his mood. It had been almost three months since he had first interviewed Biden Firth after Elizabeth's disappearance and over a month since her body had been found. He had interviewed every person with the slightest connection to the case, he had followed up on every lead. He had gotten himself involved with a woman who claimed to be able to sense spirits, for God's sake. And all the while, Biden Firth had lived on in the house where Joe was sure he had murdered his wife, driving the car in which Joe was sure he had hidden her body, living off his parents' money and hiding behind their name. Amelia Dormand wanted her son-in-law locked up for killing her daughter and Joe was no closer to doing that now than he had been the day he had given her his jacket in the restaurant of the Hotel du Pont.

Biden Firth had been lucky—but he had also been smart enough to keep his head down. Joe needed something to draw

Firth out from behind his barricade—and now he thought he had it.

Chapter 34

Joe strode down the street toward Biden Firth's house, Harry Deng hurrying to keep up.

"Are you sure this is a good idea?" Harry puffed.

"I've run out of good ideas," said Joe. "I've even run out of mediocre ideas. I'm relying on questionable ideas now."

"Wick's not going to like it." "Wick" was Joe and Harry's boss, Margaret Fraker, the Wicked Witch of the West. There had been another nickname but Margaret had heard about it and there had been hell to pay.

"She'll only not like it if it doesn't work. We don't need him to break down and confess, we just need to rattle him a little. Enough to make a mistake."

"I hear Firth's dad doesn't like 'rattling.'"

"That's why you're here, so you can confirm that it didn't get out of line."

"Great," grumbled Harry.

Joe knocked on the door of the Rittenhouse Square house and was surprised, but grimly pleased, when Biden Firth himself opened the door. Firth stood in the doorway looking at Joe wordlessly, as if he didn't recognize him.

"Good afternoon, Mr. Firth, may we come in?"

"I didn't expect you," said Firth. "There's somewhere I have to be. Is it urgent?"

"A development in your wife's case I'd like to update you on. It should just take a couple of minutes."

Firth hesitated for a moment and then stepped aside to let them enter, barely sparing a glance at Harry.

"Where's Joan today?" asked Joe as he stepped into the entrance hall.

"She's spending a few days with Sophia at my in-laws' place." Biden closed the door behind them. He turned toward them and, without meeting Joe's eyes, said dully, "What is it?"

Joe took his time answering, examining Biden. Roger was right—he looked like shit. His eyes were sunken, his lips tight. His arms hung loose at his sides but his fingers twitched as if playing some unseen instrument. He smelled as if he had not showered in some time. It looked as if Biden's defenses might be crumbling.

"Is there somewhere we could sit?" Joe asked. Biden gestured vaguely toward the parlor and turned in that direction but Joe said, "Why don't we use the library?"

Biden hesitated then crossed the entrance hall and opened the door to the library. They entered and Joe gestured to the couch. "Have a seat, Mr. Firth."

Biden stayed standing in the middle of the room. "I don't need to sit. What do you have to tell me?"

"We got some more test results on your wife's body back from the forensics lab," said Joe, holding up the manila folder he carried.

Firth's lips narrowed. "And?"

Joe flipped open the folder. "Although it's not possible to pinpoint the time of death, it seems likely that she died around the time she disappeared."

Firth nodded grimly. "I think we all assumed that."

"Yes," Joe agreed. "It was also not possible to determine the cause of death, although choking seems to be the most likely."

"I know that already. In fact, as you might recall, you are the one who told me that, several weeks ago. I'd recommend you check your records before you come to my house to re-tell me 'developments' in my wife's case."

"Yes, of course. I should have realized you wouldn't need to be reminded of those details," said Joe, a hint of condescension in his voice.

"So may I return to my plans now?" said Biden, beginning to turn toward the door to the entrance hall.

"No, not quite yet," said Joe, and caught a spasm of irritation on Biden's face. "I realize you're a busy man but I do have some information that I only got yesterday. They analyzed scrapings from your wife's fingernails. There were gray fibers there that might have come from automobile carpeting. It's used in several high end car lines—primarily BMW and Mercedes. Including last year's Mercedes E-Class." Joe flipped to another page in the folder then looked up. "That's the car you drive, isn't it, Mr. Firth?"

There was a long pause. Joe was surprised at how muted the sounds of the traffic right outside the window were. Biden's face had gone from flushed to white. "What are you saying?" he said hoarsely.

"Is it possible anyone else could have had access to your car the night your wife disappeared? You've said that your wife left by the front door but is it possible she left by the back door and took your car? Or left by the front door and circled back to the garage? Maybe she took your car and someone attacked her and then used the car to dispose of her body."

"And then returned it to my garage in time for me to drive it to the shore the next day?" snarled Biden his color beginning to heighten again. Joe fleetingly thought that if he couldn't put Biden Firth behind bars, perhaps he could give him a heart attack.

"It does seem like a long shot," said Joe mildly. "But not impossible. Especially it if was a member of the household. Perhaps Miss Davies or Miss Brouwer."

Biden's voice rose in unbalanced mimicry of his father.

"You think Joan or Esme strangled my wife and used my car to dump her body?" he asked incredulously.

"As I said, it's a long shot but one worth following up on. I'd like your permission to take a sample of the carpet fibers from your car."

Firth took a step toward Joe who took a step back. "What the fuck are you talking about?" said Firth in a ragged whisper then, in a louder voice, "What the *fuck* are you talking about?" His hands were balled into fists and Joe mentally checked the accessibility of his gun in his shoulder holster. "You may *not* have my permission to take samples from my car. You don't think it was the *housekeeper* or the *nanny*. Or the fucking *butler* in the *library* with a *knife*, for God's sake. Get out of my house! You come here telling me my wife was choked to death and then put in the trunk of a car and then you tell me you want to search *my* car? Get out of my house and don't come back unless you have a warrant! Get out *now*!!"

Joe flipped the folder closed. "Calm down, Mr. Firth, we're just following up on every lead and trying to eliminate possibilities. We're leaving." He turned toward the door but was careful to keep Firth in his peripheral vision.

"Don't come back to my house," yelled Firth as Joe and Harry left the room. "And if you want to talk to me again, call my lawyer. I'm going to be talking to the commissioner about this!"

"Fine," muttered Joe as he opened the front door. He turned to look once again at the entrance hall, where he was sure Biden Firth had killed his wife, when Firth appeared at the library doorway.

"Get OUT!" Firth said with a strangled cry.

"Good afternoon, Mr. Firth," said Joe, and he pulled the door shut.

"Congratulations, I think you rattled him," said Harry

archly.

"That wasn't quite what I had in mind," muttered Joe as they headed back to the car.

In the entrance hall, Biden Firth strode to the door, locked it, and, with trembling hands, slid the chain into place. He walked to the back of the house, bumping into the sideboard as he went, rattling the plates inside, and descended the stairs to the garage. He popped open the trunk of the Mercedes and looked in. The carpet covering the floor of the trunk was black. Booth has said they had found gray fiber. He pushed the trunk closed and then froze. The blood pounding in his ears, he popped the trunk open again. The top of the trunk was carpeted with gray.

Jesus God, he thought, covering his face with his hands, *she was alive when I put her in the trunk and she tried to claw her way out.*

Chapter 35

When Joe got to his desk the next day, there was a piece of paper—in fact, that day's page from his Philadelphia Eagles daily desk calendar—with "See me!" scrawled on it in red. With an internal groan—or perhaps it was external since The Mouse glanced his way—he headed for his boss's office and knocked on the frame of the open door.

Margaret Fraker waved him in with a hand that looked as if it should be holding an unfiltered cigarette but was in fact holding a coffee stirrer. A few spatters of coffee moistened the papers littering her desk. "Come in. Shut the door."

Joe did as he was told then stood uncertainly. He didn't have much experience being called to the principal's office.

"Sit," said Margaret and Joe did.

Margaret leaned forward in her chair and looked intently at Joe then said, with mild annoyance, "What the fuck?"

"What?" said Joe.

"That's what I just asked you." She stuck the coffee stirrer in her mouth and Joe swore he saw her inhale.

"Uh, is this about the Firth case?"

"Of course it's about the Firth case. What other case are you working on that would be worth me calling you into my office for?" Joe shrugged and Margaret sighed. "I got a call from the Firths' lawyer. He said you showed up at Biden Firth's house and accused him of choking his wife and putting her in the trunk of his car." She sat back and looked at Joe with her eyebrows up.

"I just told him about some analysis results we just got."

"The carpet fibers?"

"Yes."

"Why tell him about that before we had a chance to look into it more? Did you expect him to get all contrite and confess?"

Joe didn't reply but a flush began to spread up his neck.

Margaret waved the coffee stirrer. "Of course they'd fire me if they heard me say it but if it was some schmuck from West Philly with a dead wife, we'd just bring him in and sweat him for a while but it's Biden fucking *Firth* with his million dollar lawyers and we need to handle him with kid gloves."

"We do?" said Joe angrily.

Margaret tossed the coffee stirrer into the trash and leaned forward again. "Of course we do," she said and then, somewhat more gently, "you know that."

"Does this have anything to do with whose campaign Firth Senior is giving his millions to?" said Joe angrily.

"You know better than that, Joe. It's all about media exposure these days. We mishandle the case of that West Philly guy and who ever hears about it? We mishandle a case involving two of the biggest family names in Philly and every news outlet with a camera, a mike, or a web site is going to be all over it. Sad but true."

"There were carpet fibers from his car trunk—his trunk *roof*—under her fingernails—"

"There are tons of cars out there that use that carpet."

"He mentioned the trunk of the car before I said anything about the trunk—"

"Joe, if you mention a dead body and car fibers in the same sentence, ninety-nine people out of a hundred are going to think you're talking about the trunk."

"Shit," muttered Joe. He generally had a policy not to swear in front of women but Margaret didn't seem to count.

"You know, it's like he's charmed. Everybody thinks he did it but nothing is quite enough to arrest him for it."

"I know. It sucks."

"So he's going to get away with it."

"Not if we find something airtight to tie him to the murder," said Margaret. "But it's not going to be you finding that something, at least right now. I need you to back off for a little while." Joe opened his mouth but Margaret put up her hand. "Just for a little while. Until I can smooth things over."

Joe fussed, with increasing irritation, with paperwork at his desk until mid-afternoon when he decided he had had enough. As he jammed his arms into the sleeves of his jacket, his phone, quiet all day, rang. Reaching for it, he bumped the styrofoam cup containing the dregs of that morning's coffee and sent a stream of grayish liquid spilling across his blotter.

"Damn!" he said, fumbling in the desk drawer for napkins. He snatched up the phone. "What?"

"Uh, hello?" Joe recognized Mike Kinnear.

Joe tossed the soggy napkins toward his waste paper basket where they bounced off the edge and landed with a splat on the floor. "Damn! What??"

"It's Mike Kinnear—"

"I know. What do you want? No, don't tell me, you think I should get a search warrant. What a good idea—why didn't I think of that? No, wait, I *did* think of that and got told it was *not* a good idea. Several times." Joe sat down heavily in his chair. "Biden Firth complained and now I'm being told to lay off the case. For a *little while*," he added nastily.

"Oh," said Mike, followed by a long pause. "Well, I think it's very short-sighted of them—"

"Don't start with me," said Joe, "I'm not asking again—"

"No, of course not, I totally understand," said Mike hastily. "I could hardly ask you to do more than you've already done. I appreciate it. Really."

"Hmph," said Joe.

"Well, I'll let you get back to work."

Good-byes were exchanged and the call ended. Joe retrieved the soggy napkins from the floor and dropped them in the wastebasket. Getting Mike Kinnear to lay off the Firth case had been easier than he had expected.

Chapter 36

Late on a warm May afternoon, Mark Pironi stood on the marble step of the Firth townhouse opening the door for a prospective buyer.

"I think this is going to be perfect for your needs, Mr. Pate," he said, "fine workmanship but not an overwhelmingly large place."

"Please, call me Scott," said the prospective buyer.

Scott and Pironi moved from room to room, Scott making appreciative comments regarding the fine woodwork and practical lay-out of the house. He peered at a still life oil hanging over an antique sideboard in the entrance hall. "Beautiful decor as well," said Scott, "with all this fine artwork I suppose there is a burglar alarm?"

"Not one installed now but I'd be happy to put you in touch with someone who could give you an estimate for what it would cost to install a system," said Pironi, making a note on a manila folder. Scott nodded agreeably.

In the third floor gym, Scott pulled a tape measure out of his pocket and, with Pironi's help, took a number of measurements of the room and the equipment. ("The seller might be willing to include the gym equipment if you're interested," said Pironi.)

As they finished touring the top floor, Scott said, "I have what will probably sound like an odd request. I live in an old house now and I find that when people walk around on the floor above me it makes a terrible racket. I was wondering if you would mind if I went down to the next floor and you could walk around up here just so I can hear what it sounds like."

"Sure," said Pironi. Scott descended to the second floor and in a moment heard, faintly, Pironi walking around on the third floor. After a minute he said, "Thanks, that's good."

Pironi came down the steps. "How did it sound?"

"Very faint. Great construction on some of these older homes."

They toured the second floor and Scott make the same request—he descended to the first floor while Pironi walked around on the second floor.

"A little noisier that time," said Scott.

"Well, the third floor is mainly carpeted but the second floor has a lot of bare hardwood floors," pointed out Pironi.

"True," conceded Scott.

When they got to the back of the house, after checking out the kitchen, Pironi opened a door off the back hall with a flourish. "And an attached two car garage! Very unusual to find that in a townhouse of this era."

"Indeed," said Scott, descending the stairs to the garage. "And a workbench, very handy." He opened a door next to the two garage doors and peered out onto the alley behind the house. "Tidy," he said.

"Yes, a very well maintained house," agreed Pironi.

Scott closed the door and latched it. He pointed toward the ceiling of the garage. "Do you mind?"

"Oh, sure," said Pironi, and shortly Scott heard him walking around in the room above the garage. He clicked the latch of the outside door open again and then climbed the steps to the kitchen.

"Could hardly hear a thing!" he called out.

❖

Biden was spending a fair number of his nights away from home these days. He had largely been faithful to Elizabeth while they were married, and had been discreet about his few indiscretions. Now, however, he had given up on discretion—many Friday or Saturday nights he would go to a bar or a club and leave with a woman and take her to a hotel. Sometimes money changed hands, sometimes it did not—the experiences seemed equivalent to him. Joan was staying in the third floor apartment most nights now, so Biden felt comfortable that Sophia was being well taken care of during his absences.

Pironi had shown the house to a prospective buyer earlier in the day—"a real queen" as Pironi described him—but they had left a few hours ago and Firth had been able to get back into the house to get ready for his evening out—dinner at the country club with a acquaintance from Penn then visits to some of their old haunts. He pulled out of the garage around 7:00, leaving Joan in the kitchen with Sophia, the smoked glass of the Mercedes wrapping him in a dark, anonymous cocoon. He barely paid attention to the man with the wide-brimmed hat and knapsack, earbuds in place, who was walking down the alley.

Mike hit the speed dial on his cell phone. "He just left, let's give it a couple of minutes."

A few minutes later Scott knocked on the front door, the cell phone, with the line still open to Mike's phone, tucked into his front pocket. In a moment Joan answered the door.

"Can I help you?" she asked.

"Yes, my name is Scott Pate, I was here earlier looking at the house and after I left I realized I had lost something, I'm thinking I might have dropped it in the house."

"I'm sorry, I can't let you in," said Joan, flustered.

"No, of course not, I was just wondering if you would

look around for me, I can wait here."

Joan considered. "That would be all right. What did you lose?"

"It was a St. Christopher's medal. I had it in my pocket and I think it might have fallen out when I pulled out a tape measure. I was taking some measurements in the gym room on the third floor, I think it's most likely that I lost it there. It's silver and about this big," he said, holding is fingers about two inches apart.

"OK, let me take a look," said Joan. "Uh, would you like a drink of water?"

"Oh, no thank you, I'm fine," said Scott.

"All right, I'll be right back," said Joan, and she shut the door, Scott hearing the sound a deadbolt snapping shut.

"OK, she's on her way upstairs. I hope," he said to the air.

Behind the house, Mike opened the unlocked back door and stepped into the dark garage, then clicked on a small LED flashlight. He went quickly to the cabinet and, taking a pair of bolt cutters out of the knapsack, snapped the combination lock off. He removed the broken lock and dropped it into the knapsack, then opened the cabinet doors and shone the light inside.

There was a variety of objects in the cabinet—a number of cans of paint and other flammable substances such as lighter fluid and turpentine. He scanned the shelves, looking for something blue. A number of the containers had blue labels but his eye was drawn to two paint cans with drips of blue paint on the outside. He picked them up and, drawing a large black garbage bag out of the knapsack, carefully lowered them into it. He also noticed a blue grease gun and added that to the knapsack.

As he was closing the doors of the cabinet he heard Scott's voice through the earbuds. "Oh, excellent, I'm so happy you found it! Thanks so much for your help."

"Shit," muttered Mike under his breath. Holding the flashlight in his mouth, he reached into the knapsack and pulled out two combination locks—he hadn't remembered the color of the lock so he had gotten a red and a black one but now he noticed that the lock he had cut off the cabinet had a green dial. "Shit shit," he whispered. He decided that the black lock was most likely to pass a cursory inspection. He placed the bolt cutters in the knapsack, followed by the green and red locks—they knocked together, making a loud thunk just as he heard footsteps in the room over the garage. Mike froze. He heard the steps passing back and forth in the room above, accompanied by the click of china—the housekeeper must be unloading the dishwasher. As quietly as possible he slipped the black lock into the handles of the cabinet and snapped it shut. He put the flashlight into the knapsack and slowly zipped it shut. He grasped the garbage bag and lifted it up and as he did so the two cans of paint shifted, knocking against each other. He froze as he heard the footsteps in the room over him stop. He stepped to the side of the cabinet so that it stood between himself and the stairway to the first floor and crouched down as he heard the footsteps approach the door to the garage.

The door opened and Mike could see the shadow of a woman cast down the steps from the light behind her. After a beat the garage light clicked on. Mike held his breath. After a few seconds the light went off and the shadow on the stairs disappeared as the woman closed the door.

For a few more minutes Mike heard the sounds of the housekeeper walking back and forth in the kitchen but then he heard very faintly the sounds of a child crying and the steps receded toward the front of the house. Picking up the knapsack and the garbage bag he stole to the door and, slipping out, closed it quietly behind him.

Scott had circled the block four times before he saw Mike at the designated pick-up point. Scott pulled to the corner and Mike dropped the garbage bag and knapsack in the back seat of the Audi and then climbed in the front passenger seat.

"What took you so long?" asked Scott.

"She came back to the kitchen," said Mike. "I had to wait for her to leave. Drive away."

Scott pulled carefully back into traffic. "Did you get it?"

"I did find some blue things in the cabinet." He rubbed his hands across his face and then turned and grinned at Scott. "That worked like a charm."

"This is fun," said Scott, smiling back. "I feel like Tom Cruise in that movie!"

"Mission Impossible."

"Exactly!"

They took Walnut Street to the Schuylkill Expressway to Route 202 South, the traffic blessedly light.

When they got home Mike took the garbage bag to the garage and pulled out the items.

"A glue gun?" said Scott, raising his eyebrow.

Mike shrugged. "It was blue. I didn't have a lot of time to consider."

They stood, fists on hips, considering their plunder.

"Maybe there's something in the room of the house that is painted this color that we're supposed to find," said Scott.

"Jeez, I hope not," said Mike, "one breaking-and-entering per lifetime is enough for me." He pondered. "That would seem unnecessarily complicated, if there was something in another room, why not just send Ann the message when she was in that room."

"Maybe so the seller's real estate agent wouldn't know."

Mike looked skeptical. "Let's open them up and see if there's anything inside."

They got a newspaper out of the recycling bin and spread some pages on the garage floor. Scott got a screwdriver from an infrequently used toolbox under the kitchen sink and Mike pried the lids off the paint cans. One had only a small amount of paint in the bottom and after tipping it back and forth—the paint didn't move—Mike set it aside. The other can, however, was almost full and he used the screwdriver to stir the paint, eliciting a squawk from Scott.

"Use one of those wooden things!"

"I don't think we have one of those wooden things," said Mike. "There's something in this one."

"What?" said Scott, peering over his shoulder.

"We need something to pour the paint into."

They found an empty plastic kitty litter bucket and slowly poured the paint out of the paint can until they could see a shapeless mass at the bottom of the can. Mike reached in gingerly and, grasping the object by a corner, lifted it out onto the newspaper. When he wiped the paint away with a paper towel they could see it was a Ziploc bag.

"What's in it?" asked Scott, squatting down next to Mike.

Mike tried to clear the outside of the bag with a fresh paper towel.

"It looks like jewelry," he said.

"Let's open it," said Scott.

Mike sat back on his haunches, wiping his fingers on the towel.

"Let's not open it yet," he said. "We need to decide what we're going to do with it. Maybe there are fingerprints or something like that that the police could get from whatever's in there. We might mess it up if we try to take it out of the bag."

They both sat contemplating the bag for a time, then Mike said, "Let's put it away while we think about it."

They put the Ziploc bag into an empty Testoni shoe box and put it, along with the other items they had taken, back in the trunk of the Audi. Then they went upstairs to the kitchen and Scott poured them each a glass of wine.

"To our new occupation as cat burglars," said Scott, and they clinked glasses. "Are you going to call the police?"

"I don't know," said Mike, sipping his wine. "They would probably just arrest us for breaking and entering and not do anything to the husband." He considered some more. "What I'd like to do is take it to Ann, I think she might be able to get something from it."

"Like what?" asked Scott.

"I don't know, but I've told you about how having Beth Barboza's softball bat helped her find Beth. I'll bet that jewelry belonged to the wife and Ann could get more information from it."

"But what more information could there be?" asked Scott. "They already found the wife's body. And I would think that finding her jewelry in the house would be pretty incriminating for the husband."

"Yeah," said Mike. "I need to think about it more."

In fact, as the excitement from the success of their venture wore off, Mike realized that there was probably little he could do with their discovery. Even if he did take it to the police, it was probably inadmissible as evidence considering how it had been obtained. And it's not like they needed to find a body—Elizabeth Firth's was no doubt safely ensconced in a family vault—but Mike couldn't quite bring himself to admit that they might have done more harm than good with their adventure, and at the same time didn't want to stomach the idea of a murderer going free when they had the proof he was guilty.

He took another swallow of wine.

Chapter 37

The next morning when Biden returned home he found Joan with Sophia in the kitchen, Sophia in the high chair with a bowl of cereal in front of her. Biden kissed Sophia on top of the head.

"How's my favorite girl doing?" he said.

"She's good," said Joan. "We watched some cartoons this morning." Biden knew Joan didn't approve of his frequent absences from home but at least she didn't refer to them.

"Sounds like fun," said Biden to Sophia, turning to leave the kitchen.

"That man who looked at the house yesterday came back after you had left, he lost something while he was here."

"Did you let him in?" asked Biden sharply.

"Of course not," said Joan, affronted.

"No, of course not," said Biden. "What did he lose?"

"A St. Christopher's medal," said Joan. "I found it in the gym. He waited outside."

"Hmm. Well, thanks for taking care of that."

Biden pondered that while climbing the stairs to his room. Maybe he would take the house off the market for a while. At first he had wanted to be out of it but as the weeks went by that motivation seemed less and less. It was paid for so it wasn't costing him anything to stay. And he was getting tired of people walking through the place—first the police and then a bunch of prospective buyers, maybe even curiosity seekers. He would talk to Pironi about holding off on more showings.

He showered and changed. After finishing the breakfast

that Joan brought him in the dining room and reading the newspaper, Biden decided to go to the club and see if he could find a golf game to join. Getting his golf shoes from the bedroom and his bag from the closet in the back hall he told Joan he'd be back in a few hours and headed to the garage. He loaded the bag into the trunk and got into the car, hitting the door opener. The light from outside lit the garage and as he waited for the door to open his eye wandered across the metal cabinet and then returned to it. Something was different.

He turned off the car, got out, and went to the cabinet. Something was different but he couldn't put his finger on what it was. For the first time in many weeks he grasped the lock he had added to the cabinet months ago and began spinning the dial but before he was done entering the combination he knew what it was—it wasn't his lock.

He dropped the lock and stepped back as if he had been stung. Then, knowing it was futile, he finished entering the combination and gave the lock a tug. Nothing. His hands shaking, he entered the combination again with the same result.

He stood back, breathing heavily and staring at the lock. Then he closed the garage door and went upstairs to the kitchen.

"Joan, do you know the combination for the lock on the cabinet in the garage? I can't seem to remember it."

"No, Mr. Firth," said Joan. "I don't think I ever knew the combination."

He returned to the garage and opened the trunk of his car which still contained the bolt cutters he had bought in Tupper Lake. He applied the cutters to the lock and after some effort it gave way. He pulled the lock off and, taking a deep breath, opened the cabinet.

Where the paint can that had held Elizabeth's jewelry had

been there was now a circle of dust-free shelf.

Biden went back to the car and got in, gripping the steering wheel and staring at the open cabinet. Why had he felt compelled to keep the jewelry? Everything else had gone perfectly, how hard would it have been to throw a couple of thousand dollars of jewelry—many tens of thousands of dollars of jewelry, another part of his mind corrected—into the Schuylkill River? But he had thought the hiding place was foolproof—it had fooled the police, hadn't it? Who could have known that anything was in there? And it wasn't like the whole cabinet was ransacked, it looked like there were only a few things missing. And then it occurred to him who might have known there was something in there—Ann Kinnear.

He got out his phone, his hands shaking, and speed dialed Mark Pironi.

"Pironi here."

"It's Biden Firth."

"Hey, Biden, what's up."

"Mark, were any of the people who came to the house ever alone in the garage?"

"Not on my watch," said Pironi. "Why?"

"I bought a new GPS a couple of weeks ago and it was still in the box in the garage and now it's missing."

"Shit, that sucks," said Pironi.

"How about when that Kinnear group came, were they ever alone down there?"

"I don't think so," said Pironi, thinking. "We all went into the alley for a minute but I think we were all together. That woman had that spell in back and the buyers' realtor, Joyce, went in to get her a glass of water, I suppose that while that was going on someone could have picked it up ... but if it was still in the box it would be a pretty bulky thing to hide, I think I would have noticed something."

"How about that guy yesterday?"

Pironi was silent.

"Was he in the garage alone?"

"Well, he had this thing about hearing footsteps between floors, he wanted me to go into the kitchen to walk around to see if it was noisy in the garage."

"He cared about how noisy footsteps would be in the *garage*?" said Firth.

"He wanted to check all the floors," said Pironi. "He definitely didn't come out of the garage with a box, I would have seen it."

"How long was he down there alone?"

"Maybe a minute, tops."

"What was his name?"

"Scott Pate."

Biden gripped and ungripped his hand on the steering wheel. "Listen, Pironi, I don't want anyone walking through my house unescorted. I'm sick of having my stuff gone through and I don't want some conspiracy theorist, or some ordinary fucking *thief*, picking up a souvenir of their visit, am I making myself understood?"

"Sure, Biden, I get it ..."

"Anyway, before this even happened I was thinking of taking the place off the market. Don't schedule any more showings. I'll give you a call after I've had a chance to think about it."

"Sure, Biden, but ..."

Biden hit the End button.

He went upstairs again—fortunately Joan and Sophia weren't in the kitchen anymore or Joan might have wondered why a forgotten lock combination had put her employer in such a state—and went to his computer in the library. He did a search for "scott pate" and didn't find anything interesting, just a home address in West Chester. He pondered that for a moment and then did a search for home address for "mike kinnear." The results displayed.

"Shit," he said, burying his face in his hands.

Chapter 38

After a night pondering his options, Mike decided to drive up to the Adirondacks with the bag of jewelry. He wanted to see Ann in person since he knew that trying to explain to her why he had felt it necessary to break into the Firth house was going to be a tricky conversation best not attempted over the phone. He called her up to tell her he was coming.

"I have a couple of days with no appointments and Scott's out of town, mind if I come up?"

"Sure," she said, "we can go kayaking. Want to see if Walt's available? He might be able to pick you up tomorrow morning."

"No, that's OK, I won't mind the drive." He also didn't mind the idea of having some time to himself to mull over what plan he should propose to Ann, and how to do it.

As he neared King of Prussia where he would normally pick up the Pennsylvania Turnpike, he abruptly switched lanes and instead took the exit to the Schuylkill Expressway and Philadelphia. Soon he was driving slowly down the street in front of the Rittenhouse Square townhouse—at the end of the street he pulled into a space in front of a fire hydrant and killed the engine. Should he drive down the alley? It seemed ill-advised ... it was unlikely that he could just sneak back into the garage and replace the items. Hell, he didn't even know the combination to the lock he had put on the cabinet. He toyed briefly with the idea of just leaving the can of paint next to the back door—that would certainly bring things to a head. But he realized that now he didn't want the case solved as much as he wanted Ann out of it. He got out his cell phone, almost hit the speed dial for Scott, then tossed the phone onto the passenger seat. He could hardly decide what to do without 'fessing up to Ann and getting her input. With a sigh he started up the Audi and headed back to the Schuylkill.

Chapter 39

On the way to West Chester, Biden stopped at a convenience store and bought a map; God, he was tired of doing everything the hard way. Was it even true that they could tell if you had entered a particular address into your GPS, or that they could track your movements via data in the GPS databases? Maybe that was just an invention of the crime shows. He realized he shouldn't have searched for Pate's and Kinnear's addresses on his own computer—he hadn't been thinking straight. He didn't know what he was going to do when he got to their house, but if the disappearance of the paint can was somehow related to Pate's visit—maybe Joan hadn't locked the front door when she went upstairs looking for the lost item and he had gotten in then, or maybe he let in Kinnear who had then left by the back door—then maybe it wasn't too late. If he had taken it to the police, Firth figured he would have heard from them by now. Maybe their plan wasn't to take the bag of jewelry to the police at all—after all, there would be questions about how they had come into possession of it—but to use it some way in support of their supernatural "consulting business." Another thought struck him—maybe they meant to blackmail him! He laughed mirthlessly—they could try, but they would find that that well was dry.

The map led him to an upscale modern townhouse; he slowed as he passed it, then circled the block and pulled up across the street. What was he looking for? Not likely Mike Kinnear was going to pick that moment to get the mail ...

although, if he did, Biden thought, being seen there wasn't a great idea since Kinnear might wonder why Bob Dormand, their Harvey Cedars client, was parked in front of his house. He pulled away and drove aimlessly around until he found a pay phone inside a supermarket at a nearby shopping center. He called the number he had copied down from his internet search.

"Hello?" It didn't sound like Kinnear.

"Hi, Mike?" said Firth.

"No, this is Scott."

"Hi, Scott. Is Mike there?"

"He's not here right now, could I take a message?"

"Damn. Do you know when he's going to be back?"

"Who is this?"

"Oh, sorry, this is Bob Donald, I'm a friend of Mike's from way back. I was visiting my parents in the area and I thought I might catch up with him. I'm leaving tonight, do you think he'll be back before then?"

"No, he won't be back today but I can have him give you a call if you want."

"Sure, that would be great." Firth read a phone number off a flyer on a bulletin board next to the pay phone. "If I don't catch up with him this time I'll give him a call next time I'm in town."

"And you said the name was Bob Daniel?"

"Yup. Thanks, Scott." Firth hung up.

If Mike had gone to the police, and assuming the paint can was missing since Pate's visit to the house which seemed most likely, Firth assumed that he would have brought his boyfriend with him. If he was gone and not expected back today, maybe he was headed to the Adirondacks to see Ann. To plan the blackmail scheme—blackmail also seemed the most likely explanation.

If Mike and Ann Kinnear were both at Ann's house in the

Adirondacks, and if Mike hadn't gone to the police with the jewelry, assuming he had it, then there wouldn't be much to link an unexplained death in Philadelphia with a double homicide hundreds of miles away in the Adirondacks.

Chapter 40

Biden took the most direct route to Ann's house—up the New York Thruway—valuing speed over the ability to stay out of sight of the traffic cams. He found groups of fast-moving cars and stayed with them so he made good time without standing out. It was late afternoon when he reached Tupper Lake, the nearest town to Ann's house.

At the same hardware store where he had bought the bolt cutter the week before, he bought a box of rat poison and, at a grocery store, a steak. In the parking lot of the grocery store he rubbed the rat poison into the meat then wrapped it in the plastic grocery bag, wiping his hands on his handkerchief. Then he drove back to the For Sale house on Loon Pond.

The house looked much as it had before, if a bit more neglected. It appeared that no one had discovered the replacement locks that Biden had put on the rowboat and the dock box and he was able to unlock them with the key he had kept. It was darker now than it had been the first time he had made the trip but he was able to count the docks until he got to the one he had seen the dog on. And there it was again, still not barking but wagging enthusiastically, glad to welcome a returning visitor.

Biden rowed closer, keeping an eye out for any sign of people. He got the steak out of the plastic bag and, rowing as close as he dared, tossed it onto the dock. The dog sniffed the meat, picked it up, and trotted up the path with it. Biden rowed away to wait for the poison to take effect.

Beau made his way up the hill toward the cabin, carrying his prize. There was an odd bitterness about it but mainly there was the irresistible taste of bloody meat. Not warm — warm was better — but still good.

When he reached the cabin he took the meat to his place under the screen porch and settled in to enjoy his treat, a rising wind beginning to rattle the leaves around him. He had sunk his teeth into the meat when he heard two short whistles, one high, one low. Beau turned his head in the direction of the sound. He heard the signal again — it was the signal to "leave it" — and, reluctantly, he dropped the meat and trotted into the house.

Chapter 41

Mike stopped for dinner at an Italian restaurant not far from Saratoga Springs. Indecision was an emotion he didn't have much experience with and he wasn't enjoying it. He lingered over his second glass of mediocre wine, swirling it absently on the tabletop. When his coffee arrived he got out his phone and speed dialed Scott.

"Have you decided on a plan yet?" asked Scott.

"No. I'm stumped. I'm kind of sorry we got it."

"No, it's for the best, you'll think of the right thing to do with it. You and Ann."

"I hope so," said Mike. "Hey, let's agree that you didn't know why I asked you to go back to the house for a lost St. Christopher's medal, OK?"

"And in this new scenario, who unlocked the garage door?"

"I don't know," said Mike morosely.

"Don't be melodramatic, we'll figure it out," said Scott. "Hey, you got a call from an old friend today. Not an old friend *I've* ever heard of," he added peevishly.

"Who's that?" asked Mike.

"Bob Daniel. He's in town visiting his parents but I think he's gone by now."

"Who the hell is Bob Daniel?" asked Mike.

"How should I know, he's your friend," said Scott. "He left a number."

Mike felt a squeeze of discomfort in his gut. He pulled a pen from his pocket and smoothed his cocktail napkin on the table. "What is it?"

Scott gave him the number.

"Let me try him now, maybe I can catch him before he leaves," said Mike.

"OK, keep me up to date," said Scott. "Love you."

"Me too," said Mike, and disconnected.

He dialed the number and after a few rings a woman answered. He could hear a baby crying in the background.

"Hello, is Bob there?" said Mike.

"Who?" said the woman.

"Bob Daniel. I was given this number for Bob Daniel."

"No Bob here, wrong number," said the woman, and hung up.

A sweat broke out on Mike's forehead and he felt his heart begin to thump. He waved the waitress down and asked to get the check right away, then paid cash so he wouldn't have to wait for a credit card to be processed. He walked quickly to the parking lot, pressing the speed dial for Ann as he went. The phone rang and rang and eventually he heard, "This is Ann's voicemail, leave a message …"

Chapter 42

Biden pulled the boat up to the dock, keeping an eye out for the dog. He didn't know how long rat poison would take to kill a dog that size but he guessed that at this point if the dog wasn't actually dead it was at least incapacitated.

His steps on the dock sounded very loud, seeming to echo back from the tree-lined shores of the pond, but the wind was picking up—he was sure any noise he might make would be masked by the sighing of the wind through the treetops and the creak of the branches as they swayed.

Biden began climbing the log stairway up the hill and soon a two story cabin came into view among the trees—Biden could see lights on the first and second floors. As he watched, he saw a figure move past one of the first floor windows.

Biden fumbled in the pocket of his jacket and pulled out the gun. He had originally thought that one of the benefits of its small size was that it would make less noise. Now, he realized, the amount of noise it made when he shot her was immaterial—with the dog gone he doubted there was another living soul within a half a mile.

Ann heard the wind pick up. She checked the windows upstairs to make sure they were closed, but kept a couple of the first floor windows open to catch the breeze. She opened the door for Beau who came in, trotted down the hall, and flopped down on his bed in the sitting room.

Ann had decided to try a rather complex recipe for boeuf bourguignon and was fussing with the sauce. As she cooked, the wind continued to increase and when some papers began blowing off the dining room table she closed the first floor windows as well, keeping only the outside door open to catch the fresh air.

Ann took an experimental spoonful from the pot on the stove. She considered calling Mike to get a recommendation for what to add to make it more interesting, not to mention asking him when he was going to arrive—if he had left West Chester when he said he was going to, he should have arrived by now. There must be something to add to liven it up, she thought, and headed down to the basement pantry to assess the options, closing the door behind her so Beau wouldn't follow her.

The wind lent unfamiliar creaks and groans to the cabin, so Ann didn't hear the screen door open as Biden entered. In the sitting room Beau raised his head from the dog bed.

Biden, holding the gun in a gloved hand, had expected to find Ann in the kitchen, and the bubbling pot on the stove supported that expectation. The sitting room area was dark but a light shone from the stairs to the second floor. Biden closed the door behind him and crossed the floor as quietly as possible.

To Ann in the basement the footsteps were clear even over

the noise of the storm. "It's about time," she muttered, and, putting a can of tomato paste back on the shelf, began climbing the basement stairs as she heard footsteps above her climbing the stairs to the second floor. Her hand was on the doorknob when she hesitated. Had Mike ever come into the house without announcing himself, much less gone straight upstairs? Not that she could remember. Walt and Helen Federman would be even less likely to intrude in that way.

Feeling somewhat foolish, but thinking back on a couple of encounters she had had at the cabin with members of her "fan base," she descended the stairs again—taking care to be quiet—and looked around the basement for something she could use as a weapon. Her eyes lit upon a large cast iron frying pan that Mike had given her several Christmases ago which she decided had two considerations to recommend it— it was extremely heavy and the handle would make it easy to swing, which would be useful if the person whose steps she had heard turned out to be an intruder, and it was legitimate dinner preparation equipment, which would be convenient if the person turned out to be Mike—no awkward questions to answer. She made her way up the basement steps again, pan in hand.

She listened at the door, unsure of where the other person was. Still upstairs? And where was Beau? As far as she could remember, he had been in his bed in the sitting room when she went to the basement. As that thought passed through her mind she heard the click of his toenails just on the other side of the door, but he passed on to the kitchen before she had a chance to open the door and pull him into the basement stairwell. From what she could tell, Beau stopped at the foot of the stairs to the second floor, then continued the circuit of the first floor back to the sitting room.

She heard her cell phone ring from its charger in the kitchen, then silence as voicemail picked up.

A moment later she heard steps coming down the stairway above her. She was sure it was a man and, she thought, someone heavier than Mike. The steps passed though the dining room and into the kitchen.

Where was she? Maybe she was outside looking for the dog, but she would have needed a flashlight and he was quite sure he would have seen that. Biden glanced around the kitchen and started to turn toward the sitting room then turned back.

Stuck to the front of the refrigerator was a pencil drawing. He stepped closer to take a look and his stomach jolted as he recognized it—it was his garage. The doors, the workbench, the stairway, even the metal cabinet, it was all there. And in the center was Elizabeth, represented by only a few lines, but she was unmistakable. And she was pointing at the cabinet—pointing at the one thing that could tie him to her murder.

The psychic had done it. She had somehow found out about the jewelry—about the engagement ring that he hadn't been able to bring himself to throw into the Schuylkill River, the ring that he was going to use to torment his father on his deathbed—and she had stolen it from his house. He snatched the picture from the refrigerator, scattering the magnets that had held it there (Ann, her ear pressed to the door, jumped as they clattered to the floor), and began crumpling it in one hand but then noticed the pot bubbling on the gas stove and had a better idea.

He would teach that bitch to invade a man's home, he would burn her home to the ground—burn it to the ground with her body in it.

He held the edge of the paper to the gas flame until it

caught then looked wildly around the room. The curtains, cute little gingham things at the window over the sink—too perfect. He held the burning paper to the cloth and they flared gratifyingly. The whole fucking building was wood, it would go up like a pile of kindling.

He dropped the still burning piece of paper to the floor and whirled back to the room, then he saw a door he had missed on his first circuit through the house, a faint spill of light coming from the gap at the bottom. The door to the basement. Now he knew where she was.

Ann, crouched on the stairs, heard Biden's steps cross the kitchen and then stop in the hallway just on the other side of the door. Her hand was on the doorknob but she snatched it away as she felt a hand grasp it on the other side and at that moment she heard the whistled command that instructed Beau to attack—the fast ascending whistle followed by five quick high whistles. And then she heard Beau's paws scrabble on the sitting room floor as he launched himself at the attacker.

Biden heard the noise too and spun toward the sitting room, firing down the hallway as a huge, shaggy dog appeared, leaping, out of the darkness.

Everything then seemed to happen at once. Ann threw open the door and stumbled out, gripping the handle of the frying pan in both hands. The room in which a minute ago she had been fussing over dinner and sipping wine was chaos. She had a confused impression of man and dog mixed together, Beau's jaws clamped onto the intruder's arm, the other arm, holding the gun, flailing for balance. The momentum of Beau's leap had driven both dog and man into the kitchen and their figures were silhouetted against flames dancing at the window. Ann saw a smear of red on Beau's fur and then the gun discharged again and Beau was on the ground, writhing. Ann raised the cast iron pan above her head and stepped into the chaos.

As Beau fell away from the intruder's arm, Biden heard Ann and, turning, fired again. Ann felt a pain like a punch in her ribs but as she staggered she brought the pan down on the intruder's arm and she heard the crack of bone breaking and the gun skittered across the floor. She drew the pan back again and, swinging it like a bat, connected with the side of the intruder's head and he fell to the floor next to Beau.

Ann followed the sound the gun had made on the floor. Her fingers seemed to register every crack in the wooden floor boards and every piece of gritty dirt Beau had carried in on his paws, but no gun. And as hypersensitive as her sense of touch had become, her vision was fogging, registering only blocks of color and shape. She heard a gasping of breath but whether it was hers or the intruder's she couldn't tell. In a panic she dropped the pan and swept her arms across the floor and her wrist connected with metal. The gun slid again but she pounced on it. Fumbling it into her hand, she turned back to the intruder.

He was barely conscious, making motions to rise but lacking the force or coordination to do so. Ann looked down at her body and saw a red stain spreading slowly from under her right breast. Pressing her left hand over the wound, gun in her right hand, she crawled on her knees and elbows over to Beau.

Beau was on his side, panting, blood pooling on the floor from wounds in his chest and his neck. Ann put her hand on his head and Beau's tail thumped once, twice on the floor. The panting grew quicker for a moment and then slower and then stopped altogether.

Ann pushed herself away from the dog's body and collapsed against a kitchen cupboard. She could feel the blood pounding in her temples and seeping through her fingers—she could feel the heat of the flames above her head. The pain in her side screamed for her attention. She pointed the gun, wavering, at the intruder who was struggling to a sitting position. He tried to push himself up with his damaged arm and, with a strangled scream, fell back to the floor, his dark hair falling over his face. He tried again, seeming to be regaining some coordination, and managed to pull himself into a sitting position, propping himself against the wall on the other side of the kitchen, only a few feet from Ann. When he raised his eyes to her, she recognized the intruder as the client from Harvey Cedars.

"What are you doing here?" she gasped, through tears of pain and sorrow.

"How did you find it?" Biden snarled.

"Find what?" This man had wanted her to find a spirit in his beach house but she hadn't—what was he talking about?

"Where is it?" The jewelry must be in her house, he should get it out before it burned.

"Where is what?" she wailed, then she saw the remains of her drawing smoldering on the floor. She brought her eyes back to the intruder, struggling to make some sense of ... anything. Her vision wavered—sometimes she could see the man she knew as Bob Dormand but sometimes he became lost in a sea of murkiness and pain. "Is it blue?"

Biden hauled himself to his feet. "It's not blue, you stupid bitch, it's an emerald," he screamed. "I did it right. I did it *right*. Everything would be all right if it weren't for a fucking *psychic*!" and he lurched toward Ann.

And as the darkness finally closed on her, she pulled the trigger.

The quiet that fell was a startling blankness relieved only by the moan of the wind around the eves and the crackle of the flames above the prone bodies. The fire had reached the top of the curtains and was licking at the kitchen ceiling, a lazy dark smoke beginning to curl from the wooden beams. On the end of a beam above the window, a tiny flame sprouted, and then flared as it followed the line of caulk between the beams toward the center of the room. Shadows danced merrily on the walls.

Within the house, a puff of breeze blew, although the doors and windows were all closed. It swirled from the sitting room into the kitchen and stirred the fur on the dead dog's back. Then it rose toward the ceiling and ruffled the flame which danced for a moment but then, rather than flaring, began to fade. The breeze became more concentrated, blowing opposite the path of the flames, pushing the fire back toward the window, the flame shrinking as it retreated. It reached the window and then, like a birthday candle, winked out, leaving only the wail of the wind to mourn the scene.

Chapter 43

Mike drummed his hands on his steering wheel for a minute and then redialed Ann's number with the same effect.

"Fuck," he said hoarsely, then looked up Joe Booth's personal number in his phone's contacts list and dialed.

"Hello," said Joe. Mike could hear a ball game playing on a TV in the background.

"Hi, it's Mike Kinnear."

"Yes?" said Joe tiredly, obviously expecting another discussion about a search warrant.

"Listen, I've done something incredibly stupid and I think Ann might be in danger as a result."

"What?" said Joe, no longer sounding tired. The sounds of the ball game in the background muted.

"I was still curious about the blue thing in Firth's garage cabinet so I … I got it."

"How?" said Joe.

"I'll explain that later. Anyhow, it was a Ziploc bag of jewelry, woman's jewelry. I'm betting that it's the wife's."

"Holy hell," said Joe under his breath. "Where is it now?"

"It's in the trunk of my car."

"Holy shit," said Joe, a bit more loudly, "what were you thinking?"

"Let's agree for the moment that I wasn't thinking," said Mike. "The thing is, I think Firth knows I have the jewelry and that I'm heading up to see Ann and I'm afraid he might try to hurt her. Hell, I'm afraid he might try to hurt me but he doesn't know where I am at the moment."

"Does he know where she lives?"

"I don't know. It's not easy to find it, we've made a point of that, but it's not impossible. A couple of freaks have found their way to her house in the past. I just tried calling her and she's not picking up. I'm thinking that maybe you could call the police up there and ask them to drive by and check on her."

"Does she know about the jewelry?"

"No, I haven't told her yet."

"Does anyone else know about it?"

Mike paused. "I'm the one who was responsible for taking it."

"That's not what I asked," said Joe.

Mike sighed. "My partner, Scott, knows about it."

There was a moment of silence. "Where are you now?" asked Joe.

"I'm at a restaurant in Saratoga Springs."

"How far is that from Ann's house?"

"At least two hours."

"OK, you might as well continue on up there. Go to the Tupper Lake police station. If it's really Firth and he's after both of you, the police can keep an eye on you there. I'll call up there and see what they can do. I'll call you back and let you know what they say. Should I call you back on this number?"

"Yes, it's my cell."

"OK," continued Joe. "Call me back if you haven't heard from me by the time you get to Tupper Lake. Call your partner now and tell him to go to a busy public area and stay there until you or I give him a call. Tell him not to mention the jewelry to anyone. And don't you mention the jewelry to anyone until we've had a chance to talk. Including Ann."

"OK," said Mike. "Thanks, Joe."

"Don't thank me yet," said Joe, "you are going to be in one big hell of a lot of trouble when you get back to Philly."

Having received a confusing but urgent-sounding call from Mike, Scott opened the door of The Foundry Bar and Grill and was struck by an onslaught of noise from the mostly early-twenties crowd. He pushed his way to the bar and reached it just as a couple vacated their seats—he slipped onto a stool and put his cell phone on the bar where he could keep an eye on it. When a bartender eventually wandered within gesturing distance, Scott ordered a martini which then sat untouched as he shredded his cocktail napkin. He tried to pace himself, allowing himself a glance at his watch only every five minutes, but each time he looked he found that only a minute or two had passed. He tried to distract himself with the television over the bar but even with subtitles the show was nonsensical.

He was doing a count-down from sixty for the next look at his watch when a hand on his arm made him jump, sloshing martini onto his sleeve. He turned to find Alan, a fellow therapist at Bryn Mawr Rehab, at his elbow.

"Hey, Scott, sorry about that! Lost in a daydream, eh?"

"Yeah, a dream," muttered Scott, mopping his sleeve with a couple of cocktail napkins he pulled from the bartender's supply.

"Hey, do you know Sean? From work?" Alan gestured at a vaguely familiar-looking young red-haired man standing behind him.

"Sure," said Scott. "Nice to see you."

The young man nodded and glanced around the bar nervously. Just coming out, Scott guessed.

Alan flagged down the bartender and ordered two draft

beers. "So where's Mike? You bachin' it tonight?"

"Out of town, visiting his sister."

"Hey, I remember her, the psychic, right?" Alan elbowed his red-haired friend. "Scott's partner's sister is a psychic."

"No kidding?" said Sean, still looking distractedly around the bar.

"No kidding!" said Alan, "they even had a TV show about her. Right?" He turned to Scott for confirmation.

"Right," said Scott.

"'scuse me," said Sean, "I see someone over there I've got to talk to. Nice meeting you," he nodded to Scott and slipped into the crowd just as the bartender delivered the two beers.

Alan sighed. "Nervous someone he knows is going to see him. Hey, mind if I join you?" He slipped onto a stool next to Scott and slid the extra beer in front of him. "Since I made you spill your drink, this can be a replacement." He took a deep draft of his beer and glanced around the crowd. "I'm going to stop going for the young ones. Too skittish." He bumped Scott's elbow with his own just as Scott was picking up his glass, causing the martini stain to be diluted with beer. "So, what are Mike and his psychic sister up to these days?"

"God only knows," said Scott morosely.

Chapter 44

Maura Meece and her partner Tony Taubert made good time on their way to Loon Pond—despite not using the lights or siren—until they got to Loon Pond Road itself where the gravel surface slowed them down. They had gotten Ann's cell phone number from Joe Booth and Tony called the number several times on their way to the house but there was no answer.

When they got to the bottom of the drive to Ann's house they crunched slowly up the hill, pulled into the parking area, turned off the engine, and emerged from the car. The storm had passed but the sound of water falling from branches was loud. The windows of the cabin glowed cheerfully among the trees.

Maura snapped the strap off her gun but left it in her holster; Tony, following her lead, did the same. Tony pulled two flashlights out of the glove compartment and passed one to Maura. They located the path to the house and started down it, straining to hear any out-of-place sounds over the drip of the rainwater.

About halfway down the path Tony said, "You smell that?"

Maura sniffed. "No, what?"

"Something's burning, something on the stove maybe."

Maura sniffed again and thought she did smell something this time. They were about fifteen yards from the house and had a view of part of the brightly lit kitchen but there was no movement as far as they could see.

Maura unholstered her gun and Tony did the same. At a gesture from Maura they both stepped behind trees on opposite sides of the path.

"Ann Kinnear?" Maura yelled. There was no response. "Miss Kinnear, this is the Tupper Lake police, are you in there? The Philadelphia police asked us to check up on you." Still nothing. They waited a minute, Maura trying to see into the house and Tony peering into the woods behind them. The burning smell became stronger. "Miss Kinnear, we're coming in," yelled Maura. "With guns," she added. Maura and Tony started down the path again, Maura in the lead.

When they got to the porch Maura looked through the glass panes of the door into the kitchen and saw the body of a man sprawled on the floor, a pool of blood near his head. "There's a man down," she whispered to Tony who peered over her shoulder into the kitchen. They pulled open the screen door, the squeak of the hinges making them both jump, then pushed open the inner door and stepped into the kitchen, scanning the first floor as best they could as they entered.

The small kitchen was a scene of carnage. The man had a gaping wound in his neck, his fingers around his neck as if to try to stanch the flow of blood. A few feet from him lay a large dog, clearly dead, its fur matted with blood that mingled on the floor with the man's. Against the kitchen cabinets was the third victim, a woman in a slumped sitting position, propped up by the angle of the cabinets she had fallen against. One hand lay over a bloody stain on her side, the other gripped a gun.

Maura bent down and took the gun out of the woman's limp hand. "See if either of them are alive," said Maura, "I'll check the house." Tony was kneeling over the man but it seemed pretty clear to Maura that he was dead.

She had circled the small first floor and was on the second

floor when Tony yelled, "The woman's alive!"

"Get an ambulance!" she yelled back and heard Tony making the call on the radio. Maura completed the check of the basement and then rejoined Tony in the kitchen. He had turned off the stove and moved a pan filled with the burned remains of what looked like beef stew off the burner. Maura also noticed the charred remains of curtains over the kitchen window.

Tony had pulled Ann away from the cabinets and gotten her into a prone position with what looked like an oven mitt under her head. He had a dishtowel pressed to her side.

"Does it look bad?" asked Maura.

"Haven't any idea," said Tony, looking queasy. "It's off to the side, not in the middle, so that's probably a good thing, right?"

"That's Ann Kinnear, I saw her on TV once," said Maura. Ann's face was ashen and her labored breathing was accompanied by a slight whistling sound.

"Think she got it in the lung," said Tony. "I hope the EMTs get here quick."

The ambulance arrived about ten minutes later.

Chapter 45

As the wail of the ambulance receded, Maura pulled out her cell phone and dialed Joe Booth's number. He answered at the first ring.

"Booth."

"Hello, this is Maura Meese up at Tupper Lake. We're at Miss Kinnear's cabin—there had been an altercation, Miss Kinnear was shot, she's alive, the ambulance just left."

Maura heard a whoosh of air from the other end of the call. "Could you tell how bad it was?"

"She was shot in the torso, it's hard to say ..." Maura didn't mention that Kinnear's face had taken on the grayish, pasty look of shock victims by the time the ambulance had arrived. Maura had only seen two gunshot victims in her career and both had had that look and neither had survived. "There was another victim, a man, white, dark hair, mid-thirties ... any idea who that is?"

"Yes, I think so. Is he alive?"

"No—also shot."

"Can you send me a photo of the body so I can confirm the identity?"

"I can't really just snap a picture and text it to you."

"I'd appreciate knowing as soon as possible, could you send a picture to the precinct?"

"That should be OK. Don't mean to be a stickler but if a crime scene photo got out it would be my job."

A few phone calls and e-mails later, Joe was sitting at his PC in what passed as his home office—his kitchen table—

looking at photos of Biden Firth's body sprawled on Ann Kinnear's kitchen floor. In the wide shots he could see a dog's tail and part of a back leg intruding into the frame—shit, not the dog too, Joe thought. In the close-up shots, Firth's eyes were open, his lips parted in a snarl. Joe cropped the picture to show only the face, not the pool of blood surrounding the head, and printed out a copy. He flipped through the rest of the photos, skipping quickly over the one featuring the gaping gunshot wound in Firth's throat.

He dialed Maura's number.

"Maura Meese."

"Joe Booth. The body is Biden Firth, I've been investigating his wife's murder here in Philly."

"No kidding? The husband was a suspect, I assume?"

"Yup."

"Well, it seems like Mr. Firth has wrapped that investigation up for you—"

"Yup. But at what a price."

Joe heard a shout in the background from Maura's end, "What should we do with the dog?"

Maura called back, "Bag it and take it to the morgue, they may want to retrieve the bullets." Then, to Joe, "Uh, what should I do with the dog when they're done with it?"

"I'll come get him."

"Sure thing, I'll let them know." There was a pause, and Joe could faintly hear the familiar sounds of a crime scene team in the background. "Hey, listen, I didn't mean to be a smart ass about 'wrapping up the investigation'—"

Joe shook himself and snapped off the power on his computer monitor. "No problem. I've got to make some phone calls. I appreciate the help."

"Sure thing. I'll keep you up to date on developments."

After confirming which hospital Ann had been taken to and disconnecting with Maura, Joe called Mike and redirected him to the hospital.

Then Joe called Walt, having gotten the number from Mike, and arranged for Walt to pick him up at Brandywine Airport in the morning. He was too tired to make the drive that night—having Walt fly him would save him several hours and he wanted to talk to Mike in person as soon as possible. He also called Margaret Fraker and gave her the sketchiest of details about the death of Elizabeth Firth's husband. Then he packed an overnight bag, got into bed, and stared at the ceiling.

Chapter 46

Shortly after 2:00 a.m., in the waiting room outside the ICU where Ann was recovering from her surgery, Mike's cell phone buzzed, showing Scott's name.

"Damn!" said Mike. He answered the call. "I am so sorry! I forgot to call you back!"

"What's going on there?" said Scott. "Are you OK? Is Ann OK?"

"I'm OK. Ann was shot—collapsed lung and a chip off her rib—but so far it looks like she's going to be OK."

"Oh my God, he *shot* her? The guy who killed his wife?"

"That's what it looks like, Joe's checking. He shot Beau, too."

"*Beau*? Is he OK?"

"No, he died," said Mike and for the first time the enormity of what had happened swept over him and he felt tears come to his eyes. "He killed Beau," he said, his voice cracking.

"Oh, sweetie, I'm so sorry. I wish I was there."

Mike wiped his eyes with the back of his hand and for a minute he was seven years old again, helping his dad and Ann bury their dog Scout in the back yard. "Where *are* you?" he asked.

"I'm outside the Foundry," said Scott. "They just closed. I didn't know where else I could go at this time of night to stay in a crowd."

"It looks like you don't need to worry about it anymore, he's dead—it looks like Ann got the gun away from him and shot him."

"Oh my. Poor Ann. I'm going to drive up there first thing in the morning," said Scott.

"Let's talk about it in the morning. I'm not sure what I'm going to be doing myself, let's figure that out first." Mike had visions of himself driving back to Philadelphia to turn himself in to authorities.

"OK, we'll decide tomorrow," said Scott.

"Scott, you didn't say anything to anybody, did you?"

Scott sighed. "I'm going to forgive you for asking that because I know you're upset," he said. "Sweetie, if I told you I'm not going to tell anyone, I'm not going to tell anyone."

"I know, I'm sorry," said Mike, resting his forehead in his hand, his elbow on his knee. "What a mess."

"It will look better in the morning. You call me as soon as you wake up, or if there are any updates on Ann."

"I will," said Mike. "Scott, you're the best."

"I know," said Scott, with a smile in his voice.

Chapter 47

Walt picked Joe up at Brandywine at 8:00 the next morning and not only flew Joe to Lake Clear but drove him to the hospital as well. Joe got out his wallet when Walt pulled up at the hospital. "How much do I owe you?" he asked. He thought he might have to give Walt a down payment and owe him the rest later, having no idea how much such a service would cost.

Walt waved him away. "This one's on the house," he said.

Mike was sitting in a chair by Ann's bed and stood up when he saw Joe standing in the doorway.

"Hey, A., look who's here."

"Hey," said Ann in Joe's general direction.

Joe came into the room. "How are you feeling?"

Ann shrugged and winced.

Joe put a small potted African violet that he had picked up in the hospital gift shop on the bedside table.

"Hey, A., look at that, isn't that nice."

"Nice," said Ann.

"She's kind of out of it," Mike said to Joe. "Painkillers."

"Well, that's understandable," said Joe. He turned to Mike. "Can I talk to you for a minute?"

"A., we'll be back in a minute, OK?"

"A minute," said Ann.

Mike and Joe went down the hall to an empty visitor sitting area with a TV in the corner playing *The Wizard of Oz*. Joe turned off the TV and they sat down.

"It was Biden Firth that shot her," he said, holding up the

cropped picture of Biden's face.

"*That's* Biden Firth?" said Mike, taking the photo.

"You're surprised?" asked Joe.

"We did a job for that guy in Harvey Cedars, New Jersey, a couple of weeks ago. He said he was hearing voices in a house down there. He said his name was Bob Dormand."

Joe smiled grimly. "Bob Dormand is his father-in-law's name, and I'll bet the house he had you look at was his in-laws' house. Place on the bay?"

Mike nodded. "Why did he hire us to look at his in-laws' house?" he said, more to himself than to Joe. "And if he was going to try to kill her, why didn't he do it there?"

Joe shrugged. "I'm assuming he found out about her reaction to his house, maybe he just wanted to check her out himself. And if he had wanted to kill her there he would have had to kill both of you, and it would have been a little hard to explain how the same person who had warned some buyers away from his house in Philly ended up dead in his in-laws' shore house."

"Seems like a big risk even just meeting us there," said Mike. "I do recall Ann saying that he asked about whether she investigated crimes. Maybe he got some information during that visit that helped him find where she lives."

"Yes, I need to dig into that a little more," said Joe. He rubbed his face with his hands and wished he had some coffee. "Is the stuff still in your trunk?"

Mike nodded again.

Joe sat forward in his chair. "How did you get it?"

"Are you sure you want to know?" asked Mike.

"I don't *want* to know any of it," said Joe irritably, "but I think I'd better."

Mike shifted uncomfortably in his chair. "Maybe I should have a lawyer …"

"Mike, I'm trying to help you out here," said Joe, his voice raised enough to attract the attention of a passing nurse. In a lower voice he continued, "Consider this off the record."

"I didn't know police did 'off the record,'" said Mike.

"We don't," said Joe in a voice that suggested to Mike that he should stop screwing around.

Mike sighed. "I just need to call Scott and tell him what I'm doing," said Mike. "You can even listen to the call."

Joe hesitated, then nodded.

Mike speed dialed Scott who picked up on the first ring.

"Hey, I'm here with Joe Booth."

"What's up? How's Ann?"

"She's doing fine. A little out of it but OK. Listen, I need to tell Joe what we did."

"Are you sure?" said Scott.

Mike glanced over at Joe. "Yes, I'm sure."

"Well, OK. But remind him that Ann could have bled to death if you hadn't realized the danger and called him."

Mike thought it likely that Ann would never have been shot if he and Scott hadn't stolen the jewelry from Firth's house but decided now wasn't the time to bring this up.

"You're a trouper," said Mike.

"That's me," said Scott and hung up.

Mike told Joe the story—how Scott had toured the house with Firth's realtor to check for a burglar alarm, dropped the St. Christopher's medal in the gym room, and unlocked the garage door and how he, Mike, had removed the blue items from the cabinet and they had found the jewelry in the paint can. How he had been taking the jewelry to show to Ann, and about the call Scott got from Bob Daniel and how the number had turned out to be a fake.

"That must have been Firth too," said Joe. He drummed his fingers on his leg. "So the St. Christopher's medal in the gym room was to get the housekeeper upstairs, away from the garage?" asked Joe.

"Yup."

Joe stared at Mike for a few seconds. "That was pretty slick," he said with grudging admiration.

Mike grinned despite himself, then sobered up. "Are you going to arrest me?"

Joe rubbed his face vigorously with his hands then dropped his hands to his knees. "I don't know. I sure as hell am going to have to give some explanation for why I called the Tupper Lake police and had them go out to Ann's place." He turned to Mike. "And we need an explanation not just for the police but for Ann, too. She can't know what you did."

Mike was beginning to feel hopeful with the turn the conversation was taking. "Absolutely not."

Joe stared at him for a few more seconds. "Is Scott reliable? Could he keep quiet?"

"Yes, he could keep quiet," said Mike earnestly.

"Because if we don't tell the police what happened—note that I'm saying *if*—and it got out, we would all go to jail."

Mike nodded vigorously.

"And jail would be no fun for a cop but I can tell you it would be even less fun for a couple of gay guys."

Mike nodded more vigorously.

Joe shook his head. "What the hell ..." then took a deep breath and sat staring at the linoleum floor in front of his chair for a minute, Mike watching him anxiously. Finally Joe said, "Scott's visit to the Firth house was just a lark. He had heard you talking about it and wanted to see it for himself. You had no idea he had done it until afterwards." Joe paused. "He had lost the medal and asked you to drive him back to check for it. That will cover us if someone saw you there. Or if the police talk with the housekeeper."

"Sounds good so far," said Mike.

"You decided to drive up to see Ann, just a normal visit."

"Yes, that's what she thinks it was. I told her Scott was out of town but I can figure out a way to explain that."

"Don't make it too elaborate," said Joe. "Let's say you just wanted to get away and have some quality time with her one-on-one. She might not even remember that you said Scott was out of town. Don't bring it up if she doesn't. Let's take a page from Firth's playbook and keep it as simple as possible."

"OK," said Mike.

"Just in case they check phone records, we should have a reason that your call to me resulted in me calling the Tupper Lake police."

They both sat back in their chairs and stared into space.

Presently Mike said, "Maybe I saw him driving up there. We must have taken about the same route at about the same time."

"Too much of a coincidence," said Joe. "Plus, you would have thought you were seeing Bob Dormand, your client from Harvey Cedars, not Biden Firth."

"True, but I might well be alarmed if I saw a client who had no business in the area heading toward Ann's house. Some people do develop an unhealthy fixation."

"Still too much of a coincidence that you would have seen him on the way. Plus, it would take too long to figure out what route Firth really did take, and too much trouble to match it up to yours. But the Bob Dormand angle does sound promising."

"Hey," said Mike. "I just realized I never got the rest of the payment from him."

"That's the least of your problems," said Joe irritably.

"I know that. But we could say that I called you to find out my legal options for getting paid."

"You called a Philadelphia detective because one of your clients stiffed you?" said Joe skeptically.

"At this point you're not just a Philadelphia detective, you're a friend of the family," said Mike sweetly.

"Jesus, on top of all this I'm going to have to explain how I got involved with you guys in the first place," muttered Joe. "But that angle is at least less awful than some of the other options." He pondered for a moment. "Why would you pick that moment to call me?"

"I was drinking and getting morose and wanted to hear a friendly voice," said Mike.

"That's great, then they can arrest you for DUI."

Mike brightened. "I picked that moment because Scott had just told me about the Bob Daniel call and hearing the name Bob Daniel reminded me of Bob Dormand," suggested Mike.

"Yes, I suppose that's possible," said Joe. "So you tell me about Bob Dormand stiffing you and I know that Bob Dormand is Elizabeth Firth's father and about the last guy in the world who would hire a psychic to check out his house."

"And you put two and two together and figure that it might be Biden Firth going after Ann."

"Wouldn't I have called Ann to see if she was OK before I called the Tupper Lake police?"

"I had just called her a couple of times before I called you so you didn't need to try again."

They both sat staring at the floor for a few minutes; a young woman visiting her mother passed the sitting area and thought that the patient the two men were visiting must be very ill because they looked so woebegone.

Eventually Joe said, "It's pretty thin. But I can't think of anything better." He pushed himself to his feet. "Let's get the stuff."

They went to the hospital parking lot where Mike's Audi was parked and Mike popped open the trunk. Joe picked up the Ziploc bag from the shoebox using a handkerchief. The paint remaining on the bag was beginning to harden but Joe could pick out the muted sparkle of gems. He replaced it in the shoebox.

"What are you going to do with it?" asked Mike.

"I'm going to put it back," said Joe.

They tried the story out on Ann who didn't question it, although they realized that she was probably not the most discerning audience at the moment.

"So you weren't at the house when Dormand ... I mean Firth ... was there?" she said to Mike.

"No, sweetie, I was still on the road," replied Mike.

"So Walt was there?" she said, sounding more confused. "Why was Walt there?"

"Where?"

"At the house."

"When was Walt at the house?"

"When Firth showed up."

"He wasn't at the house."

"He must have been," said Ann. "He gave Beau the signal."

"He wasn't at the house," said Joe, looking at her quizzically.

Ann pulled herself a little higher in the bed, wincing. "Someone gave Beau the attack signal. I heard it. Nobody knows that except me and Mike and Walt. And I heard the signal when I was in the basement."

"There wasn't anyone else in the house," said Joe. I understand it was pretty windy ..."

"No, it wasn't wind!" said Ann angrily. "It was the attack signal." She gave a wheezy rendition—the fast ascending whistle followed by five quick high whistles. "Maybe …" Then she stopped, looking at Joe and Mike but not seeing them, then turned to look out the window. Finally she said, rather plaintively, "I want to go home now."

Chapter 48

Walt flew Joe back to Brandywine later that day, and to keep Walt from having to make two round trips on the same day, Joe sprang for a rental car and a night at the Microtel for Walt. The return trip was evidently still "on the house" but Joe gave Walt $100 to help defray the fuel costs.

Joe drove to Mike and Scott's townhouse to get the other articles that Mike had removed from the cabinet and to give Scott the lecture about the consequences of not keeping quiet. Scott seemed a little more excited about the illicit nature of the situation than Joe would have liked.

"You realize what would happen if the real story got out," said Joe.

"I know. Mum's the word," said Scott, making a zipping motion across his mouth.

"You wouldn't be tempted to tell the story to someone?" asked Joe.

"Oh, I won't deny it's exciting to talk about," said Scott, "but as long as I can talk about it with Mike, that's enough."

"How long have you two been together?" asked Joe.

"Oh, God, forever," said Scott with a smile.

"Do you mind doing one more, um, illegal thing to wrap this up?"

"What would that illegal thing be?" asked Scott, looking interested.

"I need an accomplice ..." began Joe.

❖

Joan and Sophia were staying with the Dormands and the police had descended once again on the Firth house. The search effort was cursory, though, since not even Morgan Firth was debating the fact that Biden had killed Elizabeth.

When Joe stopped by on the Monday after Biden's death, the only person in the house was Harry Deng, sitting at Biden's desk going through a pile of credit card statements.

"I don't know what they're hoping to find," Harry said, clearly bored. "I doubt he put the sleeping bag on his AmEx card."

"Finish up that pile," said Joe, estimating it would take Harry at least half an hour to go through the rest of the statements on the desk, "and then we'll call it a day. I wouldn't mind getting some lunch."

"There's a good pizza place a couple of blocks away," said Harry, turning over another page.

Joe left Harry in the library and turned left toward the back of the house, to the garage. He unlocked and opened the door to the alley and in a minute Scott, in Mike's Audi, pulled up and, not getting out, popped the trunk open. Joe removed a bulky black plastic garbage bag, closed the trunk, and gave it a tap, at which Scott rolled away, never having given Joe a glance during the exchange. Joe grinned—Scott really was enjoying this and, Joe suspected, the cloak of secrecy surrounding it was all part of the fun. Joe decided that Scott was probably the least likely of the three of them to let word slip of their conspiracy.

Joe took the bag into the garage and shut and locked the door. He crossed to the cabinet and opened it up. The dust was beginning to cover the spaces the paint cans had previously occupied but he could still faintly discern where they had stood. Using his handkerchief, he replaced them in the cabinet, the heavier one having had the Ziploc bag of jewelry returned to it. He put the grease gun in the most likely seeming place. All had been wiped clean of fingerprints. He pulled a lock out of his coat pocket and latched the cabinet door, balled up the garbage bag and slipped it into the inside pocket of his windbreaker, then went upstairs to get pizza with Harry.

Chapter 49

The Philadelphia Chronicle

"Firth Investments Scion Implicated in Death of Wife and Attack on Psychic"

By Lincoln Abbott

Biden Firth, son of Firth Investments founder Morgan Firth and Main Line socialite Scottie Firth, was found dead in a remote cabin in the Adirondacks on Friday by Tupper Lake police, apparently killed in self-defense by Ann Kinnear, a woman whose claim to be able to "sense spirits" was the subject of an investigation by the History Channel. Firth had engaged Kinnear in early May on the pretext of checking a house—actually the shore house owned by his father-in-law, Robert Dormand, founder of Dormand Fixtures plumbing fixtures—for spirits. That engagement enabled Firth to track the reclusive Kinnear to her Adirondack Park home and led to the altercation that resulted in the death of Firth and the wounding of Kinnear, as well as the shooting of Kinnear's guard dog.

Firth, who was evidently under some pressures due to financial commitments made to the now-popular new restaurant, Waterman's (see Greg Malone's review on page E-1), is suspected in the murder of his wife, Elizabeth Firth, who disappeared in February and whose body was found in Tinicum Marsh in April ...

Chapter 50

When Mike stopped by the hospital the next day, Ann was more alert and also more agitated.

"I have to get out of here," she said, bunching the thin hospital blanket into an accordion in her hand and then smoothing it out across her lap.

"I know you want to go home, A.—" he began, but Ann shook her head.

"I want to go home but I mainly want to get out of here."

"Are they not treating you good—?"

"Mike, think about it," said Ann angrily, twisting the edge of the blanket, "what do you think it's like for someone who can sense spirits to be in a hospital? They're everywhere."

It was a constant low rumble, like someone continuously running a vacuum a room or two away—sometimes almost but not quite resolving itself into language. Especially at night she could sense them passing in the hallway—she could differentiate at least four or five individual spirits. None of them was hostile toward her but their presence was both irritating and draining. It brought to Ann's mind old photos of people in apartments with elevated train tracks right outside their windows. Those people probably weren't concerned that the train was going to jump the tracks and crash into their home but it must have been stressful—anticipating when the next train would rumble past, steeling oneself against the sensory onslaught when it did. Thank heavens spirits were at least not as loud as trains.

In a way she was surprised to encounter so many spirits at

the hospital. Although of course occurrences of death were concentrated in a hospital, and spirits normally appeared where they had died, they also usually stayed only if the place they had died was somewhere meaningful to them—a place that, for whatever reason, they wanted or needed to stay. But as Ann let the sense of the spirits wash over her, she came to believe that these were all people who had died fairly recently—perhaps within the last year—and that none of them had expected to die. It was as if they were hanging around, waiting to wake up from a dream—in which they had dreamed they died—and, Ann suspected, they would drift away as they accepted that this was not a dream.

As it turned out, Ann was not able to leave the hospital for several more days, and when she left she was not headed home—her discharge was contingent on her having help for the next week and Mike had talked her into staying with him and Scott while she recuperated. The doctors had advised against a possibly bumpy plane ride to West Chester so Mike drove up to the Adirondacks the day before, picked up some of Ann's clothes at the cabin, spent the night there, and then drove to the hospital the next day.

Mike parked the Audi in the No Parking zone in front of the hospital doors, turned on the flashers, and trotted up to Ann's room to retrieve her. After some delays—a seemingly unavoidable part of any hospital-related activity—an aide loaded Ann into a wheelchair ("That's the rule, Miss") and trundled her into elevators and down hallways to the entrance, Mike following with Ann's belongings.

As they approached the glass entrance, Mike saw a painfully thin young black man wearing a blue oxford shirt with the sleeves rolled up, a loosened tie, and khaki pants peering anxiously into the hospital lobby. An SLR camera hung around his neck. He perked up noticeably when he saw Ann. He snapped the cover off the camera and aimed it at the still closed lobby doors.

"Shit," said Mike, drawing a disapproving glance from the aide. "Sorry. Is there another entrance?"

"Mike, the car's right there, I don't want to hang around here anymore." The aide also seemed displeased with this sentiment.

"Hey, I know that guy—Lincoln Abbott, he's with the *Chronicle*. What's he doing up here?"

"Who cares, let's go." Ann kicked up the foot rests of the wheelchair and pushed herself up with a wince.

"Miss, I can take you to your car," squawked the aide, fluttering around Ann.

"They're not going to get a picture of me in a wheelchair," said Ann, shrugging the aide's hand off her arm. "I'm OK, really, you can tell your supervisor that I was uncooperative."

"You think?" muttered the aide, giving up and stepping back.

The door slid open and Abbot snapped a couple of photos then, in a practiced motion, let the camera fall back on its strap and pulled a voice recorder out of his shirt pocket.

"Fantastic," muttered Mike, following Ann out the door.

Abbott might have been young but he had perfected the art of the subtle body block. "Miss Kinnear, how are you feeling?" said Abbott, holding the recorder out toward Ann.

"Looking forward to getting home," said Ann.

"You've been through a lot, but you managed to bring a murderer to justice—can you tell us what happened there at your cabin?"

"I really don't remember much," said Ann, trying to slip past Abbott but he slid over to block her path.

"We know there was an altercation—a gun fight. How did you get Firth's gun away from him?"

"I told you, I don't remember. Amnesia."

Mike had tossed the bags in the trunk and was coming back for Ann.

"And your dog—I believe his name was Beau—I understand he died trying to defend you from Firth's attack."

Ann stopped in her tracks. Mike saw a look of such desolation cross her face that he knew what the worst part of this whole fuck-up was for her. If only he hadn't stolen the jewelry ... He wanted to punch that little shit Abbot in the face for mentioning Beau to his sister.

Mike stepped between Ann and the whirring recorder. "That's enough," he said more calmly than he felt.

"Mr. Kinnear, our readers are concerned about your sister, they want to hear from her what happened—"

"If they're concerned about her, then they'd want you to let her go home."

Mike opened the passenger door and helped Ann in, then, ignoring Abbott's continuing stream of questions, got to the driver's side, slammed the door behind him, and hit the locks. He pulled carefully out of the hospital driveway, making sure not to make his departure dramatic. When he glanced back Abbott was snapping a few more photos.

As he drove, Mike glanced over periodically but Ann had her face turned toward the window. Finally he said, "You OK, kiddo?"

Ann rifled through the backpack she was using as a purse, located a tissue, and blew her nose. Her eyes were rimmed with red. "Yeah. Thanks for the rescue."

Mike snorted. "Some rescue. If I hadn't left the car out there ... like bait, for God's sake—"

"No, Mike, I mean it," Ann interrupted. "Don't be so hard

on yourself. I really appreciate what you're doing for me."

Which left Mike feeling even worse than he had before.

Chapter 51

Joe unlocked the front door of the Firth house and stepped aside to let Ann enter. They stood for a minute in the entrance hall.

"Do you still sense it?" asked Joe.

"Yes. It's less and less each time," replied Ann, "but this is definitely where he killed her." She walked slowly along the hall. "By the sideboard, I would guess, the sense is strongest here."

"What sense is it?"

"Fear. Terror. Helplessness, which was something she wasn't used to feeling."

"What are you looking for?"

Ann shrugged. "I'm not sure. Seems like unfinished business, somehow."

"Sense of closure?"

Ann grimaced. "I hate that phrase."

Joe gave a lopsided smile. "Me too."

With Joe following, Ann walked through the rooms, less like a person looking at a house, Joe thought, than like a person looking for someone within the house. After she had wandered through the front rooms of the first floor, she climbed the stairs to the second floor.

"You said her mother sensed her in the nursery?"

"Yes, I think so. She said she sensed her daughter when she was here visiting Sophia."

Ann went into Sophia's bedroom and standing in the center of it turned slowly around.

"Anything?"

Ann shook her head.

They walked through the rest of the second floor and the third floor, Ann moving quickly, increasingly impatient. "Let's go downstairs."

Ann led the way and, when they reached the first floor, turned toward the back of the house. She spent just a moment in the kitchen and then opened the door to the garage, flipped on the light, and descended the stairs.

Joe waited at the top of the steps, his arms folded in seeming nonchalance but his heart thumping as he waited to see where Ann would go. Ann stood in the center of the garage, now devoid of cars, and then headed straight for the metal cabinet. She knelt in front of it and tugged on the lock that Joe had fastened to the handle.

"Damn," she muttered and, letting the lock fall with a clank, turned back to the room.

But rather than returning to the stairs she froze, staring at the middle of the room, her mouth hanging open and her face draining of blood.

Joe took a step down the stairs toward her and then stopped. She looked shocked but not frightened and Joe decided it was probably best that he not interfere with whatever was happening.

In the middle of the garage stood a woman—the whole version of the woman Ann had seen at her earlier visit only in part. Every strand of the dark sweep of hair and every soft fold of her silk blouse was visible—at once clear but somehow distant, as if viewed through many intervening layers of glass. The woman stood with her arms crossed and her weight shifted to one leg, a small, satisfied smile on her face. She reached her hand out toward Ann, almost as if for a handshake, and then instead raised it in a sort of salute and then the glass started to become cloudy.

Ann reached out her own hand not knowing what to

expect and she gasped when warm fingers closed over hers. Then the vision faded and she saw that the hand that held hers was Joe's.

"What was it?"

"It was her. Like she was right here with us."

Joe glanced surreptitiously around the garage and then turned back to Ann. "Are you OK?"

Ann took inventory of herself and was surprised to find that she *was* OK. "Yes, just a little dizzy." And no nausea, she added to herself. She too glanced around the garage but the woman was gone. "Let's go upstairs."

They slowly climbed the stairs to the kitchen where Ann dropped into one of the chairs at the table. "Just give me a minute," she said sheepishly.

"Sure." Joe sat down across from her. After a minute he asked, "Do you want a cup of tea?"

Ann made a face. "Not really. I could use some coffee, though."

"My treat," said Joe, starting to get up, but Ann put her hand on his arm.

"Do you have the picture I asked you to bring?"

Joe sat back down, reached into his jacket pocket, and pulled out a photograph that he passed to Ann.

It showed a couple dressed in evening clothes, posing in front of an enormous arrangement of flowers. The man was Biden Firth—she still thought of him as Bob Dormand, the man from Harvey Cedars—and the woman was the one she had just seen in the garage, wearing the same satisfied smile.

"Is that who you saw?" Joe asked.

"Yes, that's her. So who's the woman in the photos upstairs—the ones in the office and in the little girl's room?"

"It's her mother, Amelia Dormand. Joan, the housekeeper, says Firth removed all the photos of him and Elizabeth sometime after the body was found. Joan thought it was the act of a grieving husband and didn't think to mention it but I think that once he put the house on the market he didn't want anyone coming through the house seeing the photos of him or Elizabeth, maybe especially when he knew a 'psychic' was coming. His father and father-in-law helped keep photos out of the paper, Biden kept photos out of the house. It was a long shot but you never know when someone might see a picture and make a connection that would tie him to the murder. He was lucky, all right." Ann looked at the photo of the seemingly happy couple a moment longer and then handed it back to Joe who tucked it back in his pocket. "Just what Morgan Firth needs, not only a notorious house to unload but a haunted one," Joe said, then regretted it as sounding flippant but Ann didn't seem to notice.

"No, she's gone now, she won't be back."

Elizabeth Firth had accomplished what she needed to, Ann thought, she had avenged her murder. She had won.

Chapter 52

The evening of her trip back to Rittenhouse Square, her last night staying with Mike and Scott, Ann excused herself from movie night (*The Seven Samurai*) and, armed with a glass of wine and a bowl of popcorn, went to the guest room that was reserved exclusively for her visits. The first floor of Mike and Scott's townhouse was decorated mainly in the sleek, sophisticated style favored by Mike but the second floor bore Scott's more homey sensibility. The bed was covered with an antique quilt Scott had bought at an auction in Lancaster County, a mohair throw draped over the walnut footboard. The bedside tables were stocked with a rotating offering of books with local tie-ins—a paperback describing Amish customs, a children's book featuring N. C. Wyeth illustrations—and the walls were decorated with antique maps of West Chester. Ann lowered herself into an overstuffed armchair, put her wine and popcorn on the table next to the chair, and got out her cell phone. She dialed a number she used only infrequently but knew by heart.

After a few rings the call was answered with a deep, sepulchral, "Yes."

"Garrick, it's Ann."

"Ann, my dear," said Garrick with a slight increase in warmth that would have been unnoticeable to anyone else. "How are you doing? I would have called but didn't want to intrude."

Ann assumed he meant he hadn't wanted to call her official business number and risk having to talk with Mike—

she was pretty sure he didn't have her cell phone number since it was always she who called Garrick, not the other way around.

"I'm OK. Do you know what happened?"

"Of course, I'm not completely disconnected from events in 'the real world' as they call it," he said, sounding more like the Garrick Masser Mike would have recognized.

"What did you hear?" she asked, fiddling with a frayed piece of piping on the arm of the chair.

"That you had warned potential buyers from purchasing the house where a murder had occurred."

"Yes. It was bad." She tried to think of a better word. "Saturated."

"And the murderer came for you."

"The husband, yes." There was a pause. "I went back to his house today," said Ann. "I saw her."

"Saw her essence?"

"No, I saw her clearly, the way she looked when she was alive."

"Really?" said Garrick with obvious interest. "That would be the first time for you, would it not?"

"Yes, the first time."

"But you had sensed her before, in a more amorphous form, yes?"

"Yes, mainly just the usual manifestations—mainly the sense of the emotions of the spirit—but even on my first visit to the house there were flickers of something else, like I was catching a glimpse out of the corner of my eye but when I would turn to look it was gone. And there was also a sense that she was trying to communicate with me, was trying to direct me to something."

"And did you find this thing to which she was directing you?"

"I think I would have but by the time I went through the

house the first time the police didn't have an excuse to search it anymore and when I went through it the second time, today, it ... didn't seem so important anymore." She made herself stop playing with the chair piping which she was causing to fray more. "Why do you think I saw her clearly today?"

"Was she still trying to direct you?"

"Maybe. No. I don't know. It seemed like she had gotten what she needed. But if she had gotten what she needed—which I assume was making sure her husband was punished for murdering her—why would she bother to show herself to me now?"

"What makes you think it was a change she effected?"

"What do you mean?"

"I mean, my dear, that it seems more likely that the difference was due not to this poor woman's eventual success in making herself visible to you but rather to your eventual ability to see what had been there all along."

"But why now?" Ann pursued doggedly.

"Was there nothing that happened the night he attacked you that might explain it?"

Ann thought of the whistle that had launched Beau at Biden Firth and had provided the momentary distraction that had very likely saved her life. She thought about the fire that, much to investigators' perplexity, had put itself out. She had to get home as soon as she could. "I'm not sure," she said, a waver in her voice. She cleared her throat. "I have a favor to ask you, Garrick."

"Yes, my dear?"

"Could you go to my cabin and see if he's there?"

"The murderer?"

"Yes. I don't think I can go back if he's there."

Ann heard a sound that she realized after a moment was

Garrick chuckling. "He's not there."

"But how can you be sure—" she began.

"Because, my dear, I have been to your cabin and done quite a thorough examination and Mr. Firth is not there."

Ann bristled. "You went to my house without my permission?"

"Perhaps not with your permission but not with no permission. Your brother hired me."

Of all the things Ann had heard during this episode with Biden Firth, this was perhaps the most surprising—her brother had hired Garrick Masser to make sure her home was still free of spirits. She knew what it must have cost Mike to do that.

"Oh," she said eventually. "Well, thank you."

"Don't mention it," said Garrick sourly.

They were both silent for some moments. Finally Ann said, "It's going to be a lot easier for me to go home knowing there's nothing waiting for me. I do appreciate it, Garrick."

"Hmph," he said, then, "If you decide to continue in what your brother so quaintly refers to as your 'consulting business,' then this new skill will serve you well. Mrs. Firth's death was recent and dramatic, and she needed you to perform a task for her, all of which doubtless facilitated your ability to see her, but it's a skill you can develop. You must neither push them away nor pursue them. You must let them come to you on their own terms." He gave another short chuckle. "Although perhaps I should not be coaching you, one might say you are the competition now."

"I don't think I'm your competition," said Ann modestly, pleased to be acknowledged as an equal by Garrick, a sensation that was quickly deflated when Garrick responded thoughtfully, "No, I suppose not."

They both pondered this new state of affairs for a moment, then Garrick said, before breaking the connection,

"Be open to what is there to be experienced. Remember, I never said there was *nothing* waiting for you at your home."

Chapter 53

On Monday, Mike got a call from Morgan Firth's lawyer asking if Ann and Mike had ever received payment for their engagement with Biden—a. k. a. Bob Dormand—and, when Mike told him they had not, asked what the amount due was. A few days later Mike received a check from Firth Investments.

On Tuesday, Mavis called to let Ann and Mike know that she and Lawrence were buying Flora Soderlund's house— Mavis thought Harold seemed like a spirit she would like to share a home with. They were planning a housewarming party once they updated the kitchen.

On Wednesday, Walt flew down to West Chester to pick up Ann and bring her home. On the way from the Adirondack Regional Airport to her house, he drove extra carefully, evidently feeling she was still convalescent. Ann's heart ached a little when they drove past Walt and Helen's house without making the regular stop to pick up Beau. Walt must have felt it too because he said, "He was a good boy."

When they got to the house, Walt parked with the passenger door as close to the path to the house as possible and, retrieving her bags from the trunk, took Ann's elbow as they made their way down the log steps.

"Walt, I'm OK, really," said Ann. "I've done nothing but lie around Mike's place recuperating for the last week."

"You sure?" said Walt. "You still look a little peaky."

"Yes, very sure," said Ann. "This is just my normal peakiness."

"Well, OK," said Walt, letting go of her elbow. He followed Ann down the path with her bags. At the door he held the screen door open for her while she unlocked the inner door.

The wooden floor in the kitchen was new and raw-looking.

"Helen couldn't get it clean," he said, "so I had Bruce," Walt's carpenter cousin, "put in a new one." Bruce had burned the old boards to keep them out of the hands of morbid souvenir-seekers.

"Thanks, Walt," said Ann. "Let me know what I owe him for that."

"Mike took care of it," said Walt. "Want these upstairs?"

"Yes, thanks," said Ann, feeling almost like a visitor in her cabin. The pan she had been cooking the boeuf bourguignon in was sitting on the stove, the inside mirror-like from scrubbing—a sign of Helen's ministrations, she knew. Helen had also hung cheerful striped curtains at the window, although some charring was still visible on the ceiling.

Walt came back downstairs and noticed Ann looking at the ceiling. "Lucky that put itself out," he said.

Ann nodded. "Yes. Lucky."

Walt stuck his hands in his pockets. "You sure you're OK here? Won't be scared?"

"Maybe at first but I've got to get used to it, right?"

"You want me to bring Helen by to stay with you a night or two?" asked Walt. "She wouldn't mind. Would be a little vacation for her."

"No, really, I'm fine," said Ann, herding Walt toward the door.

"Call if you need anything?"

"I promise. Thanks, Walt, I mean it."

Walt bent over and, for the first time since she had known

him, gave her a peck on the cheek. "You take care." And then he was up the log stairs, starting up the pickup, turning it carefully around, and heading down the drive.

Ann walked through the dining and sitting rooms, opening windows as she went, then climbed to the second floor and did the same. She even went into the basement, turned on the light, then turned it off and went back upstairs. She felt in some way as if she were reclaiming the cabin as her own.

With the fresh air wafting through the cabin, and the sun, filtered by tree limbs, brightening the Indian rugs scattered on the floor, she returned to the kitchen. She stood in the center of the small room and tried to slow her breathing, opening her senses to anything that might be present. Garrick's report that Biden Firth was not at the cabin had been encouraging to her but she had known she would not be fully convinced until she had had a chance to experience it—or *not* experience it, as the case may be—for herself.

She could sense nothing in the kitchen, nothing in the cabin. It would be only her own all too normal nightmares she would need to deal with in the coming months and years.

But the cabin itself was not where she especially wanted to be at the moment. Going out the front door, she turned right and descended the small hill to the fire pit. Everything was as she had left it except for an area of recently dug dirt off to one side of the clearing showing the place where, at Ann's request, Mike and Walt had buried Beau.

Ann lowered herself gingerly into one of the Adirondack chairs by the fire pit. She sat back, resting her head on the back of the chair and closing her eyes, listening for a sound different from the regular sounds of the woods—the scuffle of squirrels in the undergrowth and the slap of water on the dock—and breathing in the clear air, searching for something different from the piney scent she was used to. In a minute her breathing slowed and one might have thought she was asleep but in another minute she opened her eyes, looked around, and gave a long ascending whistle.

At first nothing happened but then, at the edge of the clearing, Beau appeared. He was not some wraith, he was the Beau she knew, large and shaggy and solid—only a slight translucence that she had never seen in his life marked him now. Her heart thudded in her chest.

"Here, Beau," she said, and he trotted over to her, stopping a few feet away and sitting, looking intently at her face. She started to reach her hand out for him but she realized that this was not something to be touched and she let her hand fall back on the arm of the chair.

The beating of her heart eventually slowed as she gazed at Beau and a tear slipped down her face.

"Good boy," she whispered, and Beau thumped his tail.

She leaned her head back against the chair again and closed her eyes and then she heard, faint but clear, a whistled bar of The Cranberries' "Kiss Me." She stiffened and her breath caught in her throat but she kept her eyes closed and in a moment she felt a breeze, or breath, at her ear. She opened her eyes and Beau was turning to trot away and, in the shadows where the clearing gave way to the woods, Ann saw a person, immensely old, gray hair pulled back from a nut brown face, the features so creased by time that only her tiny stature suggested her gender. Ann got the general impression of primitive clothing, soft folds of some kind of animal skin, but she could scarcely draw her gaze away from the woman's eyes which shone with a kind of inner luminescence even in the shadows.

Beau trotted to the figure and disappeared into the woods behind her and as the woman turned to follow, she nodded almost imperceptibly to Ann and then disappeared behind Beau.

Chapter 54

A few months later, Mark Pironi sold the Rittenhouse Square house (he no longer referred to it as the Firth house) to two doctors—Amy and Zach DeCoeur—who were relocating from Charlotte. On an overcast Sunday afternoon, Amy was in the library unpacking boxes of books when Zach came in carrying a can of paint with bluish drips down the side.

"Does this color look familiar to you?" he asked, holding up the can.

Amy contemplated it. "I don't think so," she said.

"All the other cans match something but I can't find anything to match this one."

They carried the can from room to room, comparing the paint drips to wall color, trim color. When they got to the top floor, which they were outfitting as a movie room (Zach was a huge movie fan and wanted to furnish it with old movie palace seats but Amy was unconvinced), Amy shook her head.

"I don't think it matches anything."

"Do you want to keep it?" asked Zach.

Amy took the can from him and jiggled it back and forth. "It is almost full. But I don't really like the color."

"Me either," said Zach.

They returned to their tasks—Amy unpacking books and Zach cleaning out the garage. Zach gave the can one last shake—it did seem a shame to throw away an almost full can of paint—then shrugged, opened the door to the alley and dropped the paint can into the trash bin outside the door. He closed and locked the door, setting the burglar alarm then climbing the stairs to the kitchen for a beer.

The Ann Kinnear Suspense Novels continue in

The Sense of Reckoning

After solving the Philadelphia Socialite murder, Ann Kinnear should be riding high. Instead, she's depressed and considering abandoning her spirit sensing business. To add to her problems, Ann has suffered a series of injuries to her hands—could these be the ghostly repercussions of the violence that ended her last case? Ann goes to Maine to solicit help from fellow spirit senser Garrick Masser. Ann and Garrick find more trouble than they bargained for in a tale of obsession and misplaced loyalty that has its roots in a crumbling summer hotel, international art theft, and the historic wildfire that destroyed large swaths of Mount Desert Island in 1947. Unless Ann can fit together the pieces of the past while staying ahead of whatever—or whomever—is causing her harm, her future, and that of her friend Garrick, may be very brief indeed.

Contact Matty Dalrymple and sign up for updates on published and in-progress books and upcoming events at mattydalrymple.com.

Made in the USA
Middletown, DE
02 September 2016